Autumn Return

SALLY BRICE WINTERBOURN

Autumn Return

BETHANYHOUSE

MINNEAPOLIS, MINNESOTA

Autumn Return
Copyright © 2001
Sally Brice Winterbourn

Cover design by Lookout Design Group, Inc.

Published by Bethany House Publishers
A Ministry of Bethany Fellowship International
11400 Hampshire Avenue South
Bloomington, Minnesota 55438
www.bethanyhouse.com

Printed in the United States of America by
Bethany Press International, Bloomington, Minnesota 55438

Library of Congress Cataloging-in-Publication Data

Winterbourn, Sally Brice.
   Autumn return / by Sally Brice Winterbourn.
      p. cm.
   ISBN 0–7642–2394–1 (pbk.)
    1. Cornwall (England : County)—Fiction. 2. Middle-aged women—Fiction. 3. Home ownership—Fiction. 4. Homeowners—Fiction.
I. Title.
   PR6073.I556 A95   2001
   823'.92—dc21   00-012142

I dedicate this book to:

My wonderful husband, Graham,
who has been a constant encouragement
and a patient listening ear.
I love you.

My four precious sons,
Ben, Toby, Noah, and Sam;

and the two special girls in my life,
Alison and Beth.

My dear mum,
Enid,
who has never ceased to encourage me.

And in loving memory of my father,

George Charles Brice,
now in heaven.

———

"For I know the plans I have for you," declares the Lord,
"plans to prosper you and not to harm you,
plans to give you hope and a future."
Jeremiah 29:11 NIV

CHAPTER 1

Tarran Bay

"How can you even consider buying a house you've never seen?" Lucy Summers' eldest son, Luke, asked.

"I know what I want. Tarran Bay is like a second home to me, and I admired the cottage many times when your dad and I walked to the cliffs." Lucy's voice was soft, but she had purposely leaned forward as she spoke to emphasize her determination.

"But you haven't even seen the inside! Oh, please, see sense, Mum. I'll take you down next year. We can all go—Karen, Dan, Denise, and the kids. We'll have a holiday there and look around with you."

Lucy looked at her concerned family gathered around the table. At twenty-nine, Luke was tall, dark, and yes, handsome—he had her green eyes. He was dedicated to his work as a children's social worker, but Lucy knew it was an extremely tough job. He found it hard not to get too involved with some of the more difficult cases. With his blond hair and blue eyes, her second son, Daniel, who was twenty-six, looked so much like his father, Tom, had when he was young. An accountant like his father before him,

Daniel was also very kind and caring. Tom would have been proud of their sons' growth as husbands and fathers. Lucy was pleased they had married such wonderful Christian women. She could not have asked for better daughters-in-law. Her family was a delight! And there they all sat staring at her, as if not knowing what on earth to say to keep her from leaving.

"Luke," she said patiently, "I've already told you this. I wanted to choose the house myself. And I like what I've bought. With the money I'll get from selling the house here, I can easily afford it. The money that's left over, along with your dad's pension, will allow me to live very comfortably. Please let me do this thing. If it's wrong, I can come back."

Lucy knew Luke was concerned. He was being protective because he thought she needed him to keep her from making mistakes. And, in a way, she couldn't blame him. She had often been a little absentminded since Tom's death two years ago. Her doctor had assured her that in time her equilibrium would return. But that knowledge didn't make it any easier—for any of them. Lucy just didn't know how to help her family understand she'd had two years to make her plans, and only had one life to live. She would not be curtailed at any cost.

"Leave Mum be," Karen said. Luke's wife was snuggling little Rose, who was fast asleep on her lap. The sweet baby was sucking her tiny thumb. Her long dark lashes rested on soft pink cheeks. Lucy was so proud of her granddaughter. She had hoped for a little girl herself once, but it just wasn't meant to be. Rose almost made up for it by loving Nanna, as she called Lucy, and bringing joy with her playful antics wherever she went.

"You'll be lonely, Mum." Dan tentatively interrupted her thoughts. "You know you will. You've always had so many people around you."

"That's my problem, son. I need a change. I want to paint again,

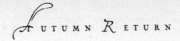

to enjoy different surroundings. I've been here for over thirty years."

"But that's why we're worried. You don't know anything else. You've only been to Cornwall on holiday. The winters are bad there. It isn't sunshine and summer all the time, you know. It rains, it snows, it's cold! I just don't think that you've thought it through enough."

"It's what your dad and I planned to do for years. We always said that if we didn't return to Africa, Cornwall would be the place for us to retire, and it was always going to be in Tarran Bay. You know how much we loved it there. Besides, I don't want to be a burden to you two. If I'm down there you won't worry so much, and you can spend your holidays with me. I'm just doing what your dad and I had planned all along."

"But Dad isn't here! And we will worry *more* when you're so far away! You can't even change a fuse!"

Lucy could see that Dan was getting exasperated, too, and she didn't want to make a scene in front of her daughters-in-law. "I've told you, I can come back if it doesn't work. There are handy men in every town. I can afford to pay them to work for me. And I'm not so old that I can't learn to do some of the things that your dad did."

Lucy stood up and started to pile up a tray with their teacups and saucers. "I'm going in two weeks, and that is the end of it. Everything is ready and waiting for me. I loved your dad and the life we had together, but I'm looking forward to moving. I need a new start. I have to learn to live alone. If I stay here, all I have are reminders of what I have lost. This may come as a shock to you, but I might still have twenty or thirty years left, and I don't want to live them in the past."

Lucy lifted the tray, now piled high, and walked toward the kitchen. At the doorway, she turned to smile at her young family. Her sons glanced anxiously at each other across the dining room table, but Lucy could see they finally realized there was no point in further argument. They might not be happy about her move, but they knew when their mother had made up her mind and wouldn't budge from her decision. Once in the kitchen, Lucy could just hear their whispers between the soft clatter of the dishes.

"You've got to let go," Denise said in her soft, slow voice. "She's never held you to her apron strings. I think she'll make a go of it. She's been so unhappy ever since Tom died. Leave her be. Perhaps starting over in a new place will help her faith come back. All we can do now is pray for her every day."

As Lucy finished up the dishes, she looked around her spacious kitchen. She liked her Edwardian house, with its tall elegant rooms and huge tiled fireplaces. But the house was hers and *Tom's*. She needed a home without constant reminders at every turn—the shelves he'd made, the floors he'd stripped, the decorating he'd so meticulously done. Everywhere she looked, Tom's handiwork stared back at her. And she cried all the time. When she was out of the house, she found that she could be distracted from reality for short periods. Often she went for lone walks in the wooded area up the hill. The natural beauty of the green, leafy trees soothed her aching heart. She loved the countryside, and she needed the sea. That was *exactly* what she needed, and moving to Cornwall was her chance.

By the time the dishes were done, Lucy's family had packed up. As they said their good-byes, they made plans for one more visit before Lucy's departure. She politely declined their help in the move, explaining she was using professional removal men and wouldn't have to lift a finger. She could tell the boys still weren't happy, but they were gracious.

It made Lucy sad to know her sons were so against the move. They seemed unable to understand her need for a change. Perhaps they thought that she was running away from them, as well as every-thing else. Perhaps she was. She didn't know. Sadly, she realized she didn't care what they thought. She was so weary with it all. To get

10

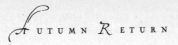

away seemed the only hope for any future for her. Luke and Danny would realize in time. She knew she should pray for them. But she couldn't pray now. She couldn't pray for anything—or anybody. She was numb.

It had been an exciting, but exhausting, moving day, and Lucy was feeling weary. At last she settled onto her white feather-filled sofa and sighed. A new life lay ahead of her. She had finally made the move to Cornwall.

No curtains hung in the windows of the cottage yet. And because it was dark, Lucy could see the little lights of the boats sparkling in the harbor, bobbing to and fro on the swell of the sea. She couldn't wait for morning, when she would be able to take it all in. She looked forward to entering every room and gazing from each window—many of which she knew had a wonderful view of Tarran Bay.

The room before her was full of her possessions, which were in complete disarray. Everywhere she looked, boxes were piled on top of one another. The sofa and an old brown leather chair were the only means of comfort and order at the moment. At least the two young men who had moved her belongings from London managed to put the boxes in the correct rooms. Thankfully, she'd had the sense to label everything clearly. Lucy wasn't always good at being organized.

Snuggled up to the comforting arm of the sofa, Lucy sipped hot chocolate and enjoyed the solitude. Back in London, in her home in Gloucester Gardens, peace and quiet had often eluded her—though she'd loved it there once. Now contentment filled her as she looked about the room. But sleep pulled at her eyelids, so she stood, puffed up the sofa's tapestry cushions, and made her way to the kitchen.

The kitchen was a cozy room, as were all the rooms in the cottage. It had a low ceiling with oak beams and—joy of joys—a deep green Aga. Lucy had never used an Aga, but she was looking forward to using it to cook her food. She felt she was cheating a little, however, since she had plugged in an electric cooker in a large cupboard—just for emergencies. The Aga's only drawback was that it had to be on at all times. At least Lucy's Aga wasn't coal fueled, as her grandmother's had been. Her oil-fired one would be much cleaner. It would be wonderful to have the kitchen warm and cozy in the winter. But she knew that in the summer, the heat from the Aga would not be so welcome.

Lucy stood and warmed her hands at the old stove, then placed a damp tea towel on its chrome handle to dry. She smiled at her reflection in the enameled surface. It seemed she was looking into a deep dark pool. Agas somehow reminded her of a comforting old grandparent—someone to snuggle up to, someone always there for you, someone who gave back.

Lucy thought about her paternal grandmother, long since gone. She was a large well-built woman with jolly red cheeks and a ready smile. Lucy had loved her grandparents dearly. She had often gone to them with schoolwork and problems, and they had always had time for her. She remembered the fabulous cakes and roasts her grandmother and mother had produced from the two ovens in her grandmother's Aga. Lucy missed her mum, too.

As she lifted one of the Aga's molded chrome lids, the heat hit her face. She gently let down the lid and turned to the sink. Thinking of the loved ones she had lost made her sad, but that was the way of life. She couldn't be sad just now. She was tired and needed a good night's rest. Tomorrow she would boil her first egg on the Aga!

After Lucy washed up her cup and saucer, she made for the bathroom. She set her wash things on top of two towels on a little stool and prepared to enjoy a soak in the pink bath. Generally, Lucy detested such old-fashioned reminders of the seventies, but somehow, here in Cornwall, in a two-hundred-year-old cottage, a pink

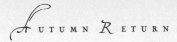

bath didn't really matter. At least it added some much-needed color to the otherwise stark white room. She thought she might stencil the walls sometime—with briar roses, perhaps. As the gentle bubbles softened her skin, Lucy began to daydream about the weeks that lay ahead of her and what she would like to achieve.

First, the white walls must be painted yellow—primrose yellow. White was so sterile and cold, yet it was what she'd asked the decorators to do. She had decided the whole place needed light until she was ready to paint the rooms herself. Yellow would enhance the wooden beams and go with almost everything she owned. After a long-ago trip to Africa, she had painted several colorful pictures, which she longed to place on the walls. They would put her personal touch on this precious cottage and make everything here feel like home.

Stepping out of the bath, Lucy pulled out the plug and wrapped a cream towel, warm from the radiator, around her clean body. She cleared the steamed-up mirror with the palm of her hand, making a squeaky sound, and looked closely at herself. People had often told her she was attractive. At fifty-five she wasn't so sure. Her hair was golden brown, with the help of coloring, and shortly cropped. Her green eyes, with their dark lashes, were probably her best feature, though they were beginning to crepe up. She had a neat nose and a small, even mouth. Lucy smiled faintly at her reflection. When she put on a little makeup—mascara and always lipstick—she felt presentable. But looking in the mirror now, she felt old, tired, and rather weak. Realizing she couldn't go back in time, she smoothed some Oil of Olay onto her face and neck, finished drying herself, and slipped a white cotton nightdress over her head.

Lucy picked up her towels, then placed them in the linen basket just inside her bedroom door. The only furniture in this room was a wrought-iron bed, an old Victorian wardrobe, a stripped pine chest of drawers, and a dressing table with an old swivel mirror sitting on top of it. In the middle of the floor were three large boxes, all full of memories, which seemed to beg for her attention.

"In the morning," sighed Lucy. She slipped into the comfort of crisp white linen and soon was sleeping soundly.

———

Lucy awoke slowly as sunlight streamed into her room, its pinkish-yellow light flowing through the east window and over the bare floor and bedclothes. As its glow warmed her face, Lucy was surprised by a certain expectancy arising within her. Most of her days had been filled with so many bittersweet memories and such aching sadness that this sudden, unexpected feeling took her unawares.

Slipping into her robe, Lucy walked across the bare scrubbed boards to the window seat that overlooked the sea. She sat down on a padded cushion and looked westward, beyond the little beach, to where the harbor lay swathed in pink. She watched as the sea began to turn gold, listening to the call of seagulls over the distant granite rock appropriately named Gull Island. Although she felt she could sit there all day, Lucy stood, stretched, and headed to the kitchen, eager to begin her first morning in Cornwall.

After her boiled egg breakfast—her first success on the Aga— and some freshly squeezed orange juice, Lucy made a list of provisions she would need. She adored Tarran Bay, but it had few shops, so her destination for the day was Redruth, the neighboring town. Paint was definitely a top priority. She needed to order carpets, too. Lucy knew she would enjoy that task. She had decided on a cream color for upstairs, where the traffic would be low. The sitting room and kitchen on the ground floor did not need carpet, as she planned to put her collection of kilim rugs on the flagstone floor. The rest of the downstairs rooms needed something dark, maybe mid-forest green. She did not want to spend her time worrying about messes her grandchildren might make when they came to visit. Rose, two, and Jamey, eighteen months, were adorable and had helped bring a

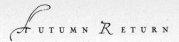

little happiness into her life since Tom's sudden death. How she wished he could have seen them. He was so looking forward to being a grandfather.

Such thoughts tormented her often—gray shadows in her mind that she could not escape. *No!* Lucy shook her head, determined to shut out the painful memories of the past.

Returning to her task, she realized she needed so much food and so many cleaning supplies that she wondered if her little red Mini had been such a wise purchase after all. Considering all the traveling she planned to do, she had thought it would be economical and easy to park in the summer months. Parking was a huge problem when the holidaymakers were around. She knew—she'd been one herself once.

———

After washing and dressing in jeans and a T-shirt, Lucy inspected the large garden. Her London garden had been the size of a postage stamp, as were most city gardens. Gardening was one of her favorite hobbies, and she looked at the beautiful scene before her with immense joy. Several fruit trees stood sheltered on a slope at the bottom of the lawn. A tall palm stood near a high stone wall. It was a fond reminder of a Greek holiday she and Tom had taken with the boys when they were young. The tail end of the Gulf Stream weather allowed many tropical plants to grow here in abundance. Lucy knew that she would enjoy the Cornish climate.

The sweeping lawn was enclosed by shrubs and bushes, offering a measure of seclusion yet allowing a wonderful view of the beach from the house. The flower beds were filled with a variety of plants, both common and unusual. Lucy had brought several favorites with her and knew she would have to get them in the soil as soon as possible.

Suddenly she remembered the hammock and headed for the garage, quickly finding the box where it was stored. It had been a present from Tom on her forty-fifth birthday, and it would look perfect hanging under the apple trees. Her garden in London had had only one magnolia tree, so the hammock had needed a steel frame. But here she could happily leave the frame in its box. She secured the hammock to two of the apple trees and got onto it carefully. The palm tree, the turquoise hammock, and the piercing blue of the early morning sky reminded her of sultry countries in far-off lands.

As she lay back, allowing the sunshine to warm her body, the memories returned. And with them came a flood of tears. She put her hands up to hide her face, a useless gesture, because no one was there to see her grief. The day Tom died had been terrible, she painfully recalled. As usual, she had been completely overwhelmed by needy people demanding her time and attention, and she felt tired and exhausted, longing for her husband to return from the office so that she could unload her frustration on him.

There had always been people from their church who needed attention, and somehow they found their way to Lucy and Tom's home. It was mostly Tom's openness and confidence in God that they needed, but Lucy had a gift for making people feel at ease. Many left the Edwardian house having been helped by her kind words and listening ears. But Lucy doubted anyone realized how overwhelmed and inadequate she often felt when people shared their burdens. Generally, the visits left her with feelings of guilt and inadequacy as she tried to sort out the problems of others. When she felt she had failed miserably, Tom would remind her that problems were God's department, not hers. He was much better than she was at leaving people's troubles at God's feet. *"Just be a listening ear. Give it to God in prayer,"* he would say.

She had been preparing supper that day when yet another knock on the door brought a deep sigh to her lips. She had opened the door impatiently and was startled to see a policeman standing on her front step. She knew immediately. Tom had been killed instantly, the po-

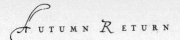

liceman told her. A drunk driver. *"So sorry,"* he'd said. . . . . *"So sorry."*

And Lucy had been sorry ever since. Now she wiped the tears from her face, brushed her hands on her jeans, and sat up slowly. The grass was still covered in dew, which sparkled in the sunshine like a million gleaming diamonds. She could make out the new cobwebs glistening on the bushes, too. She had felt like a fly caught in a web. Trapped by her desire to please people and be a good Christian. Any joy she may have experienced was now completely dead. Looking around, she noticed the leaves were turning yellow at the edges. Autumn was chasing hard on the heels of summer.

That's where I am, she thought, *in the autumn of my life, with only winter to look forward to.* With a shaky sigh, Lucy returned to her cottage to prepare for her shopping trip.

Redruth, usually so busy, was fairly quiet, which pleased Lucy, as it had been several years since she had been there, and she wanted to get reacquainted with her neighboring town. She delighted in the old market stalls under their colorfully striped awnings. Cornwall's towns emanated a charm that she had rarely seen in London. She decided to enter the paper shop first. Back in London, she had never had a paper delivered. But here, where all was to be so different, Lucy ordered a Sunday paper, with all its glossy supplements.

The carpet shop was a small, friendly, family-run business, and it didn't take Lucy long to find exactly what she wanted. The gentleman said that his son would come on the following Tuesday to measure, and within three weeks the carpets would be laid. *How efficient*, Lucy thought, remembering the two-month wait for absolutely anything back in London.

She made her way along the wide walkways to the supermarket for her groceries, her journey uninterrupted by automobiles because traffic was routed around the outside of the town. People milled around her, old and young and, of course, the couples. Oh, how it hurt to see the couples, especially the old ones. Life just didn't run the way one expected, and as she had counseled so many before, she knew she had to work through being single again. Her own words now seemed so futile against the pain, anger, and hurt that consumed her daily. How could she have ever thought to know their suffering? Jesus could. . . .

Lucy put this thought firmly to the back of her mind. She didn't want to live the Christian life any longer. She believed in God—that would never leave her. She just didn't want any part of church and all its trappings, but that often left her feeling guilty and unable to pray. An aching void lay deep inside—one she feared would never mend.

After finishing her errands, she headed back to her cottage. The ride home felt familiar, yet new, for she had never been to Cornwall in the autumn. The winding back lanes pushed their way through deep woodlands. Huge mudbanks rose higher than the Mini on either side of the lane. As she traveled through the tunnel-like roads, she felt like a mole in a hole. The way the trees formed cathedral-like arches above her head stirred something deep inside her. Was it a glimpse of joy? Lucy thought it was impossible, but still she hoped it was the start of something new—she could only hope. Curving twisted tree roots gnarled their way through the dark ivy, pushing through the countryside and out into the light. The strong sun threw shafts of filtered light through changing leaves that danced in the breeze.

Lucy turned on the local radio, then quickly shut it off. Just another boring talk show. Opening the window, she could hear the chirping sounds of sparrows and blackbirds, and the soft cooing of wood pigeons. Nature's music was far better for her spirit than anything the radio had to offer.

Dawn Cottage's white picket gates were open and inviting, just as she'd left them. Lucy liked the name of her new home. She had

always loved the dawn more than any other time of day. Even in
Gloucester Gardens, the dawn had sometimes brought solitude and
quiet, broken only by the dull traffic sounds of the M25 in the distance. She had become so used to the noise that she hardly noticed
it as she reflected on her daily readings and talked to her heavenly
Father each morning before the children awoke and breakfast was
made. Happier times!

Once more she shut her mind to the past and entered the driveway, enjoying the scrunching of tires against gravel. Unpacking and
putting away her provisions took two hours because she decided the
cupboards needed wiping with disinfectant. Of course, the cupboards were brand-new, spotless. The whole house was clean. But
giving them a thorough cleaning just seemed the thing to do.

Around two o'clock, Lucy broke for a late lunch and decided to
purchase a Cornish pasty from the Tarran Bay bakery. She ate it
sitting by the harbor, taking in all the wonderful sights. A harbor-
side lunch of delicious Cornish pasties was the first thing she and
Tom and the boys had done when they arrived on their holidays—
after unpacking their cases. She loved the familiarity of it all.

As she sat looking out to Gull Island, two boats pulled into the
bay. One had late holidaymakers on board—older people who probably didn't want the noise of children ruining their two-week break.
The other was a little sailing boat, gliding close to where she sat. A
man who looked to be in his midforties began to dock. He was wearing jeans and a typical gray-flecked Cornish sweater, which matched
his hair. As she licked her fingers, she wondered why he needed a
sweater on such a warm autumn day. Reaching the dock, he flung a
rope over the large capstone on the quayside to secure the boat.
Lucy watched him for several minutes as he covered things up and
brushed down his boat. As the people from the other boat landed
and walked past her on their way to the café, he caught her eye.

"Hello," he called. "Enjoying your lunch?"

She could only smile back and nod, her mouth full of the delicious pie.

"On holiday?"

He was apparently planning to carry on regardless.

Lucy swallowed her mouthful. "No, I've come here to live—at Dawn Cottage." While mopping her mouth with a tissue, she waved a hand toward the other side of the beach where her cottage nestled on the cliff.

"Ah, I wondered when the new occupants would arrive."

"Just me." She smiled and stood, brushing herself free from crumbs.

He sensed her uneasiness and asked, "Your name?"

"Lucy—Lucy Summers."

"Well, I'm Jack Trent. I live here at the harbor." He pointed to a large whitewashed cottage, which was very similar to her own. "I'll have to introduce you to my wife, Sue, next time we meet."

"Thank you. I'll look forward to that," she lied.

The man swung a bulky bag over his shoulder and, with a smile and a wave, started toward his cottage. Lucy quickly gathered the remains of her lunch and began her hike toward home. As she walked past the Tarran Bay Arms, which was painted a sunny yellow, and continued up the small hill to her home, Lucy reminded herself that one could not get away from people's questions. No matter where she went, there would always be people wanting to know about her life.

When she reached her cottage, Lucy marveled once again at her good fortune in finding her new home. She had purchased Dawn Cottage without even entering it. A local estate agent had sent her pictures with a long description of rooms and the views from the cottage. Lucy had fallen in love with the long narrow home. She was drawn to its eclectic charm. At one time, it had been two fishermen's cottages. Now it made one very spacious abode. The first and second stories were tied together by two small staircases, one in the

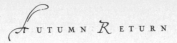

hallway, and a smaller winding one in the kitchen next to the Aga.

The cottage was painted white, the shutters and doors black. A Clematis Montana grew over the front porch and almost entirely surrounded the top windows of the cottage. Though it had no scent, she imagined the pale pink flowers sprinkling her abode with color and could hardly wait to see it in its full splendor next spring. Mr. Parsons, the previous owner, had enjoyed his garden, and Lucy had promised, by letter, that she would love and cherish the fruits of his hard work, taking it on into the future. With pleasure, Lucy entered her home eager to start settling in.

Unpacking was fun. Everything Lucy was tired of or simply didn't need any longer had been given to her family or the charity shops. And now she knew exactly where she wanted her favorite memory-filled treasures to go. She worked at this task for three happy hours after lunch, and finally her kitchen, which she had felt must be given top priority, was beginning to look the way she wanted it. She had even found time to cut a few late-blooming yellow roses and place them in a cobalt blue jug on the stripped pine table. She put away tea towels, crockery, cutlery, and utensils. Would she ever remember where she had put everything? She smiled to herself. Probably not.

A knock at her front door interrupted Lucy's contented labor. She wasn't expecting anyone and certainly didn't want the intrusion. She frowned and begrudgingly opened the door. It was Jack Trent, holding a little parcel wrapped in newspaper toward her.

"Two mackerel for your supper," he said. "They're small. Caught them myself today. Thought you might enjoy them."

Lucy had to admit she would enjoy them. "Thank you. You're very kind. Time got away from me. I hadn't yet thought of what to have for supper."

She didn't have to worry about inviting him in, for he turned immediately and made his way up her path and out the gate. Once on the pavement of tiny York stone, he turned to wave before disappearing down the lane.

Why do people have to be so kind? Lucy wondered. It left her feeling vulnerable. She didn't like feeling that she owed people something.

Tom had told her to beware of people manipulating her. It led to control. The trouble was she often couldn't distinguish between genuine need and manipulation. With a sigh, Lucy returned to the kitchen, cooked a quick meal of the mackerel—which was delicious—and cleared away her dishes.

After supper Lucy decided to do a little more unpacking before bed, but she got wrapped up in finding just the right place for all the special mementos she had gathered over the years. When she finally glanced at the clock, she was surprised to see it was past midnight. Dropping what she was doing, she rushed around getting ready for bed. *I'll pay for this in the morning.* But the satisfaction of being one more step toward a house in order was worth a little lost sleep.

CHAPTER 2

Longtime Resident

Hilda Sargeant was one of Tarran Bay's oldest residents. She kept her silver hair long, hanging straight and ending wispily just below her waist. Of course, no one ever saw it like this, because every morning she wound it loosely and gripped it to the top of her small head with hair clips. Hilda thought it looked quite nice, resembling a style of the Edwardian era.

It was early morning, and Hilda moved slowly around the well-trod flagstones of her large kitchen. She was mixing a sponge cake on top of a beautiful mahogany table, an heirloom from times past. The mixing bowl rested on a velvet undercloth of dark red, which didn't match a single item in the room. But it had covered her mother's table from as far back as she could remember, and she loved it. Hilda didn't worry about things matching, either in her home or in the way she dressed. Her main concern was that her house should be comfortable and that people should feel welcome when they visited.

Hilda loved her home. She would miss it if she, like all the other old folk of Tarran Bay—most much younger than herself—had to leave for the refuge of the old people's home in Redruth. She wanted to die in her own cottage, in her own bed.

She was ready to die and was surprised that she had lived so long—without a single day of illness. She thanked God, from a full heart, for protecting and loving her through thick and thin. Her heart swelled with gratitude that He still found work for her frail and withered hands to do.

She thought of dear Mr. Parsons. He had looked very ill when he finally decided to move. It was probably the best decision for him. The Parsons had lived next door to Hilda for over fifty years. But after his wife had died, Mr. Parsons had gone downhill quickly—so sad.

As Hilda thought about the many blessings in her life, she whipped the cake with the well-used wooden spoon. She poured the mixture into the awaiting tins, dividing it carefully and placing it in the little electric cooker located where a range had once stood.

Hilda never timed cakes. From years of experience, she knew exactly when they were ready—she knew by their smell. Waiting for the cake to bake, she tidied away and washed up all of the utensils, which she tended most carefully, as her mother would have wished. She made a cup of tea and sat down by the table in one of the three balloon-back chairs. Why there were only three, she never knew. Perhaps her father, when purchasing the table and chairs at the auction of the old manor house, had decided he only needed three. He was a practical man and never bought anything that was not useful.

The fond memory caused her to smile. What a wonderful parent he had been. Her mother, too, always busy and cheerful. Hilda remembered only great love and affection from them, and could never understand how some people would have children only to shout and torment them all their lives. Her mother had wanted more than one child, but after Hilda's difficult birth, no more came. Mum and Dad said that it made Hilda all the more precious to them.

She stood from her comfy chair by the fireplace to retrieve the cake from the oven and placed the two halves onto cooling racks. She went to the larder to get the clotted cream she was planning to put in the cake. Hilda didn't own a fridge, so the cream was stored on a cool marble shelf. Leaving the larder, she took a jar of the plum jam she had made last year. The cake filled with jam and cream would be a real Cornish treat for the new neighbors at Dawn Cottage.

As she waited for the cake to cool, Hilda went out into the garden, stopping along the way in the scullery, where she took off her tartan slippers and put on her stout brown leather lace-ups. The garden was Hilda's most special place and never ceased to fill her with great joy and a sense of God's presence. It was exactly as her father had left it. She didn't want it any other way. Wandering down the red-brick pathway to the orchard, she picked some pears and apples, placing only the best into her battered basket. The day was so warm she took off her green cardigan, laid it across the bench under the dappled shade of the Cox tree, and sat down next to it. She sat there for some time, enjoying the sun as it filtered through the leaves and kissed her face with warmth.

Her mind went back, as it did more and more these days, to the Second World War and her first tragedy. Wilfred, the love of her life, had died during the war. He had been sent to Africa, of all places, and drowned in a lake—while taking a bath! He hadn't even died in battle—so senseless and cruel.

Hilda had met Wil when she joined the choir in the next village to sing at an ordination in Redruth. They were twenty at the time, the same age—to the day. They both loved God and soon began to plan a life together, but they decided to wait to marry until they had the money to buy their own farm. Wil's father's farm would be passed down to Wil's older brother. They knew it would take years for them to save enough money, but neither minded. They sincerely wanted what God wanted, and He seemed to be saying *Wait*.

Hilda gazed out over the stone wall of her garden and beyond to the sea, which appeared dark blue at the skyline, turning green and turquoise nearer the beach where the waves foamed in again and again, creaming the beach and rocks with beauty. Several boats dotted the blue waves with their colorful billowing sails. Gull Island broke the blue expanse, and huge cliffs towered over each side of the bay. The view before Hilda had not changed for centuries. The only newer landmarks were the little seaside cottages that rimmed the harbor.

Standing slowly, Hilda made her way to the stone wall. She enjoyed the quiet scene below her for some time before a red helicopter lifted from behind the cliffs and dropped to hover above the rocky shore. She knew there was no reason to be alarmed. It was just a training day that had been well advertised for the holidaymakers to enjoy. She had seen rescues on this very beach many a time. Sometimes the trouble had been very serious, and as in most fishing villages in Cornwall, sometimes men had lost their lives.

Hilda watched the practice rescue with interest. A small crowd of holidaymakers gathered on the beach, attracted to the goings-on. As she watched, two young men were let down out of the belly of the helicopter onto the dangerous rocks beside the harbor wall, efficiently and capably carrying out the rescue drill. Once again her thoughts drifted to the past. If only someone had been there to rescue Wil. If only he had not drowned! Their life together would have been so good.

Hilda turned from the scene, momentarily sad, and walked back along the path to the fruit trees where she picked up her basket and cardigan. Taking the scissors from her basket, she cut some blooms from the flower beds, placed them on top of the fruit, and returned to her cottage.

She changed from her flowered overall into a powder-blue cotton dress, which matched her eyes perfectly. After filling the cake with cream and plum jam, Hilda decorated it with icing sugar sieved through a doily. Set on an old gilt-edged plate embellished with

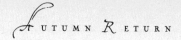

roses, it looked very pretty indeed. Everything was ready. Hilda bowed her head and prayed that her gift would be received in love and that God would bless the time she spent with her new neighbors.

———

Lucy was still in her robe when she heard a knock at the door. *Oh no, what now?* She had only been up an hour and wasn't in any state to have a visitor. *Surely not Jack again, with yet more fish!*

She wrapped the robe tightly round her body, secured it with the tie, and went to answer the door. There, to Lucy's surprise, stood the sweetest old lady she had ever clapped eyes on smiling up at her.

"I've made you a cake," said the woman in her soft Cornish accent, slowly holding it up for Lucy to take. Lucy retrieved it quickly, as the old woman's hands were rather shaky.

"Why, thank you! How very kind."

"And some flowers." She drew a glorious bouquet from a cotton market bag that hung over her shoulders.

"Oh, how beautiful."

"They're from my garden. I hope you'll enjoy them."

"Would you like to come in for tea? I'm afraid I've not been up long. I spent hours settling in last night and lost track of time. I slept until ten thirty this morning—unheard of for me!" She wondered what the old woman would think of her.

"I understand, my dear. Moving takes a lot of work. And, yes, I would love some tea."

Lucy had dreaded that answer. And now the little old lady was following her through the hallway and sitting room to the kitchen. Lucy gestured for her guest to be seated at the table and placed the flowers in the old-fashioned butler sink and the cake on the wooden drainer. She put the kettle on the Aga and sat opposite the old woman who had unknowingly intruded on her quiet morning. Her face was sweet. Lucy decided she must be quite old, but she had a good complexion, creamy with soft rose cheeks. Her blue eyes still held their color, and she had thick dark lashes.

"My name is Lucy Summers," she said, looking into the curiously beautiful blue eyes. They were so full of . . . something. . . . Light—yes, a sweet light. Her eyes quite mesmerized Lucy.

"Mine is Hilda Sargeant. I was a friend of Mr. Parsons. So sad he couldn't manage here any longer. We all tried to help, but he'd had enough. I dread the thought of ending up in a home. I live next door, though you can't see me through the bushes."

"I'm pleased to meet you, Hilda," Lucy lied. What was she supposed to say—go away, leave me alone, I don't want any friends? No, something deep inside prompted her to be kind, at least on the surface. Lucy supposed she had become very good at hiding her true thoughts and feelings. She stood to prepare the tea, and while the pot was brewing, she placed the flowers in a large white jug.

"I can't think where I've put my vases," she said. "They're probably in one of the sitting room boxes." Lucy placed the jug of flowers on the dresser and had to admit it brightened up her kitchen considerably.

"I made the cake for your family, thinking you would like a taste of Cornwall. The day he moved out, Mr. Parsons told me that you were coming down from London."

Lucy sensed that Hilda was not a busybody trying to find out about her, but that she was being genuinely friendly. "I'm here alone," was all she said.

"I see." Hilda smiled. "I live alone, too."

She didn't go on. She didn't ask endless questions or pry. She was just friendly. She talked about Tarran Bay and how she had lived there all her life—born in the same cottage and never gone farther afield than Redruth. Lucy must have looked surprised, because Hilda laughed.

"Would it surprise you to know I've never been in a car in my entire life—only the bus—or that I'm frightened to travel too far

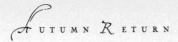

from home? I'm happy here in Tarran Bay—that's all. No need to go any farther away. Of course, I've actually been all over the world—in books. I love to read." Placing her cup in its saucer, Hilda smiled and thanked Lucy for her hospitality.

"Oh, don't go so soon!" The words came out before Lucy knew what she was saying. "Help me with the cake. I'll never eat it all myself!"

Hilda stayed another half hour and then excused herself with thanks. At the gate she turned to wave at her new neighbor. "God bless you," she said. *As you have blessed me, Lord.* Hilda had known Jesus as her Savior for a long time, and He had been a faithful friend. She clearly remembered the wonderful day she came to truly know and love Him, as if it were yesterday.

She had walked to church, holding her parents' hands, as she did every Sunday. She couldn't remember a time when she hadn't been to church. The stained-glass windows, each portraying a different parable, had always intrigued her. She knew them all and had loved it when her mother or father told and retold the stories of the Bible to her at bedtime.

But that day everything had seemed different, though even now she wasn't quite sure why. The sun shone through the colored glass, casting fabulous rainbows of color all over the stone walls and wooden pews. Hilda felt God's presence as she never had before, and that's when she truly understood God's love for her. He seemed to speak to her alone. *You're mine, child. I love you.* She heard it as though He whispered into her ear, and she had never ceased to listen to Him from that day to now. Even when her beloved Wilfred died, she felt assured he was safe in God's arms and that one day they would be reunited.

Many years later, as her mother lay dying of cancer, she once again knew His peace in her spirit. She, along with her mother and father, prayed every day that God would see them through. And He did. Her mother had shown love and kindness to people, even when she was dying and often in great pain. If children visited, she told them stories of her barefoot childhood and made them laugh at her tales of how the only teacher of her one-room school would get frustrated when her class of twenty pupils put frogs, toads, and worms in her desk drawer. And she prayed for the older people. "I came to comfort *your mother*," they would say to Hilda, "but she made *me* feel better."

One year and two days after her mother's death, her father died, too. Hilda was convinced it was because he missed his dear wife, but the old doctor had told her not to be silly. It was a heart attack that took him. Hilda had never cared much for that doctor and secretly rejoiced when he announced he was retiring. He wasn't very positive when he told her about the new doctor who would take over for him.

"You won't like him," he had said. "Coming here from London with newfangled ideas. Think they know everything, Londoners do."

But she had adored Gordon from their first meeting in his office because he loved God and had told her so. He asked the secret of her long life and why, except for the occasional checkup, there wasn't anything on her medical card.

"Prayer," she told him in her matter-of-fact way. And he believed her, though he confessed he'd be out of a job if everyone were like her. They laughed together, and she admitted that it hadn't always worked when she prayed for others, especially her parents. She didn't understand but explained that she knew God had His plans for His children, and much could be learned through trials.

Gordon often walked her to church. He told her he didn't mind. He didn't care much for cars, either. Boats were his passion—and windsurfing. He had told her once that he believed God had put him on this earth to save lives. While Hilda thought Gordon was a gifted doctor, she told him that though she believed God still healed people, she felt He was more interested in saving souls! Gordon had

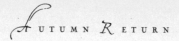

smiled his usual cheeky smile at her and agreed she was probably right.

As well as being the local doctor, Gordon also led a small group at her church. Hilda loved to listen to him encouraging the people who came to his home. Gordon Seymour was a very special man, and Hilda loved him like a son. She often wondered why such an attractive man was still unattached. He was always busy, and she had considered the possibility he was trying to erase something from his life. Perhaps keeping busy meant he didn't have to dwell on his pain. A sudden gust of wind blew a cloud of leaves and dust against Hilda's legs and brought her back from her musings. *What a fine man—a caring doctor and a good friend.*

As Hilda reached her gate, she noticed the roses covering the archway were in need of deadheading. Autumn had almost arrived, and a great amount of work needed to be done. She proceeded down the path, looking to and fro as she went, stopping, touching, breaking off dead leaves and flowers. Even in autumn, Hilda was drawn to the peace and charm of her garden. *Thank you, Father, for the beauty of your natural world.*

Hilda intended to pop over to the vicarage later that afternoon to do a bit of gardening with the vicar. So as she entered the cottage she decided to rest up and read for a while before lunch. Sitting in an old red Rexene chair from the thirties, she picked up her book and opened it to the place she'd left off.

She was reading a biography of Mary Slessor, a missionary to Africa who had been born in the mid-eighteen hundreds. With God's empowerment, she helped change the course of the spiritual and social lives of whole tribes.

As she finished reading, Hilda found she had tears on her cheeks. *What an amazing life. I hope I can make even a small measure of a difference in the lives of the people around me.* She put down the book and closed her eyes to pray. *Please, loving Father, use me. Show me how to help my new neighbor, Lucy, for she seems so sad. Is she running from something?* Hilda felt she could hear God say *Yes, love her.* She knew it would mean spending time in loving prayer and patient ministry. *Help me to be patient with her, and help her find you.*

Hilda then prayed for Vicar Todd, for all the people she knew at church, and finally for all the villagers who didn't yet know Jesus as their Savior and Lord. "Amen," she said firmly, then rose to make some lunch.

CHAPTER 3

Vicar Todd

Vicar David Todd sat amid the mess of his study. He liked everything his housekeeper, Mrs. Philips, did—including the crisply starched linen tablecloths and the flowers she placed in vases in the kitchen and beside his bed. But his study was off limits. It was the only room he wouldn't let her touch—no, not with a barge pole.

Here, all was his and his alone. In grander days, the room had been a dining room. Vicar Todd always ate in the kitchen, so he had turned this large room with its French windows and high ceilings into his study—the place he retreated to read God's Word and fashion it into a message for his parishioners. His sermon for Sunday, "My Sheep Know My Voice," was finished. He marveled that after nearly fifty years he could still find something new to share with his flock. He always prayed before preparing his thoughts and found that God spoke anew through His Word every week, giving him something refreshing or sometimes something difficult to impart to his congregation. And the message always seemed to help the right people at the right time. That was God's doing, not his.

Vicar Todd turned his leather-buttoned swivel chair around to look away from his large paper-laden desk to view the garden. Hilda would arrive soon. He looked forward to her visits every day, especially the time they spent talking and praying over tea and . . . *cakes!*

Jumping to his feet, Vicar Todd rushed to the kitchen. He made cakes or cookies every day for tea when they finished gardening. Today he planned to make cupcakes with white icing and place a cherry on the top of each. He and Hilda would each need two, and he decided to make six more for the new family that had just moved into Dawn Cottage. He planned to visit them the following day. After setting out ten flowered paper cases, he made the batter with the help of his electric mixer, splattering his pale blue shirt and black worsted trousers as he did so. When he had placed the cakes in the oven, he quickly took a cloth to wipe the batter off his clothes and then began to wash the dishes. Vicar Todd loved to cook. He had taught himself after his wife, Betty, had died, and he was quite proud of his culinary achievements. *Betty would be so pleased to see what a good cook I've become.*

They had met while Vicar Todd was at theological college. He had spent five years of his life teaching in a grammar school but had never felt fulfilled in that vocation. He believed God was calling him into the ministry, and the certainty simply wouldn't go away. At the age of twenty-four, he left the schoolroom and went to college, where he met Betty, who was working as a secretary. They fell instantly for each other and, after two years, were married in a little church in Betty's home village, just outside Bude.

As Vicar Todd iced the little cakes and placed a cherry on the center of each one, he smiled at the memories of Betty. Her eyes had been a lovely pale blue, with blond lashes. Her blond hair had been very curly, hanging to her shoulders. Only after they had married did she wear it shorter. She was the daughter of a gentleman, and it showed—though her breeding meant nothing to her. Her innate sense of style was not forced or showy, but fashionable. He consid-

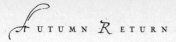

ered himself fortunate, because most vicars' wives were so dowdy in those days. Her confidence in God gave her an inner peace he relied on whenever their lives got hectic or they faced difficulties.

She had been so full of fun and was always busy planning adventurous things. Twice-yearly picnics were held for the parishioners, one on the beach in May and the other on the moors in September.

At the beach she was always the first into the water, splashing and swimming with the parish children in the rolling waves, no matter what the weather was like. She would take the younger children to the special pool that had been hewn from the rock many years before to make a safe place to swim when the tide was out. Oh, the creatures she had helped them find in the rock pools. They would play happily for hours with little homemade nets.

Then, there were the treasure hunts in the vicarage garden. Betty, Hilda, and Wilfred, who at the time was the head teacher of the Sunday school, would spend days planning these Sunday school adventures. They always managed to find little treats for the children to enjoy. He and Betty had wanted several children of their own, at least four. But none came, which brought them great sadness. So Betty focused all her love and attention on serving others.

Her concern for the poor touched Vicar Todd's heart. She often took huge pots of homemade soup to women whose husbands were out of work or sick. Every Christmas she somehow convinced wealthy people from her hometown to give boots to the poorer children of the village. It was all done discreetly, so no one would feel embarrassed in any way, just grateful for the provision. She was a listening ear, a baby-sitter, someone to do the shopping or cook a meal for the elderly. Her genuine love for God, and therefore concern for others, was a constant source of inspiration for him.

On dark and starry nights, she would place Strauss recordings on a wind-up gramophone and set it on the terrace outside the French doors. Then she would coax him into waltzing around the vicarage garden. He could still picture her floating across the lawn in a beautiful emerald silk gown with sequins sewn all over the bodice. Such wonderful fun she had brought into his rather dull life. To the end of his days, he would never understand why she had chosen him.

The memory of the tragic boat trip still brought tears to Vicar Todd's gray eyes. Betty had planned a day of fishing with two other women, friends from St. Ives, in an old borrowed motorboat. She had left early that fateful October day clothed in a heavy pair of flannel trousers, several sweaters, a navy woolen jacket, green Wellington boots, and a bobble hat of different colored stripes a village child had made to thank her for some kindness she had shown. Her fishing gear was in a sacking bag over her back. She had looked enormous, although she was, in fact, rather small. And as she kissed Vicar Todd's cheek, she had assured him her catch from the sea would provide a splendid feast that night.

He never saw her alive again. What had started out as such a beautiful, still—though cold—day suddenly turned treacherous, with winds raging from the north. Betty's two friends had died with her as the boat crashed on the rocks near Hayle. Three husbands mourned together. Three husbands picked up the pieces of their broken lives and went their separate ways. Vicar Todd had lost touch with them over the years.

The viewing of the body had broken his heart—the very sea she had loved so much had taken her so cruelly. In the midst of the pain of his loss, the realization hit him—he had no family, no parents or children to comfort him. He felt so alone. But he gave his sorrow to God. Then, as he sought God's presence more and more, very slowly a deeper love for his heavenly Father had overtaken him. His parishioners were also a great comfort. He never ceased to thank God for their love toward him. They were his family now. . . .

Vicar Todd placed the finished cakes into a tin with pansies on it and went back to the study for his black gown. Taking it from the hook on the back of the door, he threw it over his head with gusto. He rarely went out without it. It was a part of him. He was the

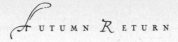

vicar—a role he loved. He ran his hands through his hair to brush it into place. It was thick and curly, and still quite brown, though streaked with gray. He was thankful it didn't take much looking after, just a trim once a month at the local barbers.

Entering the garden through the open French doors, Vicar Todd walked across the worn York stone patio toward Hilda. She was already perched precariously on a wooden ladder, reaching up with her secateurs to cut the withered blossoms off a large pink rosebush that had long since flowered.

"Hello, Hilda!"

"Hello, David," Hilda said without turning from her task.

"What a beautiful day." As he reached his friend, Vicar Todd steadied the ladder as she stepped down.

"Yes, a lovely *week*, actually. I didn't think we'd enjoy an Indian summer after such a dreadful August. The poor holidaymakers, with all that rain."

"Well, that's why we should thank the Lord we live here all the time. At least we can make hay while the sun shines!"

Vicar Todd took the ladder, folding it to more easily carry it farther up the garden. It was a huge site, mostly laid to lawn, with large shrubs and a rockery at the lower end along the tall Cornish rock wall. A cobblestone pathway wound its way around the perimeter of the garden among huge conifers and rhododendrons. Vicar Todd and Hilda made their way to the last rosebush in need of attention. It still had a few fragrant yellow blooms on it. Vicar Todd worked more slowly than Hilda, because he wasn't the expert she was—and she told him so with a laugh.

Vicar Todd enjoyed Hilda's company very much. He had almost asked her to marry him many times. He had first considered it about six months after Wil had drowned in Africa, not long after his own wife's death. It seemed strange that they had both drowned. He never dwelt on it, though.

At the time he thought it too soon after Betty's and Wil's deaths to ask her. Then he wondered what the bishop and his parishioners would think. When her mother became so ill and died, and her father passed away soon after, proposing to her just didn't seem right . . . and so it just never got done. As it was, they saw each other every day, but many were the times when he would have liked to kiss her cheek or give her a hug. *Silly old fellow. No sense wishing for that which never was and never will be.*

"Shall we have tea?" he asked as he carefully stepped from the ladder and folded it for the last time.

"I'm ready for it," Hilda said.

Reaching for her secateurs, Hilda took the lead back up the cobblestone path toward the kitchen door. She stepped into the welcoming room, and while the vicar put his ladder in the shed, she sat down in a comfy red velvet chair beside the Potterton gas boiler, which heated the entire vicarage and supplied Vicar Todd with plenty of hot water.

When Vicar Todd came in from the shed, he plugged in the electric kettle and placed a teapot, milk jug, and blue-and-white bone china cups and saucers on the table. He took four little cakes from the pansy tin and placed them onto two plates, handing one to Hilda.

"How delicious." She smiled up at him. Hilda loved Vicar Todd but never imagined he loved her. Otherwise he would have asked her to marry him. She supposed it was enough to see him every day. On Sundays he always came to her cottage after church, and they usually shared a roast of lamb or beef and enjoyed wonderful conversation. Yes, she was content with her lot, but sometimes she wondered what might have been.

"Who shall we pray for today?" Vicar Todd asked as he poured the tea. He stirred it and handed it to Hilda.

"The new neighbor, I think. I met her this morning. Her name is Lucy Summers."

"And what is she like?" Vicar Todd inquired, sitting back into his worn but comfortable chair.

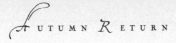
"Oh, nice. Yes, very nice. There's something amiss, though. I couldn't quite put my finger on it. There was sadness in her eyes." Hilda took another bite of the cake and wiped her mouth with the linen serviette, so stiffly starched by Mrs. Philips. "She lives alone."

"Lives alone? I thought we were to have a family there. Shame— we could do with more children in the village." Vicar Todd looked Hilda in the eyes. "A widow?"

"I really don't know. She's in such a muddle at the moment. She was trying to sort out the kitchen when I arrived. She's changed everything, you know."

"Modern times, my dear."

"I didn't notice any pictures or anything, so we'll have to be patient and wait to get to know her slowly. Anyway, we must pray for the sadness to depart from her."

"Of course. And how are the Trents?"

"They are all fine."

"I haven't had them over for tea in a while. Have the twins started school yet?"

"Yes. I saw Sue bundling the girls into the car this morning. They looked so sweet in their uniforms. I do love the little straw hats and blazers. They chatted to me through the window, but I can hardly understand a word they say. They always seem to talk over each other. I just smile at them and nod when it seems appropriate." She looked down into her half-full cup.

"It's a shame they have to go to Redruth for school these days," Vicar Todd said, interrupting her thoughts. "I suppose it had to happen. It was a sad day when the school closed."

"Oh, it was terrible. I cried!" Hilda didn't look up from her cup because she had colored up a little. The passing of the old ways was difficult for her to accept.

"Well," Hilda said, after a time of companionable silence, "perhaps we should pray."

Vicar Todd nodded, and they bowed their heads.

CHAPTER 4

St. Ives

On the day she moved into the cottage, Lucy had asked the removal men to put her green table and slatted wooden chairs on the cobblestone terrace outside the French doors of her sitting room. She was certain it would become a favorite spot of hers.

Now, as she enjoyed her lunch in the glorious noonday sun, Lucy knew she had made the right decision. The scent of grass and sea heightened her spirits. As she threw crumbs for the birds onto the freshly cut lawn, she began to feel strangely excited at the thought of her plans for the cottage. She had been preparing for this new season of her life for a long time.

All the construction work had been completed before she arrived. She had simply sent pictures and requirements to the builders through the estate agent. Everyone had been marvelous in carrying out her wishes for the changes she wanted. The kitchen was perfect. Most of the furniture was made from old timber—solid pine. Instead of being built in, it was free standing. Lucy liked this new idea, as she could move the pieces wherever she wished. The builders had seen to all the plumbing for the washing machine and sink, and had done a very good job of it. They had also done some tiling for her, splash backs and the like. Wrought-iron rods had been put up in every room for the curtains to hang upon.

Lucy had made the curtains herself. Back in London she had spent a day at Brent Cross Shopping City and found the exact cream muslin she required. Then, with great pains, she stenciled a border of eggshell blue ivy leaves along the edges. She braided some of the cloth together for tiebacks and was very pleased with the results. After carefully starching and ironing each piece, she placed lavender bags here and there among the folds and packed them in a sturdy box.

Now that she had finished the kitchen, Lucy planned to spend the afternoon arranging her bedroom and unpacking the rest of her cases and trunks. With that intent, Lucy rose quickly to her feet, disturbing the little birds. At first they flew off in all directions and finally ended in a flock, dipping and diving, up and over and around the bay. She smiled as she picked up the plate and glass and made for the kitchen.

"Thank goodness for the sunshine," she said into the fragrant air. Setting the dishes on the wooden kitchen drainer, Lucy placed a large slice of Hilda's cake on a plate and took it to her bedroom.

At one time she would have prayed for a person who had taken such pains to be thoughtful to her. That was then. She couldn't pray for anyone now. She had just given up. Many of her prayers had been answered over the years—but no more.

Shaking the thought from her head, Lucy climbed the little winding staircase that circled from the kitchen to the landing above. The cottage had four large bedrooms, all with magnificent views of the sea. It also had a small room suitable for a study, but she didn't know what she would do with it quite yet. So she had placed Tom's guitar and her computer in the corner and shut the door firmly, as

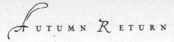

if to shut out the past. Everything was new. Everything had changed.

Eventually, Lucy planned to use one of the bedrooms as a sort of studio—the light was perfect for painting. She hadn't touched a brush since Tom died and had no inclination to do so yet. But one never knew . . . with views such as these to inspire her. She glanced through the window out onto the clear blue waters and the scudding, white-clouded sky. The black granite cliffs, with their dark velvet moss, yellow lichen, and tufted green grasses, were so tranquil today—breathtaking in their majesty.

Moving from the window and along the hall, Lucy entered the bedroom she had chosen for her own. In London her bedroom had been a place of refuge. As the boys were growing up, they had always brought friends home, so the house was often full of noise. It was happy noise, but Lucy needed peace and quiet, so she escaped to her bedroom. She liked to read, sew, and simply relax there. Though she knew her surroundings were very different here, she hoped her new room would have the same ambiance as her old one.

One thing was certain, the views from her new bedroom far surpassed those in London. One window faced inland and the other west, toward the sea. Their placement allowed her to view the sunrise or the sunset from her bedroom. Dawn Cottage was halfway up the hill, so she could see the sea and the cliffs, and Gull Island rose from the center of the harbor like a huge granite head. The sea was a deep turquoise today and devoid of boats—so peaceful.

Still unable to believe she was finally living in Tarran Bay, Lucy drew a deep breath and finished the last delicious crumbs of her cake. *Tom would have loved it here.* A pain drew itself across her heart. *Don't think of him. I must stop remembering.*

Placing the empty cake plate on her bedside table, she made for the box that held her linens. As she untied the string and opened the folded lid, the sweet scent of lavender filled her head, and there on the top of the pile of linen lay her beautiful muslin curtains, all ready to hang. She pulled them gently from the box, shaking them free of folds, and laid them on the bed. Placing large brass rings to the heading tape, she threaded the iron pole through the rings and hung them in place. Hooking the tiebacks to the wall, she gathered the curtains into soft folds. The salty sea breeze, scented with just a hint of heather, gently billowed the fabric into the room. Once she finished both windows, Lucy stood back to admire her handiwork. The look of the pale blue ivy leaves against the cream muslin was exactly what she had hoped for.

Turning back to the box, she pulled out her linens to make the bed. She had chosen a pale blue pinstripe, with blue piping trimming the pillow slips. Lucy sighed with delight. *It's perfect.* As she lay back on the wrought-iron bed she and Tom had purchased for their thirtieth wedding anniversary, Lucy decided she had just enough time for a bit of a read before supper. She propped herself up with many pillows. The bed was beautiful, but so uncomfortable when trying to read. She knew a padded headboard would be more practical, but she wouldn't consider getting rid of the bed.

As she read, her mind slipped delightfully sideways. Lucy found it increasingly difficult to stay focused and soon drifted off to sleep.

Sometime later, Lucy woke with a start to the shrill of the telephone from the hall below. Stumbling down the staircase, Lucy scrambled to get her thoughts together. As she picked up the receiver, she made a mental note that she needed to have a bedside phone connected.

"Hi, Mum. It's Luke. I thought I'd give you a few days before phoning. How are you settling in?"

"Luke, how lovely to hear your voice. I'm fine. Well . . . exhausted, really. I fell asleep after putting my curtains up and had to rush to the phone when you rang."

"I thought you sounded out of breath. So you've put those flimsy things up, have you?" Luke had laughter in his voice. "Everyone will see in!"

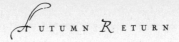

Lucy knew her son was playing with her. He had Tom's sweet sense of humor.

"No one can see in the second-story windows except, perhaps, a nosy seagull. I want the sunlight to filter through." She sat down on the chair beside the hall table. "How are Karen and my little Rose?"

"They're fine. Can't you hear them?"

Lucy could indeed hear mother and daughter laughing in the background.

"They're playing hide-and-seek." Luke paused. "Mum, thanks for the money. You really didn't have to do it."

"I know. I wanted to." Lucy didn't spoil her boys. They were both doing quite well financially. It was just nice to give them a gift occasionally. "What will you do with it?"

"We're going to buy a computer."

"Oh, Luke," she exclaimed, exasperated with her son. "Why buy a new one? I told you to take mine—or is it too out of date?"

"No, Mum. It's not. I just think you'll write again, that's all. I have always loved your stories."

"I'll never write again," she replied softly.

"Well, I beg to differ. You should try. Anyway, we are buying a computer, so you can do what you wish with yours."

"Well, I did tell you to do what you want with the money. I'm glad you found a good use for it."

"We did, and thanks again."

Lucy heard Luke take a deep breath before he proceeded.

"What are you going to do tomorrow, Mum?"

"If it's nice, I'm going to St. Ives." She knew why he had asked, but she didn't want to talk about it. Her feelings were too tender right now. She didn't know how to communicate what she was going through without sounding bitter. "Must go, darling. I still haven't unpacked my clothes."

"You'd better get on, then. Love you, Mum."

"Yes, I know. It's a great comfort to me. Thanks, Luke. Love to everyone."

Lucy replaced the receiver and went back upstairs to fetch the empty linen box. As she climbed the stairs, she felt a burst of motherly pride. Luke was such a good son. It was sweet of him to remember she might be feeling low. The next day would have been her and Tom's thirty-fifth wedding anniversary, and she so badly wanted him there to celebrate it with her. She hoped Luke understood that she appreciated his concern but wasn't ready to talk about her deep loss.

She made a chicken stir-fry for supper and enjoyed it while listening to a very interesting radio interview with a couple that was traveling in Indonesia. They were trekking through the deep jungle with two children under seven. Lucy thought that they must be mad. But the children were also interviewed and seemed to thrive on it. She smiled to herself, thinking that her boys would probably have loved it, too!

After supper she finally got around to unpacking her clothes, shoes, coats, and bags. It seemed to take forever to organize everything, but she was glad to finally have everything in order. It would be easier to decide what to wear now. As she considered her wardrobe, Lucy decided she really needed some new outfits. Most of her London wardrobe wasn't warm enough for the cold Cornish winters. She placed her shoes in racks underneath the clothes and realized that she also needed a pair of walking boots. Her sneakers would do for now. Finally, Lucy put her rose-covered hatboxes on top of the wardrobe and stood back to see how nice and orderly everything looked. At last everything was where it should be. Now she could truly rest. And after a hot soak in the bath, she went to bed early.

———

Lucy was up with the lark, or perhaps with the seagulls would be more accurate! Even before arriving in Tarran Bay, she had de-

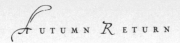

cided that if it was a nice day, she would go to St. Ives to reminisce about the good times. It would be difficult—but it had been thirty-five years! An hour later she decided it was going to be a beautiful day, so she prepared for her outing. She found her picnic basket in the garage box. She and Tom had bought it many years ago. It was old now, and a bit misshapen. But Tom had mended the handle with rope, and Lucy simply loved it. The basket had a little lid on the top, fastened with a leather thong. The inside was lined with green gingham. She sighed as fond memories of picnics with Tom came flooding back. Just as quickly as they had come, she busied herself with her preparations.

Since the day was already getting warm, she put a bottle of sparkling water and a bottle of elderflower cordial in the holders on the back of the basket. She bundled up a leg of chicken, a buttered nutty brown roll, a little container of salad, and a banana and put them in the basket along with two ice packs from the freezer. While unpacking the night before, Lucy had set her pink swimsuit and a large beach towel aside, and now she put them into her flowered backpack. She decided that she would pack her painting supplies, too—just in case. St. Ives had never failed to inspire her in the past. At the last minute, she remembered her royal blue changing robe and pushed that in, too. She was ready to be off.

Lucy knew from experience that to find a convenient place to park in St. Ives, you simply had to get there before nine. She was there early and quickly found a space in the car park near the train station, which nestled beside the cliff above the beach. Taking her things from the little boot of the Mini, Lucy walked down the hill past the artists' cottages. They were all painted white and had yellow, pink, and blue doors to brighten her route over the tiny cobblestone winding walkways to the beach. Among the rocks she found a sandy place made smooth and clean by the receding sea. Lucy took out a rush mat and laid it close to the smooth rocks so that she could rest against them to read.

She took out her changing robe. It was at least forty-five years old. Her mother had made it so she could change clothes even if a changing room was not available. She had used it on so many beaches, mostly the English coastline, but also Africa and Greece. As she slipped it over her head and slipped into her swimming costume, she could picture those beaches so clearly—such beautiful memories.

Because the sun wasn't hot enough for swimming yet, she decided to read for a while. She had chosen a lighthearted novel, which wasn't really her style, but she thought it might be nice for the beach. It was enjoyable, without making one think about issues. However, after a few minutes she felt restless. So she laid it down and decided to rest for a bit.

As always, when she closed her eyes her thoughts turned to Tom.

They had met through a Baptist youth group. Tom was two years older than Lucy, and they married at twenty-two and twenty. They were both Christians and prayed about absolutely everything—well, Tom did. Lucy generally just followed along.

After they had been married for four years, a visiting missionary, Ruth Lange, introduced them to the distress of the children in Mozambique. Ruth had started an orphanage in an area where most children lost one or both parents before the age of five. Tom and Lucy were certain God was directing them to minister to the needs of the war-ravaged country. They discussed it with their minister, Robert Hemmings, who suggested they take a year off. He said the church would support them while they helped Ruth in her work. They had no doubts about their decision.

Trained as a primary school teacher, Lucy easily fit into teaching responsibilities at the orphanage. Tom was an accountant, which proved to be useful to the mission. However, his compassion and his ability to make something from nothing became the greater assets. Plumbing, electrical—you name it, he could usually do it.

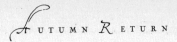

They hadn't been prepared—even though they had read every single article and letter Ruth sent them. They were shocked to see the devastation of incomprehensible poverty, compounded by the atrocities of a senseless civil war. It broke their hearts to see the sorrow in the eyes of the people, particularly the children.

Though they originally intended to stay for one year, it was closer to two when they left. They might have stayed forever, if only . . . Lucy wiped a tear from her cheek. When she realized she was pregnant, she felt overwhelmed—caught between two worlds, not knowing which way to turn. She felt sick and exhausted most of the time. The morning sickness dragged on into the afternoon of each day. It was so debilitating, she couldn't teach any longer. The heat became her enemy, and as she lay on her bed, she was tormented with thoughts of losing the baby. The hospital facilities were so primitive—unsanitary conditions, few instruments and supplies, and doctors who had such poor training it seemed they did more harm than good. She just couldn't risk losing this baby. She explained to Tom that she simply couldn't face having a baby there, or bringing it up in such deprivation. Tom thought differently. He felt that God would protect her and the baby, but she wasn't convinced. A sense of despondency enveloped her, and neither Tom nor Ruth could break through its hold to comfort her—nothing was ever the same again.

So Lucy returned home to give birth in comfort and kindness, cleanliness and love, leaving the war and her precious orphans behind. But Africa was never far from her dark, shadowy thoughts. She remembered the faces—yes, every single one—the beautiful teeth, the dark eyes so full of sorrow. She and Tom had made a difference—until Lucy had insisted they return home.

There probably would never have been a right time to have a baby if they had stayed in Africa. And she did want children, always had, ever since she was a young girl. She had tried so hard to stay, but there was war and things were so primitive there. Eventually,

49

she pushed it to the back of her mind and told herself she had handed it back to God. But, deep down, the guilty thoughts were always there. She had failed Tom—and God, too.

Then, miraculously, after years of self-doubt, it seemed Lucy was going to have the chance to make things right. Only a month or two before Tom died, he had told her he believed God was calling them back to Africa. The work would be different, he had said. God hadn't revealed His plan, only that they should prepare for the change. They prayed about it and left it with the Lord to show them the next stage.

Tom had never been wrong before. Why would God tell him to prepare for Africa and then take him from her? Tom had been just fifty-five when he was killed. It wasn't right! No longer able to bear the memories, she cried from her depths. *Oh, God, help me.*

The sun was getting hotter, so Lucy decided that it was time for a swim. With childish abandon, she ran toward the water and straight into its icy blue depths.

Lucy had always approached the sea in this manner, preferring to get the deed over quickly. Once in the icy, tingling water, she took some deep breaths and reveled in the wonderful sensation of water enclosing her body as her arms pushed up and outward through the foaming waves. How she loved this feeling of weightlessness. It exhilarated her. She swam the breaststroke for over half an hour, back and forth along the shoreline. The sea was so calm Lucy could see through the clear water to the seabed. Little fish swam in small shoals beneath her.

The swim refreshed her, but she was tired. She dried herself with her towel and lay down on one of the large rounded rocks that jutted up from the sand. It was so warmed by the hot sun, Lucy felt her body would melt right into it. Ripples of water ran down her flesh, rejuvenating her, strengthening her, and at last she was ready for lunch. As Lucy sat up she noticed the beach had few people on it. She could see a lone windsurfer out near the harbor coming around

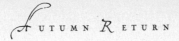

the rocks. Only a slight breeze stirred the air, but it was enough to help the small brightly colored craft on its way. She took out her feast and ate and drank slowly, enjoying each mouthful.

After she finished her late-afternoon lunch, Lucy felt a little chilled, so she put on her clothes. But she wasn't ready to leave yet, so she settled down again and contemplated the scene before her.

The water, bathed in the golden afternoon glow, was beautiful—she simply had to paint it. Out came her paints, brushes, water carrier, and paper. First she sketched the scene, then added the color wash, and finally painted in every detail. Lucy was thrilled with her work and relished the thought of enjoying this hobby once again. Would she put in the windsurfer? Maybe.

She painted for some time, trying to capture the wonderful golden hues, the mood of the shadows, and the reflections of the cliffs on the water. She loved the way the sea became a beautiful turquoise color above the deep, sandy seabed. It seemed the day would go on in peaceful silence forever, the other bathers long since gone. At last, as the sun set, the sea turned as red as a field of poppies. It was magnificent and so quiet except for the gentle lapping of the incoming tide, which had nearly reached her before she noticed and quickly gathered her belongings. She stood just a little way up from "her place," watching the waves as they removed all evidence of her day. It was done. It was her memory, and hers alone. It had been her place of solitude from beginning to end.

Lucy turned and strolled slowly up the beach, her toes sinking into the delightful softness of the warm white sand. She felt more content than she had in months. Her day hadn't been so bad. He was there, her dear Tom, wrapped up forever in her own sweet memories.

CHAPTER 5

Gordon Seymour

Gordon Seymour, Tarran Bay's only doctor, had lived and worked there for almost seven years. Normally he loved his place in life very much, having made some close friends through the church, but today he was anxious. He had received biopsy results that were not good, and he was going to have to tell Sue Trent, one of his closest friends, that she had cancer. At least Jack would be with her. It was at times like this that Gordon caught a glimpse of some of the blessings he gave up when he chose not to marry. Having a spouse to love you through the hard times had to make life easier to bear.

He put the thought to the back of his mind, jumped onto his red-and-blue Windsurfer, and sailed out, moving the sail to and fro in the gentle breeze. The wind carried his little craft from the beach to the harbor and around the head of St. Ives. Gordon loved to sail and windsurf, especially after a hard day in his surgery, and St. Ives harbor was a favorite sailing spot of his. After several hours he headed back. Only a handful of people were on the beach, but then it was never crowded in September when a normal pace of life returned to Cornwall.

Pausing to rest a moment, he saw a woman sitting close to the rocks painting. He couldn't see her face, but for some reason, he couldn't take his eyes from her. What he felt wasn't attraction—just curiosity. She looked serene and, at the same time, rather lonely. As he watched, she put down her belongings, tidied everything away and for a long time stood watching as the sea covered where she had been sitting. Only then did she make her way up the beach and into the car park, where she loaded her things into a little red Mini and headed toward the town.

Suddenly, Gordon realized the time. It was almost six o'clock. Sue and Jack were going to be at his surgery in thirty minutes! *I'll never make it.* He rushed to get back to the beach, and after packing his equipment and changing into a navy track suit, he whisked his old blue Morris Traveller homeward. Gordon arrived late for his first evening appointment. Tardiness was not at all like him. He was normally very prompt. Gordon seriously considered the possibility he was unconsciously avoiding the difficult news he had to deliver. A bit flustered, he headed into his surgery.

Mary, his young nurse, was normally very sweet and gentle. To-night, though, her expression told him he was very late, she was very cross with him, and no, he could not have a cup of tea—because she was just too busy! Gordon smiled apologetically and made for the little room that served as his surgery. What he had to do was not going to be easy. Sue was a wonderful woman, a dear friend. She had gone through a lot in the past few months, a round of coughs, summer colds, a bruised ankle, and two children with chicken pox. Gordon braced himself, for there was no easy way to break this kind of news.

When Gordon looked up in response to a soft knock at the door, he was surprised to see Sue standing all alone in the doorway.

"Sue. Where's Jack?"

She hesitated for a moment. "A huge crisis came up on a project

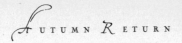

he is working on—so he had to go to Exeter. He thought he would be back, but he called an hour ago and said it would be later tonight." She sat down across the desk from Gordon. "He felt terrible, but I told him there was no reason to worry." She fiddled with the clasp on her handbag. "There isn't any, is there. . . ? Reason to worry, I mean."

Gordon stood up and moved around the desk to sit next to Sue. He hated this part of his job.

———

Later that evening, Gordon sat down on his sofa, thankful the deed was finally done. Sue had sat there pale, clutching her knees so hard that her knuckles turned white. She had put up a brave front, but Gordon knew she was shaken up. He answered every question— advising her what he would do if it were his decision. But in the end he told her to go and speak to Jack so they could decide together. He had offered to postpone his next appointment to walk her home, but she had refused. She needed air and time. He understood.

Gordon stood to place a large log on the fire he had kindled in the grate. With one hand, he took his mail from the black coffee table and picked up his coffee with the other. His room was sparse, just the bare essentials—a box-shaped sofa of thick navy corduroy, two matching chairs, a table, and a TV in a cabinet. A large rug lay over the rush matting that covered the entire cottage. Bright modern paintings hung on every wall. Gordon had acquired quite a collection, mostly from galleries in St. Ives. His friend Mark owned a gallery, and he'd shown Gordon what to look for in a good painting. Returning to the sofa, Gordon sipped his black coffee and began to sort through the mail.

Yes, there was the one he had waited all day to open. It was airmail from Kenya—a letter from his sister Jane. He put the scalding drink onto the table and opened the blue envelope.

Dear Gordon,

Hi, Janey here! How are you? We all hope you're well and happy back there in Cornwall. When are you going to come and visit? Why do you leave it so long to write back? Naughty boy!

He knew she was joking. She was always joking and asking endless questions, which he always forgot when he wrote back, so they never were answered. Gordon chuckled. He imagined his forgetfulness was a great source of frustration for her. But she was right—he should try harder. Jane had been a surprise baby, born when Gordon was already a teenager. Most of what he knew of her as an adult came about through letters. He knew it was important to stay in touch.

Mum and Dad are fine. I'm watching them as I write from my garden. Their garden backs onto ours—couldn't be more perfect, could it? I think Dad really misses the hospital. Mum still goes in three times a week. I'm so glad they finally bought the bungalow. I never thought they'd go for it. It's so much better having them where I can keep my eye on them.

Gordon's parents had gone to Kenya about twenty-five years before, just as he was finishing up at the University. Gordon's father was a surgeon, and his mother a nurse. They felt God needed them there—so they went along with Jane, who was only a child at the time. Their church back home, along with periodic payments from grateful patients, was their only means of support. They built a hospital from nothing. While living very simply, they spent all they had on the building and maintenance of the hospital. Their work made a huge impact on the country, and the people of Kenya loved them for their selfless dedication.

Jane came to think of Kenya as home. She met Harry, a handsome black pastor, there and married him. They had two boys. John was now ten, and Mark was seven. Gordon loved the little letters that often accompanied their mother's, and the beautiful, childish

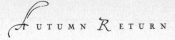

paintings—animals and the gorgeous scenery of their homeland. He had many of them framed and hung them on the waiting room walls to cheer his patients.

He had been to Kenya several times to visit, but not for many years. The lads had been very young on his last visit. He had helped in the hospital and loved it. But it didn't seem to be the right place for him to settle. Deep down, he knew this must have broken his parents' hearts. Though they had only hinted at it a few times, he was certain they were disappointed when he did not join them in their work. His choice to set up practice in England probably seemed selfish to them. He never could explain why, but he was certain it was where God wanted him.

> *Gordon, please come soon! Think about it for springtime. Come and see the new baby! There, that got your attention. Can you imagine—at my age? It's due at the end of April, and we're all very excited. I'm hoping for a girl this time.*
>
> *Well, must dash, as Harry will be home any minute now and wanting his dinner. The boys send their love and kisses. Oh, please come.*
>
> *Love you,*
Janey and Co
XXXXX

Gordon reread the letter several times. It wasn't one of her epics. Maybe he would go in the spring. It might be just what the doctor should order for himself. He put the flimsy blue airmail paper onto the table and switched on the television.

But before he even noticed what was on, his mind wandered back. His parents had sacrificed a great deal for him to go to the university, and he knew they wanted him in Africa when he had finished his schooling. He had let them down. He had been selfish. And worse than that he had been foolish. He had walked away from God and made some big mistakes during his time at the university, and he was still paying for them. No—he wouldn't dwell on the past. The future was important, and his future was in Tarran Bay.

He stood, switched off the unwatched television, and went to make some toast. But he couldn't get his sister's invitation out of his mind. It would be good to see the family again. The boys would have changed so much—and a new baby! Maybe he should visit. Perhaps he could be of more use in Africa.

He loved his life and knew he would find it difficult to leave this special community of people who had taken him into the very fabric of their lives. He was as much a part of Tarran Bay as those who had lived there since birth. He owned a fifteen-foot motorized fishing boat and went out in it whenever he could, catching fish for himself and his friends. He also had the use of Mark's small sailing boat, and in the springtime he would take himself off to Jersey for two weeks, enjoying the solitude after so much work with people. Yes, it would be very hard to leave. But was that an acceptable reason for deciding to stay?

Gordon finally took a shower and went to bed. He was reading a book about a missionary doctor in Ethiopia, which led him to think about his parents once again. Had he made the right decision to stay in England? He had often struggled with this question. The call to missions was an honorable one, but God needed His people in their own hometowns, not just abroad. He was the only doctor in the village, and the people really needed him. He thought again of Sue and what she would have to go through in the next few weeks. She and Jack and the girls needed him now, and that was just one family in his care. Gordon placed the book on the bedside cabinet, looked up at the low-beamed ceiling, and prayed.

Father God, thank you for your love to me. How can I ever repay you? Thank you for being there when I needed your grace and wisdom with Sue. Give her the strength to cope with whatever is necessary. Please help her and Jack at this time. Bless the girls, Lord. Find some-

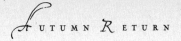

one who can help with the twins—someone who they will enjoy being with. Oh yes, and, Lord, please show me whether Kenya is for me. I just want what you want. Thank you, Lord. Amen.

He switched off the light, but sleep eluded him for some time.

CHAPTER 6

The Caller

As Lucy drove through her gates, her car's headlights shone against a man in a black robe. The sight made her shiver, and her mind raced. Though frightened at first, within seconds she realized who it was. *Oh no, the vicar.*

The man turned toward the light, and as the little car came to a halt on the driveway, he moved to open the car door for Lucy.

"Thank you," she said politely, thinking *Why me? Why now? And for goodness sake, what for?* Once more she had to find the nice inner person—the person she wished she was, not this frightened, miserable wretch she knew was the real her lately—and root her out to the surface. She took her belongings from the boot of the car and invited the vicar in. The vicar insisted on carrying her basket and followed her to the kitchen, where he gave her a pansy tin gift.

"I thought I would come and introduce myself," he said as he made for the comfort of her granddad chair—un-invited. "My name is David Todd. I am the vicar of St. Luke's—the church at the bottom of your lane." He looked around her kitchen thoughtfully. "I like your changes."

Lucy turned to smile at him and shook his hand. "My name is Lucy Summers. I'm pleased to meet you. I only changed the kitchen and asked the painters to paint all the walls white. I couldn't make up my mind what colors to choose. I'm afraid I found all that brown rather gloomy."

"Yes, indeed. I don't think old Parsons had a clue about decorating. Loved his garden, though. You've inherited a gem there. Lovely view!"

Lucy agreed with the vicar but didn't say anything. She had indeed inherited a beautiful sanctuary, but perhaps it wasn't going to be the place of solitude she was expecting. *Is it common practice for these people to drop in unannounced? If so, I won't get a moment of peace.* Her heart began to sink.

"I visited Mr. Parsons today. He's very ill. I think he knows it won't be long for him now. It's so sad. He just never really recovered after his dear wife passed away."

Lucy placed the kettle on top of the Aga. *So many go through the loss of a loved one,* she thought sadly. She knew grieving was part of life, and her heart went out to the old man. She turned to empty her picnic basket onto the drainer. The vicar seemed to sense her unease and changed the subject.

"Had a picnic I see. Lovely day for it. Most unusual to have such nice weather for so long."

"Yes, it's been a nice start to my new life here. I went into St. Ives today. It has fond memories for me." She placed the tin he had given her onto the table and opened the pansy lid.

"Oh, how lovely. Cherry cupcakes!"

"I made them myself," the vicar said proudly. "I love cooking. Do you?"

Lucy smiled at the old man. He had a wholesome, friendly face and didn't seem to be prying.

"Do you want the truth?"

He nodded. "Of course!"

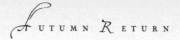

"I think I am a good cook, but I hate cooking. Do you understand?"

"Yes, I do. Betty was like that. Betty was my dear departed wife. She was so good at everything else. She did teach me a little, but I've taught myself since she died . . . I had to!"

Lucy put out the teapot, pottery mugs, milk jug, and sugar bowl, then poured the tea. She took two plates from the dresser and placed a cake onto each of them.

The vicar glanced at her old brass-rimmed school clock that hung above the mantel. "I'm sorry to be calling so late. I stopped by earlier, but you were out. When did you get into town?"

"A week ago. I stayed at Mrs. Bryant's Bed-and-Breakfast."

"Mrs. Bryant runs a very good bed-and-breakfast. She and her husband are valued members of our church. She's very popular with the holidaymakers, too. I think it's the extra sausage she gives them for their breakfast!"

Lucy smiled. Mr. and Mrs. Bryant had been extremely kind to her. They had invited her to church, but she wouldn't commit herself.

"I hate sausages!" she said at last with a smile at the kindly old man.

"I've never met anyone who didn't like sausages before."

"There's a first time for everything!"

An awkward pause followed in the conversation, and Lucy hoped the vicar would decide to head home.

But instead he went on to a new subject. "So, did your move go smoothly?"

"It went very well—once I was able to get into the cottage. I expected to get the key the day after I arrived, but the builders hadn't finished the work. And do you know—they wouldn't let me into my own house until it was completely finished! They said they wanted to surprise me—didn't want me to see the mess. I spent the time getting reacquainted with Tarran Bay. I suppose the walking did me good! I didn't even have time to look around my own cottage before the removal men arrived. But they were very quick about it, did a fine job."

They talked about nothing of consequence for quite some time, and Lucy really wished the vicar would leave so she could wash the salt from her weary body and sit down for a good read.

"Have you met Hilda yet?"

He wasn't going to give up so soon.

"Yes, my first full day here. She brought me a cake, too. I shall get very fat if this continues! She is very kind."

"Yes, a fine woman." He paused, as if he were pondering something. "Well, I hope you'll be very happy here." The vicar stood and patted Lucy's back gently. "It's getting late, and I must be going."

Lucy stood from the table to see her visitor to the front door. "Thank you . . . thank you for your thoughtfulness—the cakes and everything. It was kind of you, and they were delicious."

After the vicar left, Lucy tidied away, not wanting any supper. The little cakes had filled her up. The vicar had forgotten his tin, and on the table next to it lay some pamphlets. She looked through them. They were all about St. Luke's. First the Bryants, and now the vicar. Lucy absolutely was not ready for church yet. She supposed it was his job, though. At least he didn't ask endless questions about where she stood on the religious front. The truth was that Lucy simply didn't know anymore.

She had been brought up in a beautiful suburb of London. Fields and woods lay in one direction and the town in another, all in walking distance. Her mother and father were wonderful Christians. They went to church regularly, gave of their time, and invited waifs and strays for dinners. Their home was always full.

Lucy had believed in God ever since she could remember. When she was thirteen her father had asked if she was ready to give her life to Jesus, and she said yes because she truly loved God and wanted

to go to heaven. She was baptized, but little seemed to develop in her personal relationship with God. She just continued to follow her parents' lead—going to church, getting involved.

When she met Tom, she continued going to church, getting involved. She remembered the Bible study group he led. She had loved to hear him quote the Bible. He had the ability to define and clarify theology concepts in such a way that they became easy to understand and practical. Yet there was something about his relationship with God she just couldn't grasp. He tried to explain it so many times, and she truly wanted the same closeness for herself, but it never came. She did everything right. She struggled to be a "good" Christian. She could sing and pray, listen and care, and open her home to lonely, and often difficult, people. She had even written songs—and meant them. But something was missing—she knew it with all her heart. And when Tom died, everything washed out from under her, and Lucy had no idea how to adjust to facing life on her own.

As she lay in the bath, she wondered if the vicar knew Jesus as Tom had. He seemed to. The phone rang, interrupting her thoughts, for which she was grateful. She climbed carefully from the bath, grabbed a towel, and ran down the stairs.

"Hello, Mum."

Lucy was pleased to hear her younger son Dan's voice. She wrapped the green bath towel tightly around herself and sat on the chair beside the table with her wet hair dripping around her shoulders. She patted it dry with the corner of the towel.

"Oh, Dan, how lovely of you to phone. How is everyone?"

"They're fine and send their love. Have you settled in? What's the weather like?"

"Danny, you're obsessed with the weather. It's been lovely. I went to St. Ives today. You remember, the place by the rocks where we built that huge sand castle for your Lego dragons to live in?"

"Yes, Mum." Of course he remembered.

She knew he loved Cornwall, loved the memories of his holidays there. He just didn't think it would work for her to live there for the rest of her life. Lucy understood his concern, but she would prove him wrong—she would prove them all wrong.

"Mum, thank you for the money. We really needed it. The car's done in, so we're going to buy a newer one. The money will really help."

"Oh, it's my pleasure. I've got enough now. Never be afraid to ask if you get stuck. I'll always be here. It'll be yours one day anyway. You may as well let me see you enjoy it."

"Mum, you will need it. What if you want to come home?"

There he went again. Dear Danny.

"Darling, this is my home now. Come and see it at Christmas. I'm sure you'll be pleasantly surprised."

He finally submitted. "Okay, Mum. We want to come for Christmas. But it seems months away."

Lucy answered enthusiastically that the time would fly.

Jack and Sue Trent

Sue Trent was in shock as she left Gordon's surgery. It was a pitch-black night, and it would have been difficult to make her way even without the tears. How could this be? Sue could not grasp the reality of Gordon's news. She hadn't considered the seriousness of the lump. She had been so convinced in her heart that it was just a benign cyst.

I was so sure everything would be okay. When she found the small lump, Sue had felt a moment of fear. But after the biopsy, she convinced herself she had nothing to worry over. Though she wasn't terrified, she was relieved when Jack insisted he accompany her to her appointment with Gordon. But business had called him away and kept him away. She knew it wasn't his fault. He would have canceled the Exeter trip if he could have foreseen he would be late— or that the news would be so bad. She hadn't realized how much she needed him until now.

A mastectomy! Sue hadn't even considered that it might come to this. *Oh, Jack, what will we do?* She wrapped her padded coat around her like a quilt for comfort. Her mind began to race every which way. What would Jack say? How would he cope with the children, if. . . ? "Oh, God—please help me." The cry was from the bottom of her heart, but she did not feel the peace she sought. She couldn't go home yet, not to an empty house. She'd dropped the girls off with her friend Sarah, who'd said she wasn't to worry and that she would have them until Sue or Jack was ready to pick them up. Almost subconsciously, Sue made her way to the vicarage. She had to tell someone. . . . Picking up the twins would have to wait a little longer.

When Vicar Todd answered her knock at the door, Sue could tell he was surprised to see her on his doorstep.

"Sue, how lovely to see you . . ." He trailed off as she stepped into the light of the hall.

She was sure she looked a sight, and he could probably tell she had been crying.

"Are you all right?"

Sue shook her head but couldn't get the words out.

"Is it Jack or the girls?"

Again, Sue shook her head, but she could only stare at the vicar, her eyes welling up with tears.

"Well, let's sit down. And you tell me when you're ready to talk."

Vicar Todd led Sue into the sitting room and motioned for her to sit in the chair by the roaring fire. Then he sat across from her, waiting for her to speak. Sue looked about her. A rolltop bureau, which was open and full to the brim with the vicar's papers, had a small chair in front of it. Sue could tell she had disturbed him from his accounts. *I must be quick with this. Vicar Todd is a busy man.* But try as she might, the words would not come—only the tears.

She sat taut as a wire on the edge of her chair staring into the fire. She couldn't bring herself to look into the vicar's eyes. Why couldn't she speak? Why was it so hard to put what her heart was feeling into words? She knew she could tell him anything. It wasn't the first time Sue had sat in this room asking for help. Having tried

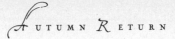

to get pregnant for five years to no avail, she had finally gone to the vicar in desperation. They had prayed together, and within two months she had come to him with the exciting news of her pregnancy—and later they rejoiced when the Trents found out twins were on the way. Yes, Vicar Todd's prayers were full of power. But *this* was too hard for her to talk about! How could she even say the word *cancer*?

Finally, the vicar cleared his throat.

"What is it, Sue?" he asked gently.

Sue blinked away a few tears.

"I've got . . . cancer," she whispered.

Vicar Todd leaned forward in his chair, took off the brass-rimmed glasses he used for reading, and rubbed his eyes with his free hand. "Cancer? Where? When did you hear?"

"Just a little while ago. I had some tests—a biopsy. It's in my breast." She paused, bowing her head and beginning to cry once more. It was so hard to continue. It seemed impossible to say the words. But it helped when she looked into her vicar's kind eyes. "The doctors are concerned it may be spreading quickly, and they want to remove it immediately—next Thursday!" *How could this be happening? It all seems so unreal.* "I could go with surgery to only remove the cancer, but Gordon believes I need to have a mastectomy. I don't know what to do—it's my *breast*!"

A part of Sue was shocked she was discussing such personal things with her vicar, but she really didn't care.

"So where is Jack? Does he know?"

"Well, he knows about the lump, but not that it's cancer. I was so convinced it was benign. I suppose I should have taken it more seriously, but I thought it would be routine. Jack planned to come with me to meet with Gordon, but a meeting in Exeter went much longer than he expected. If I'd thought for a minute it would turn out like this, I wouldn't have let him go. . . . I don't know how to tell him. I can't believe this is happening to me. . . . I'm in no pain."

69

At last she sat back, allowing the comfort of the chair to ease her tense body. She pulled a feather cushion around and under her arm. Vicar Todd found her a cotton hanky from the bureau drawer and patted her shoulder as he gave it to her.

"I would trust Gordon's judgment on this, Sue. He is a marvelous doctor, and he knows what would be best in these situations."

"I know. He has been wonderful to me. When he told me about the cancer, we *both* ended up in tears! He's like a brother to me and Jack." She blew her nose and started to cry again.

"Would you like a cup of tea?"

"Oh yes, please. If it's not too much trouble."

"No trouble," he called over his shoulder, already halfway out of the room. Suddenly, he felt very tired. Vicar Todd had been to see old Mr. Parsons in the morning. It broke his heart to see how thin and weak the poor old chap was. Probably well aware of his failing health, Mr. Parsons had asked him to sort out some legal documents concerning his estate. Vicar Todd had been busy going over the papers when Sue arrived. He never liked packing too much into a day and was beginning to regret his visit to Lucy. It could have waited, but how could he have known what the evening would bring?

In the privacy of the kitchen, while waiting for the kettle to boil, Todd did what he was best at in times such as these. He prayed. *Father, I don't know what to do. Please help me to be a comfort to Sue. Give me sound advice for her, and give her peace.*

While the vicar was in the kitchen, Sue was quietly thinking about her situation. How would Jack react? Would he still find her attractive if she decided to have her breast removed? Would she die? The twins were only five. How on earth was she to cope without them being anxious?

Needing a bit of relief from her thoughts, Sue looked up at the

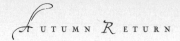

crowded oak mantel. In the center, a picture of Betty she'd seen so often but never *really* noticed before caught her eye. Betty had been so beautiful—she looked like a starlet of the thirties in the picture. Sue had never asked Todd much about his wife. She just knew she had died too young. *Will I die? Am I ready, Lord?*

Sue lifted her hand to her left breast and then released it quickly as the vicar returned with a tray. He placed it on the little oak occasional table, then picked up the whole caboodle and set it beside her. He poured the tea, stirred it, and handed her the mug. As she cupped the mug, a sort of comfort began to spread through her. Though she had a long way to go, Sue knew that God, good friends, and her family would get her through this crisis.

"I think I am going to have the operation, Vicar—if it's necessary. I need to speak to Jack first, though. And there's always the possibility that God might heal me." She looked at Vicar Todd in hopeful expectation. "If not, He can help me through whatever may come. But would you pray with me?"

Vicar Todd smiled, stood beside her, and placed his hands gently on her bowed head.

"Loving heavenly Father, we come to you with this problem because we know that you alone have the answer. I ask you to heal Sue, in the name of Jesus. And now, Lord, I ask that you fill Sue with your precious peace. Give her the strength to tell Jack, and help him to be a great support to her at this time. Amen."

"Thank you. You helped me so much. I couldn't go home to an empty house. I needed to talk to someone. I feel a little better now." Her immediate need was taken care of, and now her thoughts turned to Betty. "Vicar, would you tell me about Betty? I've never asked. I can't think why."

Vicar Todd sat down again and looked up at the picture of his lovely wife on the mantel.

"She was wonderful, Sue—absolutely wonderful. I have to admit I never understood God's timing on that. . . . Like you now. I have to accept these trials that life brings to be mysterious, and I have to leave them in God's hands. I suppose I did wonder, once or twice"—he smiled as if to indicate it was actually many more times—"why I couldn't have had her with me a little longer."

Vicar Todd went on to explain what a wonderful woman Betty was, and how the tragedy had happened. He told her everything. And when he was finished, he thanked her for asking. Sue was surprised he would thank her, and he seemed to notice her reaction.

"Not many people ask me about how I feel. The truth is, folks usually come to see me when they are in need. I appreciated the chance to talk about my life for a moment." He hastened to assure her he was glad she came to see him with her concerns. Ministering to others was his calling, and he loved it. "I hope what I've shared helps you see that I do understand a little of what you are going through."

"I had no idea," Sue said at last. "It must have been terrible for you, Vicar. I'm so sorry. Thanks for telling me about Betty."

"My pleasure, my dear. I love to talk about her. She lives on in my old heart!"

"And I will remember how much it helps when others ask how *you* are doing."

"Thank you, Sue. But don't you worry about me. You just take care of yourself—and your family. Don't forget, I have Hilda. And we'll be there for you, any way you need us."

"Of course. Thank you." Sue rose quickly. "I need to get going. I want to be settled when Jack gets home." She needed to pick up the girls, too, but she decided to go home first and wash her face. She thought she must look a terrible mess by now and didn't want the children worried in any way. "I do appreciate you, Vicar."

"I know you do, my dear, and I am grateful for that."

Vicar Todd insisted on walking Sue home, holding her arm all the way to her cottage on the harbor. The clouds had rolled onward

and the moon was shining brightly on the sea. It made a silver shaft of light that reached the beach. *A roadway to heaven*, he thought. More and more, Vicar Todd found himself looking forward to meeting his Maker. He and Sue watched the scene for some time before walking on. As they walked slowly up the quayside, he was keenly aware of the familiar sound of the waves crashing with vengeance against the harbor wall. When they reached the Trents' cottage, he opened the gate and kissed Sue's cheek.

"Would you like me to go in with you?"

"No, I'm okay. But you can pray. And thank you, Vicar."

"My pleasure, Sue."

As he walked slowly home, Vicar Todd pondered how the community could help the Trents. Perhaps with cooking, or someone to look after the girls. If only Betty were here. She would know exactly what to do. His heart felt uncharacteristically heavy as he turned from the cottages that made up the harbor enclosure. The lights from inside them and from the well-lit pub didn't serve to cheer him as they usually did on his way homeward. His empty home seemed so unwelcoming at times such as these.

Not quite ready to return to the solitude, he decided to call on Hilda. It was a bit late, but he doubted she would have already retired for the night. He made his way slowly across the beach, hands deep inside his trouser pockets, scrunching pebbles beneath his boots. Around the bay he went and through the cleft in the cliffs—dark, mysterious, shadowy. He was not afraid of the dark. Although he was feeling a bit melancholy, he knew God was there to protect him. His heart warmed a little at the thought of being with his friend.

Hilda was obviously surprised to see him at such an hour. She seemed a little uncertain it was him as she peered slowly around the door.

"It's only me, Hilda. I need a chat. Is it too late for you, dear?"

73

"I wondered who would call so late! What on earth is wrong? You look terrible!"

"I feel terrible," he answered truthfully as he entered the warmth of the hallway and followed Hilda to her tiny sitting room.

"Sit down, and I'll make us some hot chocolate. Then you can tell me all about it."

Vicar Todd sat beside the fire and propped his feet up on an ottoman. He would never do such a thing anywhere else—he was the vicar. But, somehow, Hilda's cottage felt like his second home. Beside the fire, the only light in the room came from a lamp with a pink silk shade. It stood behind Hilda's favorite chair. Her book was open on the side table, and her glasses sat neatly on top of it.

He called to Hilda through the open door. "Shall I put some more coal on the fire?"

"Yes, bank it up for the night, please?" The fire kept the water hot and the house warm, so at this time of year Hilda left it burning in the grate at all times. She entered the room with two steaming mugs, one of which she gave to the vicar.

"Thank you, Hilda."

"My pleasure. And thanks for tending to the fire, David." Hilda sat forward in her chair. "Now, tell me. What's troubling you tonight?"

"Sue just called on me. I was surprised to see her so late—and alone. She looked dreadful, Hilda, and I could see she had been crying." He found it difficult to say the words. "She told me she has breast cancer."

"Oh my, no! Not Sue."

Hilda felt the tears prick at the corners of her eyes. She swallowed and took a hanky from her cardigan pocket.

"What will she do?"

"I don't know. I told her to talk to Jack, to tell him all her worries and fears. Unless the Lord heals her, I believe she will decide to have a mastectomy."

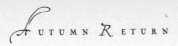

"Oh, dear God, no." Hilda's hand touched her cheek in shock. "I don't understand it. Why does God allow these tragedies to happen, and to such wonderful people?"

"It's the age-old question, isn't it Hilda—the one we all ask God more than once in a lifetime. I don't think these trials always come from God. All I know is that He promises to turn every difficulty His loved ones face into something good."

"Yes," sighed Hilda. "I always struggle with my faith at this point, and then God does some miracle or other, and I wonder why I ever worried."

One of their silences fell heavily between them. Vicar Todd watched Hilda as she sipped her drink. He noticed the furrow between her eyes. He had seen it there many times when they were working through a difficult situation. He rubbed his own drawn forehead with the back of his hand as she looked up at him.

"What did Gordon say she must do?"

"He said she should have the operation as soon as possible. I think she said next Thursday. She was so afraid—it nearly broke my heart."

"How will she cope with the twins? They are so lively—they need their mother." The anguish in her heart was evident.

Vicar Todd leaned toward her. "Don't jump the gun, my dear. She isn't dead yet!"

"I'm sorry, David. My mind races. I just get angry sometimes. I mean, look at us. We've had our lives. Why doesn't God take us and let her live?"

"You and I both know God isn't bound to work the way we expect. I am wondering what He will teach us all from this experience. What you and I have to do is think how we can help the Trents through this difficult patch. Betty was so good at ministering to others in need. I'm afraid I need your help, Hilda. What can we do that's practical?"

"Well, I don't mind having the twins, but they are a bit of a handful."

"Then we must share them. We could have them over for tea, take them to the park—that sort of thing."

"Yes, I think we could cope between us. The Sunday school team might have some materials for us to keep them occupied."

"Like what?"

"Paper, crayons, books—plenty to keep them busy for a while."

"Oh yes. I see. I have lots of old games at the vicarage. We could play with them, too. It might be fun for us."

"Yes, it might. I do love their antics."

Out of the blue Hilda asked her friend, "Do you miss Betty, David?"

Vicar Todd was a bit surprised by her question—two questions of the same sort in one night—but he was glad to speak of Betty anytime.

"It's not so hard as the years go by, but I have always felt that a part of me died when she went home. She was such fun to be with. I never expected to marry. It was such a wonderful surprise—that someone like her would love an old fool like me. I loved her so much, and then she was gone."

"Were you angry?"

"Who with?"

Hilda smiled. "You know I meant God, but you never seem to get angry with Him like I do!"

"I question His ways; that's the difference. I don't always agree with Him, but He is always right. I put my trust in that, and it helps me through the day."

"I was so angry when He took Wil away from me. I just couldn't see any rhyme or reason for it. A total waste—my love gone forever! I knew I would be alone for the rest of my life when he died. I just knew, and I felt cheated."

"I do understand." Vicar Todd rested back into the chair. "You

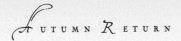

forgave God in the end, though, didn't you?"

"Yes—I love Him. He forgave me so much. It took time, though!"

Vicar Todd finished his drink. Hilda was feisty. That's what he liked about her. She had spirit, and didn't beat about the bush when she wanted to say something. She was honest—the most honest woman, apart from Betty, he'd ever met. He swept his hair back from his forehead with his hand and leaned forward to place the mug on a tray. "I think we should pray now, Hilda. Let's ask God what to do!"

They bent their heads, and Vicar Todd prayed first.

"Loving Father, we come to you to ask what to do for Sue, Jack, and the girls. We need your guidance and grace. We pray for ideas, Lord. We also ask you to give grace and peace to Jack and Sue during this difficult time. We ask that you would be a great comfort to them. We trust you for them, Lord. Amen."

Hilda softly cleared her throat. "Dear Lord, please look after the twins. Help us to look after them when their mummy is in hospital or needs a break. We want to do your will, Lord. Do shine your light on the path. Amen."

They slowly opened their eyes and looked up at each other.

"I nearly forgot to tell you, Hilda. I went to visit old Parsons this morning. He's very frail now and asked for my help getting his papers into some sort of order."

"He didn't cope very well after Florence died."

They looked at each other in silence. Vicar Todd knew they both understood how hard it was to carry on after a loved one dies. At last he took the tray of mugs to the kitchen and placed it on the sink drainer. He turned, kissed his friend on the forehead, and said he would see himself out.

As he left Hilda's home, Vicar Todd realized he hadn't told Hilda about his meeting with Lucy. He prayed for the sad woman, glad he'd made the effort to meet her, in spite of his busy day—and night. He hoped Hilda would sleep well. He thanked God for her. Somehow she replaced almost all he had lost when Betty died, and he really couldn't bear the thought of losing her. He should have told her—told her that he loved her so much. Perhaps one day he would find the courage.

Wearily, Hilda took to the tiny winding staircase and made for her bathroom. After washing she got into her nightgown and made her way down the landing to the bedroom. Before switching on the light, she went to view the bay. She always enjoyed this time of the day. The moon was now small and high in the sky, and clouds gathered on the horizon. Many bright stars sparkled in the heavens tonight, and she watched in wonder at her Father's creation. At last she put on the light, sat at her dressing table, and took out the few hairpins that held her bun in place. Her soft, silver-white hair fell softly down her back, and she began to brush it in long, even strokes, as she had done since she was a child. Looking in the mirror, she imagined herself young again. She thought about how she would feel if she were in Sue's situation—about to lose her breast. She shuddered. What a terrible trial to face. And what if she died?

Hilda wondered again why God didn't take her instead. "Lord," she began to pray, "take me, not Sue. I've had my life. The twins and Jack need Sue. Please, let her live."

Hilda knew in her heart of hearts that to try to manipulate God was terrible. But she also believed He knew her heart, and she may as well verbalize what was inside. At last she laid down the silver-backed brush her mother had given her on her twenty-first birthday and got into bed. As her head rested at last on the pillow and her eyes closed, she remembered a precious memory she hadn't thought of in years.

Wil had taken her for a picnic just before he left for war. They had taken a basket of food covered with a red-and-white checked cloth to the top field of Wil's father's farm. The wheat was ripe and ready for harvesting, and it gleamed in the sun like a mirror of gold. He took her to the middle of the field where he knew they would have complete privacy and a wonderful view of the sea. The wheat was just above Hilda's knees. She held out her hands and stroked the soft spiky heads of the waving harvest with her fingers like a comb until they reached the spot Wil had selected. He trampled down some of the wheat and spread a navy blanket on the ground for them to sit on.

Hilda unpacked the large willow basket that her father had made for her mother, and they began to eat.

"I love this place. Do you like the view, darling?" Wil asked his wife-to-be.

"It's so beautiful, Wil. Look at the color of the sea today." It was emerald green in places near the rocks. "Can you see the sailing boat coming around the rocks?" She pointed to the beautiful boat with billowing cream sails.

"Lovely day for sailing. Big boat—I don't recognize it." He stretched back on the blanket. "One day, Hilda, I shall buy us a boat."

Hilda laughed. She thought it would be fun to sail away with Wil. She had been terribly sad since he had received his conscription letter. He had to fight, and that was it. She was so afraid she would lose him. She simply adored him and believed with all her heart it was God who had brought them together. They were perfect for each other. Wil was no great talker, but even in the silences, they understood each other. She looked out to the sea, above the wheat that swayed gently in the breeze, and wondered if, when Wil bought them a boat, they would take their children out in it.

After their meal, she had her head in Wil's lap. He took the hairpins from her bun and stroked her soft, shiny hair, and she began to cry.

"Don't torment yourself, Hilda. I brought you here today because I want you to know two things, and I want you to keep them hidden in your heart until we meet again. The first is that I think you are the most beautiful woman I have ever met and that I will love only you until the day I die. And the second thing is that, whatever happens now, I trust God with all my heart, and you must trust Him, too. He is a faithful God—a God of refuge and strength—and I know that I can trust Him to love and care for you forever. While I am away, I won't worry about you. I will miss you." He looked down into her eyes. "But I won't worry. You are in safe hands, and so am I. Do you understand?"

Hilda could only nod, and then he kissed her. It was the last private kiss he ever gave her. She never forgot it.

Hilda knew what he'd said about God was true. She would trust He had a plan for Jack and Sue, and she could rest in that knowledge and trust Him for their future, whatever it would be. She turned once more in her bed, snuggled deep down under her blue silk eiderdown, and slept very peacefully.

———————

When the vicar left Sue at her front door, she had her hand on the knob ready to open it, but she just couldn't do it. Even though it was very chilly, she sat down on the steps and cried once more. How would she tell Jack? It had taken them so long to find each other—was this where it would end?

Sue had met Jack at her Keep Fit class in Redruth. She worked as a physical education teacher in the local secondary school. Sue had been brought up in an orphanage until she was eighteen, when she found a job and a flat. She lived for nearly seventeen years in her flat, alone, and was quite contented. She loved the children in her care, though, and often felt sad that she'd never married and had some of her own.

After a local lady gave up her Keep Fit classes, run by the council, Sue grabbed her chance and got one started in the church hall

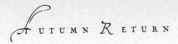

on Wednesday evenings. She also attended the Methodist church where her classes were held but didn't like it very much. The congregation didn't have many people of her own age—mostly very old ladies. They were kind to her, of course, but she missed the friendship of younger Christians.

She was attracted to Jack the first time he came to her class. He was handsome, in a rugged sort of way, but she was surprised he would join a Keep Fit class, which was mostly full of women! During the first class Jack explained that he sat at a computer most of his working day and felt a Keep Fit class was just what he needed. Sue was a little suspicious of his motives, however, and when he asked her to go out for dinner after his second class, she turned him down flat.

Jack continued to be polite and friendly—and an enthusiastic member of the class. Sue felt her attitude toward him changing, and she was thrilled when she overheard him telling someone at the door that he would pray for them. She immediately engaged him in a conversation and soon discovered he was a dedicated Christian. Sue had long since forgotten how she managed it, but somehow she maneuvered Jack into asking her out again, and they were inseparable from that time on.

The people of Tarran Bay had welcomed Sue from the moment she entered Jack's life. They were like the family she had never had. And after a wonderful wedding on a hot June day, the little Methodist church in Redruth sent Sue off to her new home in Tarran Bay with their blessings. The couple decided to live in Jack's home rather than moving to a new one, which thrilled Jack because he had lived there for so long and felt comfortable. Sue didn't change anything, just added her belongings, which seemed to fit in so well.

Sue and Jack tried without success to have a baby. They both had tests, which found nothing wrong. Jack had been very ill as a boy and had suffered through some difficult tests and treatments. As a result he didn't like doctors, or hospitals, or anything to do with illness. Sue knew he only endured the infertility tests because he loved her so much, and they both wanted children. One day Sue went to see the vicar, and she'd asked him to pray. The rest was wonderful history!

And now a new page of their history was being written. Sue knew Jack needed to be told, and she needed his arms around her. Praying that he would be home soon, she stood and opened the door. She was shocked to see Jack standing by the kitchen sink with his back to the door.

As she wavered in the entryway, Jack turned from the kitchen sink. "Where have you been? I was—"

Suddenly Sue's knees felt weak. She stumbled slightly and fell against the doorpost. Jack rushed around the table, knocking into a chair, which rocked gently back into place as he took Sue into his arms.

"Sue, darling. What's wrong?"

She needed him to know. She needed him to help bear the burden. But her voice was soft and ragged. "I've got . . . cancer."

"Cancer? Where?"

"In my left breast."

"No, it can't be. How is this possible?"

Jack held her through another bout of tears. She sobbed and sobbed, saturating his shirt. His arms would not let go. It was just what she needed.

"Oh, Sue, I'm so sorry. I knew I should have been with you tonight. I wish I had a nine-to-five job. It's so frustrating. I could have canceled . . ."

"Jack, I know. Please don't worry. I know how busy you are. I really didn't think for one minute it would be so serious. But Gordon was wonderful. And I talked with Vicar Todd."

At last Sue pulled away from his hold and looked up into his watery eyes.

"I have to ask you what to do," she said at last.

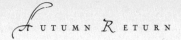

"I don't understand."

"Gordon said I need to have a mastectomy. He said I shouldn't just have the lump removed. It might not be enough. He said we should discuss it together and see him tomorrow. He was so kind. Oh, Jack! Will you still love me?"

He pulled her into his arms, even tighter now, and kissed her hair.

"Oh, Sue, how could you think a thing like this would change my love for you?"

"I know you love me. It's just . . . Well . . ." She struggled for the right words, but they wouldn't come.

"I can cope," he spoke for her. "We must face this together. If it means surgery or you not being here with us, then it's an obvious choice." He leaned down and they kissed.

"Daddy, we're ready. Come read us a story."

Their moment had been interrupted by two precious gifts from God who were calling from their bedroom.

"I got home earlier than I expected, so since you weren't home I went to pick them up. They've had their baths. Do you want to help me tuck them in?"

Sue grabbed Jack's hand and dragged him toward the girls' room. "With all my heart—I wouldn't miss it for the world."

Carly and Kasey were snuggled in their wooden bunk beds, ready for their story. Sue marveled again at the beautiful girls God had given her and Jack. The twins were identical—blond curly hair and sparkling blue eyes. Even she had trouble telling them apart at times—until they spoke. Their voices were very different, and their personalities were as opposite as night and day. She loved this part of the day and sank into the comfy chair by the beds while Jack snuggled in to tell the girls a story. First he told them about the Good Samaritan. Then he read them a story from their favorite book, *My Naughty Little Sister*. Soon hoots of laughter filled the room.

"That's what Carly would do," Kasey said as the story progressed.

"Oh no it's not. It's what you'd do," her sister responded, leaning over her bed and bending down to look at Kasey underneath her. She stuck her tongue out at her sister, at which Jack insisted he would not continue unless they behaved like proper little girls. Finally Jack said it was time for prayers, then sleep.

Carly and Kasey were eager to outdo each other as they traded off requests. "God bless Mummy."

"And Daddy."

"The cat."

"Uncle Gordon."

"The vicar," and so on and so on.

They lengthened their prayer list so much, with teachers and new friends, that Jack finally had to stop them by saying, "God bless everyone!" in his loudest daddy voice. Sue could hardly keep from laughing out loud.

After tucking the girls in and kissing their rosy cheeks, Jack and Sue went downstairs to the kitchen.

"Can you eat something?" he asked softly.

She nodded. "Believe it or not, Jack, I'm starving."

CHAPTER 8

The Weekend

Night had long since departed, but when Lucy awoke the sky was still dark. The rain, crashing at her west window, rattled the latches as if desperate to get inside. She jumped from the bed and sat on the window ledge to take a closer look at the view. She could hardly see anything for the rain. *Good day for painting some of those white walls*, she thought, wrapping her robe tightly around her waist.

After breakfast she put on some old jeans and a pale blue shirt of Tom's that had seen other painting days, taking comfort in wearing it. She threw a raincoat over her head, rushed out to the garage to get a tin of paint, a roller, and brushes, and rushed back in, looking a bit bedraggled as she shook out her raincoat and hung it on the back of the utility door. She had already covered the furniture with dust sheets, so she put on Vivaldi's *The Four Seasons* and plunged into the task at hand. As the fierce intensity of the chords of "Winter" filled her head, Lucy felt an aching void—cold, dead, with no hope for the new life of spring. She had to stop herself from dwelling there too long, reminding herself that her life was in *autumn*—and the *beginning* of autumn at that. She had plenty of time before winter came. As she listened to her favorite piece, she realized winter had its charms, too.

By lunchtime Lucy had finished the laborious task of taping and painting the edges and detail work with a paintbrush. So she snatched a sandwich and an apple and started with the roller. She put on some Puccini and for once forgot the rain, the time, and the bittersweet memories.

By five o'clock the job was finished, and Lucy stood back quite delighted by the results of her hard work. She decided to take the pansy tin back to the vicar before preparing supper. So she washed and changed, donned her coat and grabbed her umbrella, and headed out to face the storm. Even with the umbrella and coat, Lucy was a sorry sight by the time she reached Vicar Todd's door.

"Well, what have we here, Hilda?" the vicar shouted over his shoulder into the open doorway of the sitting room. "A drowned rat, I think!"

"You sound like Toad from Toad Hall!" Lucy said, smiling as she shook her umbrella out into the rain before placing it in the old-fashioned stand in the large hallway. The vicar took the tin and her coat. While shaking the worst of the rain from her coat, he told her that Hilda was in the sitting room and that she should go in and say hello. As Lucy entered the warmth of the lovely room, she saw Hilda sitting by the fireplace.

"Come and see what we have here," Hilda said to her. Lucy peeped over the top of the sofa to see two identical little girls with golden curls stuffing their pretty faces with cake.

"Well, well. What fun!"

"We've come for tea," said one.

"We're having cakes!" piped the other, grinning up at Lucy. Their tiny mouths were stuffed full of food.

"These little angels belong to Sue and Jack Trent." Hilda put her hand on the curly head of the twin on the right. "This is Carly."

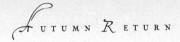

She shifted her hand to the other twin. "And this is Kasey. I often have trouble telling them apart, but today I think I'm doing quite well."

Lucy bent down to study the little girls' faces. "I am very pleased to meet you."

"Us too!" the twins announced together.

"And I believe I will be able to tell you apart, as long as you don't move around."

Hilda laughed. "Don't count on that. They are full of energy—like two spinning tops."

The vicar came in through the doorway with a clean cup, saucer, and plate and told Lucy to sit in his chair by the fire to warm up.

"We've played snakes and ladders and ludo," he told her. "And guess who won?"

"We did! We did!" sang the girls excitedly, and in unison.

"After tea," said Hilda, "they're going to color in their coloring books and make a nice picture for their mummy."

The twins immediately jumped up at this suggestion and, with crumbs flying everywhere, ran to the table by the window. It was laid with their books and crayons, ready for use. The vicar handed Lucy a cup of hot tea and a plate.

"Do help yourself, dear. As usual, I've made far too much!"

"Thank you. How nice." She took an egg roll with cress.

"Jack's wife, Sue—have you met her yet?" the vicar inquired in whispered tones.

Lucy shook her head and explained she had met Jack, but not Sue. "This is the first time I've met the girls!" She smiled over at them.

"Well . . ." The vicar was whispering very softly, and Lucy could hardly hear above the noise coming from the direction of the window. "She's just found out she needs a serious operation, so Hilda and I thought we'd have the girls for the afternoon to give Jack and Sue some time together. I found out after I saw you yesterday. She came and told me late last night."

The girls were chattering with delight at their artistry, and the noise seemed to be a bit disturbing for Hilda, so Lucy thanked him for the information, excused herself, and went over to join the girls in their fun. To calm them down, she drew some pictures of a cat and a dog. She showed them how to make the dog's tail look as if it were wagging.

"You're the new lady, aren't you," said the twin Lucy believed to be Kasey. "My daddy gave you two fishes, didn't he! Have you thanked him yet?"

"Yes, she has." Suddenly Jack's head peeped around the door. "And don't be so cheeky!"

"I only asked," replied his daughter, looking just a little crest-fallen.

He looks okay, Lucy thought, wondering what on earth could be wrong with his wife. Lucy left before Jack and the girls did, explaining she must put the freshly painted room back together before morning.

Vicar Todd led her to the hallway. "See you at church?" he asked, raising his right eyebrow at her and smiling with a face full of expectancy.

She had to smile back. She couldn't do anything else! "Maybe! Thanks so much for the tea."

"My pleasure." He helped her into her still-wet coat and bid her farewell as she entered the engulfing rain.

Hilda took the girls into the kitchen, where she asked them to help her with the washing up. She stood them each on a chair and let them get on with it while she put the dishes away. After assuring himself that Hilda had the situation under control, Vicar Todd took advantage of the time alone to see how Jack was doing.

"It was such a shock, Vicar. I don't need to tell *you*, though, do I? Sue said you were very shocked yourself. To be honest, I feel sick.

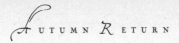

I can't believe I wasn't there for her—when she found out, I mean. I look at her drawn face and wonder, why us? Why now? I wish I had an answer."

"I know, son. It is always so difficult to see the light at the end of a twisting tunnel. Believe me—it is up ahead. And don't berate yourself for not being there when she found out. It wasn't the ideal situation, but God was with her. While it is wonderful to have the comfort of loved ones, His comfort is what we need the most in crises.

"Thank you, Vicar. I know that is true. I am so thankful we can rely on Him to get us through this mess."

"What have you decided to do about surgery?"

"Well, Sue thinks she would like some more prayer. But she is ready to go ahead with the mastectomy, if necessary. I think it's the right decision. She has asked Gordon to make all the arrangements with the hospital for her."

89

"I think it's the right decision, too. I will make time for prayer after the service tomorrow. Make sure to be there, won't you?"

"We'll be there." Jack looked toward the kitchen, from where they could hear Carly's and Kasey's wonderful laughter. "I think Hilda needs our help!"

"Before we enter the war zone, let me pray with you, Jack."

"Thanks—I need all the prayer I can get at the moment."

Vicar Todd asked Jack to sit down and then placed his left hand on Jack's bowed head. He held his free arm heavenward.

"Loving heavenly Father, thank you for this time to seek your face. We love you, Lord. We come humbly into your presence and ask that you comfort Jack while Sue is in the hospital. Bring your peace into their home and may your love flow there in abundance during the next few weeks. Give Jack understanding for his wife and patience with the girls. Bless this family, Lord. They need you. In Jesus' name we pray—Amen!"

"Amen," Jack said. He stood and hugged his dear vicar and

friend, and they went to see what damage had been done to the vicarage kitchen!

───────────

When Lucy returned home her cottage sat in darkness, as she had forgotten to leave on any lights. It didn't worry her, though. She felt incredibly safe in Tarran Bay. She switched on the hall light, shook out her wet things, hung them above the radiator, and went into the freshly painted sitting room. As she switched on the light and saw the new color, she was very pleased. Even without the furniture in place it was a lovely room, with a window facing east and French doors facing west. Lucy even liked the smell of fresh paint.

Whipping off the dust sheets, she went to her boxes in the corner of the room. They were placed near the window seat with the view of the front garden. Out came feather cushions of all shapes, sizes, and rustic colors. She had made some, collected some from junk shops, and bought others. She arranged some on the window seat, which already had a pale mustard pad of piped velvet on it. Then she found her rust, cream, and black Indian throw and placed it on the back of the sofa. Before she arranged her furniture, she placed her huge antique kilim rugs down on the flagstones. A small oak dining table, which Tom had cut the legs off, served as a coffee table in front of the fireplace. To finish it all off, Lucy placed a wooden bowl of potpourri and a thick church candle in the center of the table.

Lucy stood back to admire her work. It was exactly what she had hoped it would be, except for the bare walls. She had left the hanging of her paintings until last, as she knew the pictures would pull the room together. She couldn't help liking them, not so much because she thought she was an exceptionally talented artist, but because the paintings were all of the Africa she loved. They were a constant reminder of her time there. Bringing to life the good

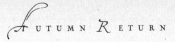

things—the extraordinary people, the amazing colors, and the precious, precious children.

When all was completed, Lucy sat wearily on the sofa with a glass of freshly squeezed orange juice. She curled her legs beneath her and enjoyed the roaring fire. Looking around at her paintings, she was overcome with scenes from the past, and her thoughts turned to Tom, as they often did when she was quiet and alone.

When she and Tom had landed at the airport in Mozambique, Ruth Lange had been waiting for them, wearing a welcoming smile as she stood beside an open truck. They had to sit in the back of the truck with their belongings, while Ruth sat in front with her African driver, whom she had introduced as her teacher, Matthew. It took over two hours to reach their destination over uneven, muddy, and potholed roads. Lucy was exhausted. The flight had taken nearly ten hours, and now they had to endure this bumpy journey in the back of a steel-floored truck. Her spirits were muddled. She knew God wanted her here, but everything was rather alien, and she wasn't certain she would like it—at all!

At last they arrived at their destination, and after looking over the large compound, Tom and Lucy were shown to the room that would be their home for the next few months, or years—who knew? The room was part of a block of six rooms, set among the dry bushes. Lucy truly believed she was prepared for things to be tough, but as they stepped into their new home, a swarm of flies flew frantically about her, and she felt like bursting into tears. The room had a window at one end and double lockup doors at the other—it was not at all what Lucy had expected. Two single beds covered with clean, though worn, quilts lined the walls, and each bed had a little cupboard beside it. A rail in a crevice with a curtain across it served as the only place for hanging clothes. The "kitchen area" consisted of an electric kettle placed on a table with two chairs and some plates and cups. A baby bath and two buckets, underneath the table, would serve as their sink and "bath." A single bare light bulb hung from the black corrugated-tin ceiling.

"We'll get used to it," Tom said, putting his arms about his young wife. He held her close and kissed her.

Lucy doubted she would ever adapt to living conditions so primitive, but after a good night's sleep, with their beds pushed together under mosquito netting, she was surprised to find she felt much better.

They had no time for settling in as she had hoped—too much needed to be done. Tom went to help Ruth with some legal documents, and Lucy went with Matthew to the open-air classroom and sat, listened, and learned. Soon she was teaching a class of eighty, unable to believe she could enjoy it so much. Back in England she had struggled with a class of twenty-five.

The children were as good as gold, and they understood Lucy quite well because English was the second language at the orphanage. Lucy helped them improve their English and taught them mathematics and geography. She had a huge easel under the trees, and they learned quickly. On Fridays they were given paper and pencils to write up what they had learned.

Equipment was scarce, as were the tools, which Tom found extremely frustrating. Supplies would be sent from England on a regular basis, but because of the run-down transportation system, as well as frequent confiscations by warring factions, the supplies hardly ever reached the intended destination.

In spite of the good work they were doing, Lucy found herself spiraling down into despondency. She felt as though she was barely hanging on. The living conditions were pitiful, health care was non-existent—even negligent—and she often heard gunfire in the distance throughout the day and night.

One afternoon, as Ruth, Lucy, and Tom were escorting some children back to their classes after lunch, they stopped short when twenty soldiers entered the gates and stood under the compound's few scorched trees. They were loud and drunk and carrying rifles.

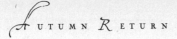

Ruth, so tiny and unassuming, was at the front of the procession. She wore a washed-out red cotton dress and a very battered straw hat to shade her eyes. Once it had seen better days, but now it allowed the sun to filter through in spots on her face.

Turning quickly to Tom, who was close at her heel, she mouthed that he should let her do the talking—not surprising, because Tom did not know their language very well. However, Lucy was startled when the men spoke in perfect English. The soldiers mocked Ruth, jeering at her. She stood straight and waited until they finished, though they continued to point their guns at her. The little children snuggled around Lucy's body for comfort. She was petrified but summoned a weak smile for the sake of the children who stood close to her.

At last Ruth spoke, telling the angry young men that she took no sides in the war and that she was only here to look after and love their orphans. The leader's only response was to hold up his rifle. Lucy thought she was going to faint and reached for Tom's arm to uphold her. The leader fired his rifle high into the air, and the others copied him. Then, just when Lucy was sure she could not possibly hold herself together, the soldiers finally left the compound with shrieks of cruel laughter. Ruth and Tom rushed to bolt the gates behind the angry men. Lucy turned and quickly ushered the children to their classes in a strange and very silent procession.

Later that evening, Ruth paid Tom and Lucy a visit.

"How are you doing?"

Lucy, who was sitting in the chair next to her bed trying to read, knew Ruth's question was directed toward her. She looked at her friend, put in her bookmark, and rested the book on the blue counterpane. "To be honest, Ruth, I was terrified. I don't know if I can handle living here. How did you stay so calm?"

"I was petrified," Ruth replied.

"Well, it didn't show," Tom said, looking up from his work. Pieces of radio were scattered all over the table. He was trying to build a radio from the parts of two old ones.

Ruth sat on the bed near Lucy.

"Has something like this happened before?" Tom asked.

"I often see confrontations in town or out on the road. But I have never been the target before. This is the first time an incident has occurred in our compound. For the most part, I think people appreciate our work with the orphans and don't give us trouble."

"I thought I would faint," Lucy said.

"So did I. My knees were so weak, I could hardly stand." Ruth smiled. "But I reminded myself that God was with me. I asked Him to give me wisdom, and He told me to keep quiet until they finished speaking. I was still shaking, but I felt His power in me as He assured me, *I will never leave you nor forsake you, and I will be your strength in weakness.* I felt a moment of hate toward those men—for putting us through such a frightening ordeal. But that would do me no good. My hatred would only hurt me and the work of the orphanage."

Lucy found Ruth's words difficult to accept. She'd seen the malice in the soldiers' eyes and knew she could not forgive them for the fear they had brought to the hearts of the children. Ruth was a far better Christian than she would ever be, which saddened her greatly, making her wonder if she would be able to cope with life in Mozambique.

"Now, to better news!" Ruth announced that Paul and Sara—other workers on the project—were leaving for the United Kingdom for a year, and she asked if Lucy and Tom would like to stay in their bungalow on the other side of the compound. It would be more peaceful over there and would give them more room. Lucy and Tom's room had been rather noisy at night, since they had teenage students living on either side of them.

"Oh," Lucy cried, "how wonderful!"

Tom winked at her from the other side of the room as a big grin crossed his handsome tanned face.

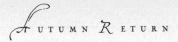

Ruth rose wearily to her feet and made for the door. As she reached for the handle she turned to Tom. "I'll send something for you to put your belongings on to move over to the bungalow. See you there in the morning."

Lucy folded her flimsy print dress about her knees, drew them up under her chin, and rested her small smiling face on them. Joy filled her heart as she looked over at Tom. Tom came over, knelt beside his wife, and kissed her cheek.

"God knows our needs, Lucy." Taking her hand in his and giving it a little kiss, he suggested, "Let's go for a walk." They both loved the stars and moon out here in Africa, and as dusk settled itself like a cloak over the bush, the fading mauve light cast long, surreal shadows over the compound and turned the harsh daylight colors to soft pastels. The birds quieted as they settled for the night, and the peace was palpable. Lucy could not think of a more perfect moment in her entire life, and she was amazed it had occurred on the same day that she had encountered the most difficult event of her life. They held hands and wandered slowly to the boundary gate, where Tom held Lucy in his strong arms and kissed her forehead.

"God is sovereign, Lucy. We must learn to trust Him every day. Our lives are in His hands, and He will take care of us. When trusting Him becomes a reality, life will be easier to cope with."

"I know, Tom. But I think your faith is stronger than mine."

"It can cope for two. . . ."

They watched as the night sky darkened and the brightness of the moon and stars began to dispel what had been a difficult day for Lucy. But she wondered secretly if Tom's faith truly would be enough for both of them. At last, under a filigree of shadows cast by the light of the moon through the trees above them, they headed back to their room.

Tom and Lucy woke early the next morning, eager to begin their move. When they opened the double doors, they were surprised to see a huge wheelbarrow waiting on the pathway. They quickly piled their few possessions high on the one-wheeled removal truck. Lucy laughed when she saw how strange Tom looked trundling his burden to the opposite side of the compound. When they arrived at their new home, Lucy could barely contain herself—the bungalow was gorgeous. It was very small, with only one bedroom. But it was clean, whitewashed inside and out, and had running water—if only for one hour a day.

In their first room in the compound, Lucy had gotten used to bathing from one bucket of water, first washing her hair and then using the water to bathe in—and Tom used it after her! But with a bungalow to call home and an hour of running water every day, she felt very pampered indeed!

Lucy lay on the comfortable bed in the bungalow, with its pink woolen blankets and soft pillows, and thanked God with all her heart. But at the same time, she struggled with her need for such luxuries, when all around her life was spare. The children—sad, lost, and rejected—had only two blankets and a mattress on the floor of the dormitory to sleep on. But eventually she shut this thought from her mind and enjoyed her baths in five inches of water and stealing the occasional candlelit meal alone with Tom.

Lucy enjoyed the outside of her bungalow as much as the bungalow itself. Behind it stood huge fir trees that whistled as the wind rushed through their branches. Below them a garden was piled high with rocks, and a hollow had been hewn to pour leftover washing-up water to attract the little bright-yellow weaverbirds to drink and play. Their shrill chattering never ceased. Cacti and bougainvillea, all bright pinks and mauves, brought color and life to the dry, dusty earth. It was such a lovely place to sit in the evening. Lucy and Tom enjoyed the little home very much and carried on with their individual work. They both learned quickly and soon fell into the routine

of helping Ruth with all the needs of the orphanage. Everything felt so right that they confidently extended their original one-year commitment for an indefinite period of time. Their home church was thrilled with their decision and committed to continue their support.

One evening Tom acquired a cow and arranged for a local butcher to cut it up for him.

"We're going to have a brier!" he said as he entered the kitchen with a beaming smile on his handsome face. The orphanage didn't have the luxury of fancy barbecue equipment, but the brier, a huge metal drum with a grate over the top, served the function wonderfully. Back in England, they had always enjoyed entertaining at home, and the idea thrilled Lucy.

They invited all the children and workers and served everyone in the large garden. After the feasting, they sang choruses around the fire that glowed in the brier until late into the night. Lucy loved the way the Africans danced and sang. They really put their hearts into it.

97

When they had been in Africa sixteen months, Lucy began to feel ill—constantly tired and nauseated. The doctor soon confirmed she was pregnant. How could she stay now? The lack of proper sanitation, the water shortages, and the constant struggles with diarrhea were making her life unbearable. A new life was too precious to risk under the area doctors' care. They were unskilled and made too many mistakes. This was her baby. She had to protect it!

Lucy felt a constant sadness surrounding her all the time. She couldn't face staying in Mozambique any longer. Tom was reluctant to leave, but after weeks of begging, Lucy managed to persuade him she could carry on no longer. So after less than eighteen months in Africa, they made their way back home to England, and soon everything was back to normal—as it had been before Africa. Lucy had endured a deep sadness, but it was all tidied away, tucked and tied deep down inside her. She knew better than to bring it to the surface.

As the large log she had laid in the hearth settled and sent sparks flying, Lucy's mind came back to the present. She loved the way the dancing flames of the fire seemed to be alive. It was a comfort just to sit and watch it change, glow, and finally die in the hearth. *It was too soon. Did I do something wrong? Was God punishing me? Why does He take loved ones from us before their time? Doesn't He care that it leaves a gaping hole in our hearts that can never be filled—never re-placed? How can He be so cruel?* She hated that she still harbored these questions and pushed them away behind the locked door of her heart once again.

Lucy thought again of Jack's wife and wondered what was wrong with her. Perhaps she should pop around to them—take a cake or something. Jack had, after all, been so kind to her on her arrival. No—she mustn't get involved so soon. She simply mustn't get too close. Getting close might mean getting hurt! Lucy switched on the television to distract her thoughts and watched an old movie until bedtime.

CHAPTER 9

Sunday

The next morning Lucy was enjoying a late, leisurely breakfast when she was startled by the ringing of St. Luke's bells. It seemed so loud she felt as if someone had built the belfry in her attic, but she supposed it was because the church was only at the end of the lane. *It must be nearly time for the Sunday service.* She tried to ignore the bells' clamor, but it seemed to be calling her name. She didn't want to go to church, but the vicar had smiled so sweetly, and Hilda too.

Where had she put those pamphlets the vicar had given her? There they were on the dresser—the service started at eleven o'clock. She glanced at the old clock, with its friendly brass-rimmed face—she had twenty minutes. As she climbed the staircase from the kitchen, Lucy wondered what she was doing. She hadn't gone to church for so long—why now? Was she being manipulated once more? *No, it's my decision. I'm in control.*

Lucy quickly donned a pair of cream cotton trousers, a black leather belt, black boots, and a black cashmere sweater. After tying a pretty red scarf around her neck, she went downstairs to find her Bible. She was ashamed when she couldn't find it. At last she found Tom's. She held the soft leather book in her hands and opened it to see all the red underlining and well-thumbed pages. *I will be with you always*, jumped out at her. Lucy shut it with a snap. She didn't want to take the hard reminder of Tom, but she knew she couldn't go to church without it.

Picking up her shoulder bag from the sofa, she went to the hall to put on her coat. It was slightly damp from the day before, but since it was still raining, she didn't care. Using her umbrella to battle against the wind and rain, Lucy made for the church and arrived only a few minutes late.

Vicar Todd was still greeting people in the archway. He welcomed her with his warm smile. "Glad you could come."

Lucy was surprised by the laxness. Her church in London had always started on time.

She nodded a smile and headed for a seat at the back of the little church. At least fifty people were milling around and talking with one another. It seemed to be a lot of people for such a small community. She saw Jack sitting with a slim, attractive woman, his arm around her shoulders and the twins sitting next to him. Her heart went out to them. Several people came over, shook her hand, and introduced themselves. She couldn't remember a single name. When the service started, she felt a little uncomfortable. She was not used to the formality of the Church of England service, but she knew one or two of the hymns and sang along.

After the children were led out to Sunday school—the twins gave her a cheeky grin as they passed her—the vicar started his sermon. He began to talk about confronting our fears. He said that often God puts us into situations to help us to be overcomers.

"People often mistakenly assume the things that God allows in our lives are His way of showing His anger," he said. "Remember, it is God's kindness that leads us to repentance, as Paul tells us in Romans. It is his wonderful kindness and grace that He extends to

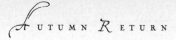

us that helps us face the things of which we are afraid. God wants to show us that He is with us in everything we go through, and that He is able to keep us safe through the storms.''

Looking around at his silent congregation, he carried on with passion in his voice—the sort of passion Lucy had heard her husband use so often.

"Jesus told us His sheep know His voice. The point is—do we listen?''

Lucy realized that much in the vicar's sermon applied to her struggles. She knew she should be working harder to get through this difficult time. But she didn't know how. To tell the truth—she didn't feel like it. When her thoughts returned to the vicar's words, he had finished the sermon and was talking about the Trents.

"We need to pray for Jack and Sue, as Sue will be having an operation on Thursday. We will be praying for them in the vestry after the service, and if anyone would like to join us, they are most welcome. I've placed a sheet of paper on the table by the door where you can put down your name if you think you can help with cooking the odd meal, baby-sitting, and such, for at least a month. Please carefully consider how you could help out this dear family.''

Lucy left quietly during the last hymn. She didn't want to get involved in any difficult conversations. She glanced at the paper with *Help for the Trents* written at the top and signed up—still the same old Lucy. She considered turning around to erase her name but decided against it. She would have to cope with the consequences of getting involved later. These people needed help. As long as she could keep them at arm's length, she thought she might be okay.

Outside, the air was cold, and though the rain had ceased, the sky looked heavy and dark, brooding for yet another downpour. She took the long way around to her home—across the harbor wall and over the beach. A man was walking his dog close to the water's edge, tossing a piece of driftwood for his canine friend to catch and return time and time again. Three children played stepping-stones across the stream that meandered gracefully down from the cliffs and across the beach on its homeward journey to the sea. Lucy wrapped her coat snugly about her and sat on the rocks. The cliffs were high and majestic—soft green turf and flowering heather clung to the granite. She remembered each cave and crevice and looked forward to exploring them once again.

The rain returned, falling in a gentle mist around her, but she was reluctant to leave. They would be praying for Sue and Jack now, and once she would have joined them. Lucy stood and buried her face in her scarf, the hot stinging tears flowing in contrast to the cold pelting of the rain. When the rain began falling more heavily, and she could hardly see Gull Island, she decided it would be foolish to stay. Pulling her collar up around her neck against the wind and opening her umbrella, Lucy left the sound of crashing waves and the cry of the seagulls and walked slowly homeward, crunching the pebbles beneath her feet.

After the service, Vicar Todd asked Sue to sit in the vestry, and Jack stood beside her. A dozen people, all close friends, surrounded them to pray and give their support in any way they could. Sue admitted she was nervous about undergoing the operation but felt God's peace. She knew He would be with her. Jack expressed his fear but knew he had to be strong because his wife needed his love and comfort and a shoulder to lean on. He asked for strength and wisdom to give her the support she needed. Then each one prayed, asking God to guide the surgeon's hand, to give peace and comfort to Jack and Sue, and to bring about a speedy recovery.

CHAPTER 10

The Operation

The doctors at Redruth General Hospital were so kind. The specialist talked to Jack and Sue for over an hour, explaining every detail of what would be happening. He told them reconstructive surgery was available if Sue wanted it, though it was expensive. But Sue felt she needed to get through the mastectomy before she considered other operations. He did not rush them and encouraged them to ask any questions they had. Afterward, Jack and Sue asked God to be with their family throughout Sue's surgery and recovery, and that He would allow Sue to see her girls grow up. They felt assured God would answer their prayers. Two days later the preparations were finished, and Sue went down for surgery.

When Jack entered her room after the operation, Sue was hardly aware of him being there. She was still groggy from the anesthesia. She could tell his heart was breaking as he questioned the nurse about the tubes coming from her, filling slowly with ugly blood-filled liquid. She wanted to tell him she was all right but couldn't find the words—or the energy to speak them. As he sat encircled by the curtains, weeping silently into his handkerchief, she could do nothing but drift into a drug-induced sleep.

In the morning the nurse told Sue that Jack had left to see the girls before they headed to school. Sue still felt a little groggy, but a cup of tea, along with some buttered toast, helped. She felt pain when she moved and did so only very slowly. After breakfast two nurses washed her and gave her more medication. She fell back onto the stiff pillows in weary exhaustion and asked God to be with her and give her ordeal some purpose. The woman in the bed next to her stirred and moaned restlessly. She looked to be in her early thirties. Sue assumed she had been weeping, because as she turned toward Sue, she could see that the woman's eyes were very swollen and red.

"How are you feeling?" the woman managed to ask Sue while mopping her eyes with a tissue she pulled from a little pink square box on her bedcovers.

"Groggy," Sue answered honestly.

"They've taken my breast off." The woman continued, as though Sue hadn't even answered her.

Though her face was red from her tears, Sue could see she had an attractive face. Her eyes were dark brown, and her dark hair curled around her shoulders. She wore a pretty blue cotton nightdress.

Sue smoothed the blanket and crisp starched sheets over her stomach.

"Yes, me too."

"Have you seen it yet—the stitches, the scar?"

"No, not yet."

"Are you afraid to look? I was. It looks strange—horrible!"

Gail went on and on, relentless in her tactless questions. Suddenly, Sue's heart went out to the woman. Perhaps she didn't have a husband like Jack to tell her it didn't matter, because it was she he loved, not her body.

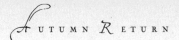

"I'll cope. They showed me some pictures of what to expect. I want to live, that's all. . . . I have twins who need me!" Sue hoped that mentioning her family would change the subject. She was learning to trust God, but it was still hard to talk about her faith. Finally a nurse came over and started talking to the woman. Relieved, Sue readjusted herself in her bed. She just wanted to sleep and sleep. Then the pain would go—the pain inside, as well as outside.

At about nine o'clock, Jack called to see how Sue was doing and asked if she would mind if he didn't return until after supper. Another emergency had come up on the project he was working on, and he needed several hours to work it out. Sue said she was doing fine, that he shouldn't worry, but that she would be anxious to see him when he returned.

Vicar Todd arrived at half past eleven with a huge bunch of rust-colored chrysanthemums from his garden for her. She was pleased he had come. His face always brightened up a gray day!

"Oh, Vicar, how lovely to see you." She couldn't sit up just yet, so he bent and kissed her cheek.

A nurse quickly came over and asked if she could help with the flowers. "I'll put them in a vase for you," she said cheerfully.

Vicar Todd passed them to her with thanks.

"So how's my girl?"

"Sore, but I'll survive!"

"You will survive, Sue, because you're a fighter." He made himself as comfortable as possible in the plastic chair beside Sue's bed. He told her how blessed he had been when Lucy put her name down to help her family, because he knew it was a difficult thing for her to do. Sue said that she had been overwhelmed with the offers of help. Even Mark Holding—more a friend of Gordon's—had said he would take the girls to the cinema in St. Ives sometime.

"People need to be needed, Sue. Sadly, a lot of people don't realize they miss out on a lot of joy and fulfillment when they don't look around for opportunities to give a helping hand."

"I expect you're right, Vicar. How's Hilda?"

"Hilda is fine. She's having fun with the girls. You should have seen the mess they made of my kitchen on Saturday. There were soapsuds on the ceiling, as well as the floor! Still, it cleaned the flagstones for Mrs. Philips!"

"Oh, please don't make me laugh, Vicar. It hurts!"

Vicar Todd stayed for half an hour. He prayed for Sue and said he would call again. She felt more peaceful after his visit and was grateful to have such a wonderful father figure to lean on.

———

Lucy picked up the twins from school. She had been given directions by Jack and found the place easily from his map. It took her back—all the chattering, mothers bustling, cars parking, and doors slamming. The girls seemed genuinely pleased to see her waiting at the gates with all the young mums. They talked nonstop to the car, in the car, and out of the car!

At last, in the comforting warmth of the kitchen, Lucy shed them of their coats, hats, scarves, and mittens and laid the garments on the Aga to warm. While the girls sat at the table, Lucy made them hot chocolate and jam on toast. They loved it and ate ravenously, though still chattering away. *Like little weaverbirds*, Lucy thought, smiling across the table at the girls. They were delightful, but what on earth would she do with them for four hours? What would she do with them *all next week*? In a moment of weakness, she had offered her services for two weeks. Jack would have them on the weekends, with the help of Todd and Hilda. Suddenly Lucy wondered what she was doing. She was getting involved so soon. Was she beginning to make the same mistakes again?

"How's our mummy?" they asked.

Kasey continued, "Daddy came home to see us off to school. He said Mummy was done with the 'peration, but he did not talk to her because she was still sleeping when he came to see us."

"I don't know how your mummy is yet," Lucy replied honestly. "I expect we'll hear when your daddy picks you up. In the meantime, would you like to make Mummy a present?"

"Oh yes!" was the excited reply.

Lucy was discovering the girls often spoke in unison.

"Well, first we'll need to go to the beach to collect shells."

"What for?"

"You'll see!"

Lucy took the warmed clothing from the Aga and helped the girls into them. Once they were wrapped up warmly, the little party of three headed for the beach. They turned left at the gate onto the lane, which led them past two modern bungalows. Lucy loved this walk. She had loved it for years and truly couldn't believe it was now at her own doorstep. The grassy banks were edged in bracken, yellow gorse, and heather. Lucy bent down to make certain the girls were still well bundled. It was cold and blustery—quite a contrast to the week before—but at least the rain held off. When they entered the beach through a cleft in the cliffs, Lucy noted the sea was out. "Oh good, now we can go to the secret place!"

"The secret place! Where's that?" asked the girls excitedly.

"You'll see."

Lucy held the girls' little mittened hands in her own and brought them around the cliffs on the left of the beach to the caves. In one of the caves was a bath that had been cut from the rock. When the sea came in, it filled with fresh seawater, which stayed there all day. Another of these strange baths lay just around the corner in a deep cave, which you could only find through a tunnel when the sea was out. Lucy had heard some eccentric old ladies had had these baths, as well as the little swimming pool that nestled on the right side of the beach against the harbor wall, hewn from the rock in Victorian times. She didn't know if this story was true, but she loved the romance and mystery of it.

"This isn't a secret place," Kasey said. "I know it's here, and so does Carly—and Mummy and Daddy do, too!"

After spending hours with them, Lucy was learning to tell the girls apart. The placement of their eyes and the curve of their mouths varied slightly, and Kasey was definitely the more outspoken of the two. "I'm sure you do. I just think it's a sort of secret, because the sea won't always let you visit it."

"Ooh, yes! That's true, isn't it, Carly!"

"Yes," Carly said slowly, rather in awe of the expedition.

"Now, girls, we must collect some shells. We won't need many, so choose only very nice ones."

"We haven't got anything to put them in," Kasey said.

"Oh yes, we have," Lucy said, pulling out a plastic shopping bag from her coat pocket. They stayed for some time, scouting the chilly rock pools, until all three decided they were very cold. Dark blue clouds on the horizon were heralding the night, and they were ready to make for home with their bag full of seashells.

Back at the cottage, coats once again placed on the Aga, Lucy sat the twins at the table in the kitchen. She had covered the table with a navy-and-cream flowered plastic cloth from Laura Ashley, and on it she placed a little white box that had once held a paperweight. The table held a tub of Polyfilla, an old knife, some green velvet, a bottle of glue, and some white cotton wool.

"What's all this for?" Kasey asked, as the two girls eagerly placed their elbows on the table to peer closely at the mysterious objects in front of them.

"We're going to make Mummy a little trinket box."

"What's a trinket box?"

Lucy sighed. All these endless questions! They were so sweet, though—easy, fun.

"It's a box to put nice things in. Now, let's get started."

Giving Kasey the bottom of the box, she spread some Polyfilla onto the lid and showed Carly how to cement the shells on it in a pretty pattern. She then showed Kasey how to glue the velvet around

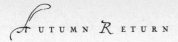

and inside the box. Kasey was not the neatest worker and got glue everywhere, especially on her hands. But Lucy was ready and quickly cleaned up with a wet cloth. When it was finished Lucy went to the cupboard and took out a little glass jar filled with sugared almonds. She opened the lid and told the girls to take out three almonds each while she laid a little mound of cotton wool inside the box.

"Now put them onto the cotton wool," she said patiently. "And you may each take one for yourselves while I make you some tea. Then we'll make Mummy a card."

As she prepared the tea, Lucy smiled at the twins from the Aga. It had been such a pleasant afternoon. She made them beans on toast with grated cheese on top and strawberry yogurt. The twins eagerly consumed their snack with a glass of cold milk and were soon ready to make their mummy's card.

Lucy had brought her paints and oldest brushes down from her studio and laid them on the table. She gave them a piece of paper that was folded down the middle.

"We're going to make a butterfly card," she told the girls.

She asked Carly to paint the shape of half of a butterfly on one side of the page, and then let Kasey fold and squash it. The children had obviously not done this before and squealed with delight at the finished product.

"We need to let it dry now. Would you like to see the rest of my cottage?"

"Oh yes, please," said the girls in unison.

Lucy took them over to the sink to wash the paint from their hands and then began the tour of inspection. They jumped on beds, hid around corners, looked in wardrobes, and made Lucy laugh— something she hadn't done very much of in a long time. She hesitated at the study, but the girls were in before she knew it.

"Oh, Lucy, do you play guitar?" Kasey said, strumming the instrument's strings.

"Not anymore," she said, slowly shutting the door behind them. "I used to play and sing when I was in Africa. But that was a long time ago."

Lucy felt the familiar despondency return. Her heart was heavy and she felt near tears. But the girls did not seem to notice her despair, and soon their happy chatter cheered her up once more. They made their way downstairs, and the girls put some glitter on the wing tips of the butterfly and wrote—with a little help from Lucy—in the card. Finally, they wrapped the present, which Lucy had put on the Aga to dry out. Lucy glanced at her watch. There was still half an hour to go, and she was out of ideas to keep the girls busy.

"We want a story now," Kasey said, who didn't mind telling Lucy exactly what she wanted.

Lucy racked her brain. She no longer had any of the boys' children's books. At last she remembered her African stories. "I do have some stories I wrote myself," she said. "Would you like to hear them?"

After a bit of digging in the desk in the study, Lucy found two of the eight stories she had written after coming back to England from Africa. The girls were very excited, and they soon had Lucy curled up on the sofa—with one of them snuggled on either side—just like three cozy cats they were. In front of a glowing fire, she fascinated the twins with tales of African children—children not so well off as themselves, children who played different games and ate different food, children who sang, though they had nothing. She described the colors of Africa and the plants and the many wonderful birds and animals. The time went by quickly, and Lucy found she loved remembering!

The girls continued their silence at the end of the stories, but finally Kasey said, "Sing us an African song, Lucy."

So she did. She sang in Shona, *"O Mwari Waka Naka"*—"God Is So Good." As she sang, the inevitable tears, which she blamed on the heat of the fire, began to roll over her cheeks.

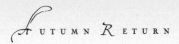

Later that evening, after picking up the girls and taking them to Hilda's, Jack came to visit Sue bearing an armful of red hothouse roses wrapped in cellophane and encircled with a gold bow. He placed them on the bed as he kissed his wife.

"How are you?"

"Do you want an honest answer?"

"Of course."

"I feel lousy, and I'm so tired."

"It's part of the healing. You must sleep all you can."

"It's so noisy in here, though." Then she lowered her voice. "And that poor woman next to me doesn't stop talking." She pointed secretly with her finger in Gail's direction. Jack got a bit of an odd look on his face, and Sue knew he was going to quickly change the subject. Sometimes he was better than her at looking after people's feelings.

"Well, then, it looks like you have a window and a decent view!"

Sue managed a smile for her husband, who placed a little parcel and envelope before her while he went to find a vase. She knew the package was from the girls because it was wrapped most strangely in pink paper with *get well* written all over it and stuck together with bits of cellotape all over the place. When she unwrapped the gift, she found a little cardboard box with shells covering the top. The outside and inside were covered with green velvet and, in a little nest of cotton wool, lay some colored sugared almonds. Jack came back with a steel vase and smiled at her, winking as he passed the bed, and placed the flowers on the window ledge.

"They made it themselves," he said proudly. "Lucy's a real gem!"

"It's beautiful!" Sue didn't try to hide the tears from him. He handed her a tissue, then she opened the envelope. They had made a card, too. It was a beautiful butterfly. Inside it read:

> deer mummy
>> get well soon
>>> luv
>>> carly and kasey
>>> XXX

Jack placed it with his card next to the roses and sat down beside his wife. He took hold of her hand and stroked it gently. As they watched people gathering to visit other patients on the ward, they talked a little of what she was feeling. Sue felt better after talking with Jack, but soon she could not keep her eyes open, and she drifted off to sleep.

———

Three days later Sue had her first bath. She asked the nurse if she could do this alone. After undoing the dressing very slowly, she looked at the scar for the first time. It was a neat, slightly swollen, straight scar. A little frightening at first, but she'd get used to it in time. Washing very carefully, she familiarized herself with this change to her body. She looked—she touched—she faced the awful fear that had become a giant to her. And found, to her surprise and relief, that this particular giant was as small as a mouse! She knew deep within that she would cope, Jack would cope, and the flesh was temporary. But her soul—the most important of all—was safe in the hands of Jesus.

———

Slowly, Sue got to know Gail. One afternoon she was roused from a drowsy afternoon sleep by weeping. It was Gail again, standing at the end of Sue's bed looking out onto the cold gray day. Sue sat up slowly. She had a slight infection so was still attached by IV tubes to the medication bags that hung from a steel stand beside the bed.

"What's wrong, Gail?" she asked gently.

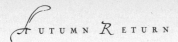

"I'm so depressed, Sue. What is there to go back home for? I wish I had died."

Sue carefully got out of the bed.

"Don't say that, Gail. If you're here, you're here for a reason. I think you will make an excellent recovery." She walked with her stand and stood beside Gail and put her arm around her shoulders gently.

"I can't think of one reason why I should be here. My husband doesn't care."

A loud *Shhh!* came from one of the other patients who had just had surgery and wanted some peace and quiet. Sue whispered to Gail that they should go to the dayroom.

As they walked slowly up the corridor together, followed by their steel stands with swaying medication bags, Sue saw a humorous side to her situation. They looked like something out of *Star Wars*, with their C-3PO units beside them! The dayroom was nicely, though sparsely, furnished with comfortable chairs and a television that was never turned off, which drove Sue mad. She liked to read and found television such an intrusion. They sat down opposite each other in a quiet corner of the room.

"I do wish I were dead, Sue. I really do, except I'm afraid of what's out there!" She looked out of the window at the dark clouds. Rain ran in long rivulets down the huge hospital windows.

"What do you think is out there?" Sue asked diplomatically. She had been in this situation before.

"Well, nothing, I hope!"

"Nothing? Oh, how awful. I believe God is out there, and I look forward to going home to Him. But not until He decides it is time. I believe He has plans for His children. And His plan for me isn't over yet!"

"Do you *really* believe in God, Sue?"

Though Gail's tone was incredulous, Sue thought she detected a note of hope.

113

"Yes, I have put my trust in Him for many years now, and He has never failed me."

"Huh—looks like He's failed you now, though, doesn't it!"

"No, Gail. I don't think so. In the Bible, it never says that life on earth would be easy. It just promises peace in every situation, if we trust God."

Once more Gail questioned her. "Do you read the Bible?"

"Yes, every day if possible. I couldn't get through the day without it!"

Gail sat quietly and looked at her hands resting in her lap.

"If there *is* a God, why are there so many horrible people about?"

Sue smiled at the same old question.

"I also believe in Satan, and that he causes havoc here on Earth. Thankfully, when we become a Christian, God protects us."

"Well, He's not doing a very good job with you then, is He? It doesn't look like your getting cancer is very protective."

Sue knew that Gail didn't mean to be unkind. She was questioning, and Sue was pleased for the opportunity. It was what she had prayed for.

"Gail, if I hadn't got the cancer, I wouldn't be in here to tell you about God, would I? I don't believe for an instant that God causes cancer, but He is using this trial for His good. And I think God wants you to know Him for yourself."

"Do you? Well, I don't. What would He want with someone like me? I'm nobody special."

"That's where you're wrong, Gail. You are very special to God. Every person on this earth is special to Him, and He will find a way of reaching out to everyone, somehow."

Gail was silent for a moment. Then she turned to look at Sue through tear-filled eyes. "Well, maybe there is a God, but I doubt He would protect and love me the way He does you." She faltered.

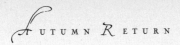

"I've done some terrible things, Sue. I don't think God would have liked some of them."

"That's the whole point, Gail. God sent us His Son, Jesus, to rescue us from sin."

"Did He?" Gail leaned forward.

At that moment Sue knew without a doubt that her relationship with Gail was the good God would create as a result of her cancer. Gail couldn't say Sue didn't understand how she felt, because Sue knew exactly how she felt. Only God had the power to use the pain and heartache of cancer for good.

"Yes, God has a wonderful plan to rescue all of us. He loves you, Gail, and wants to give you a new life, a life worth living, an adventurous life. I can't tell you how exciting it is being in His safe hands."

"You make it sound like a fairy story."

"Well, it isn't. It's very real."

"So what do I have to do, then?"

"Well, first you have to believe that you are a sinner, who needs to be saved."

"Oh, I know I'm a sinner all right."

"Well, then, you ask Jesus to forgive all your sins, and ask Him into your life. And He comes in and washes you clean from whatever wrong you have done."

"You really mean that?"

"Yes, I do. But it comes with a cost."

"What's the cost?"

"You have to promise to love God with all your heart, and soul, and mind, and to follow Him for the rest of your life."

"To be honest, Sue, I think I need to think about all this."

"Quite right. You need to know more, and there isn't the time here. When we're both better, and at home, I'd like you to come visit me at my cottage. We'll have coffee, and I'll show you where all these promises are written in the Bible."

Gail smiled for the first time since Sue had met her, and she looked very beautiful!

"It's settled then. We must exchange phone numbers before we leave."

When they returned to their room, Sue began to pray silently for Gail, and as she did she felt a wonderful peace descend on her. It washed over her and bathed every part of her body with a tranquility she had never known before. "Oh, Lord," she whispered, "I do love you." At that moment she knew that God would sort Gail out. She would try to be there for her, but it was God who would transform her into what He intended her to be.

———

The next time Vicar Todd came to see Sue he commented on her progress—physically *and* emotionally. She explained about Gail and asked him to pray for her. She also told him about the gratitude she now felt in her heart toward God. "I am so grateful, Vicar. Gail needed to hear about God, and my ability to understand her pain— because of my cancer—made everything easier to bear."

Vicar Todd patted her hand as it lay on the bedclothes. "God knows His plans, Sue! Wonderful plans He has!"

How Sue loved the vicar!

CHAPTER 11

The Visit

On Saturday Lucy decided not to go to church for a while. Even though she enjoyed her new friends, she wasn't ready for all the pressure and conviction that attending church brought on. Maybe soon, but not now. She had plenty to fill her days—including Sunday mornings. The gardens needed tending, and after the success of the African stories with the twins, she was eager to illustrate them.

She spent the whole morning in the garden, putting in the plants she had brought down from London. After lunch she planted over one hundred daffodil bulbs in large groups in the flower beds and two hundred crocus and snowdrop bulbs in sweeps in the lawn. The air was cold about her, but she didn't notice. At least the rain had ended. There was nothing she liked more than planting new life into her garden, and she knew she would spend the winter looking forward to the spring arrivals with great anticipation.

In the early evening dusk, Lucy lit a bonfire and burned all the dead leaves and branches. She enjoyed tending the huge fire. As she poked it occasionally with her pitchfork, she was momentarily sad her boys weren't there with her.

She remembered many a cold autumn day when the whole family worked together to clean up the yards and garden and then spent hours in the evening tending the fires. As the fire died down, feeling a little lonely, Lucy left her fond memories behind to go indoors to make some supper.

Suddenly, she remembered she had promised to phone Jack concerning arrangements for the twins the following week. Jack took over on the weekends but needed help during the day the rest of the time. She dialed the number, and Jack answered.

"Hello, Jack. Lucy here. I just wondered what you'd like me to do for you this week."

"Well, something's cropped up, and I have to go to Truro on business on Monday. Do you think that if I drop the girls at school you could pick them up and take them to see Sue? They want to see her as often as possible, and I think it's good for Sue, too."

"That sounds fine. I'll need directions to the hospital."

"Yes, I've drawn you a little map. I'll put it in one of the girl's pockets. I should be back early enough to visit Sue and pick the girls up at about seven-thirty. Will that do?"

"Yes, of course, that's fine. Will the girls know which ward to go to?"

"Yes, they've been there twice now."

"How is Sue?"

"Remarkably well. It's amazing, really. Lucy, thank you so much for your help. The twins really loved their time with you."

"It's my pleasure. The girls are fun."

Lucy popped into Hilda's at eleven o'clock on Monday morning. She asked her if she would like to come over after tea to help with a project she was going to do with the twins. She stayed for a cup of tea, but since Hilda was in the middle of her washing, Lucy insisted she needed to be off. She made a hasty retreat, leaving Hilda with

118

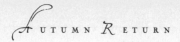

her arms up to the elbows in foamy suds.

She then made a quick trip to the shoe shop in Redruth and asked if they could let her have a few boxes for her project with the girls. They kindly obliged, and once more Lucy marveled at the differences between Cornwall and London. With everything purchased for the craft she had planned for the girls, Lucy headed for the school.

As usual, the girls—especially Kasey—did not stop talking for the entire trip to the hospital. Lucy had brought flowers and fruit for them to give to their mummy, and they were intent on arguing about who should give what. When they reached the hospital, Lucy split both the flowers and the fruit so they could offer duplicate gifts to Sue. Lucy had not met the twins' mother yet and was a little nervous as she walked down the corridor. But she needn't have worried at all. Sue was looking remarkably well, and she smiled with delight at the sight of her beloved twins.

"Thank you, Lucy. It's so nice to meet you," she said as she carefully opened her arms to the twins, who were clambering onto the bed.

"I am pleased to meet you, too." It was difficult to hold a polite adult conversation around the girls' chatter. "And you, how are you feeling?"

"Not as bad as I thought I might. I've made it over the first hurdle."

The girls took over after that. They wanted some time with their mummy, and after unceremoniously dropping their gifts into their mother's arms, they started in about every detail of their day.

Wanting to give Sue and the girls a bit of privacy, Lucy looked out over the uninspiring view of buildings that made up the hospital. She was glad to see some trees with a few leaves in the last of their glorious autumn red and gold dress left on them. They helped break the monotony. She turned and gazed about the ward, which held four patients, all looking very ill and worried. The room was nicely decorated, even boasting some rather lovely landscapes of local beauty painted, she guessed, by local artists. Lucy noticed the trinket box on the cabinet beside Sue's bed. Lucy wondered how many more of the girls' crafted treasures were placed with pride about the Trent home.

"Lucy," Sue interrupted her thoughts, "how are you coping with the children? If they are naughty, please tell them so."

Lucy smiled into the woman's blue eyes and shook her head. "They're no trouble, really."

For the first time, Lucy took the opportunity to study Sue. She had small, neat features, and lovely golden curls framed her face perfectly. Lucy could see where the girls got their looks. Yet, she seemed pleasantly unaware of her attractiveness. Lucy noticed that Sue looked a little drained, so she decided to set up a diversion for the girls. She took two coloring books, which she'd found in the supermarket, and some waxed crayons from a box in her bag. Since the room had no table, she settled the girls on two chairs and helped them place the books and crayons on the window ledge.

"Do something pretty for Mummy," she said.

When she returned to Sue's bedside, she was resting wearily on the stiff hospital pillows. It seemed Sue was still in a lot of pain—and very tired—so Lucy decided their visit needed to end soon.

"Like little sparrows they are, always singing." Sue spoke lovingly of her little girls.

"They get bored." Lucy smiled, wondering how Sue felt without her breast. She tried hard not to look at the place where it had been.

"I hear you may be out soon?"

"Yes, I'm worried how I'll cope. I'm still very sore." She shifted awkwardly on the bed.

"Hilda and I discussed it today over tea. You don't have to worry. Several people want to help you out. We're going to make up a rota."

"You're so very kind."

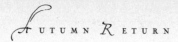

"Not at all. It's payment for the mackerel!"

"I heard about that."

They both laughed.

The girls began to squabble over the crayons, both wanting red at the same time.

"I think it's time we left Mummy. I have a new project for you to do after tea," Lucy told them.

"Oh good!" Carly cheered. "I want to do the gluing. I'm good at it. What will we make?"

"You'll see! Now, let's get going."

Both girls presented their mummy with a colored picture, a big kiss, and a promise to be good for Lucy.

"Thank you for all you've done," Sue said.

"Don't mention it. It's my pleasure," Lucy said, then gathered up her bag and left with the twins.

It was dark by the time they got home. *Winter is on its way*, thought Lucy as she put the lamps on in the sitting room and allowed the girls to watch a cartoon until teatime. She lit the fire for them, though the heating was on, and went to prepare boiled eggs and toast fingers. Hilda arrived at six o'clock. She was as excited as the girls about what the project might be. They all sat around the table, the girls kneeling up on the green pads to get a better view. Lucy then produced four shoe boxes filled with an assortment of objects: pieces of material, empty matchboxes, some leftover bits of her new carpet, glue and scissors, paints and brushes, and a sharp knife—the latter of which the girls were told not to touch.

"What are we going to do?" sang Carly and Kasey together, sounding exactly like the *Wooden Tops*—a favorite children's program—which took Lucy back to her own childhood.

"We're going to make a doll's house," she said matter-of-factly.

"It will have four rooms: a sitting room, a kitchen with a staircase, one bedroom, and a bathroom."

"Oh, Lucy," Hilda said, her face lighting up, "what fun!"

Lucy set Hilda cutting a large window at the bottom of each box—each with a cross shape insert, making four windowpanes. Once this was done, she put the boxes on their sides to make the rooms. She showed the girls how to make the furniture for the house. She helped them glue matchboxes together for chests of drawers, craft a bath from a margarine tub, and cut cardboard to make beds, tables, and chairs—the sky was the limit! Lucy explained they would make one room a day, and then when all was ready, she would make a front and a roof for the doll's house.

The children were so engrossed with their folding and gluing they hardly said a word. Lucy played some Beethoven softly in the background. The music had soothed her many times before, and as she looked at the new people in her life, its mood touched her again.

They quickly finished the kitchen. It had a little sink, made by cutting the bottom from a yogurt carton and setting it into a stack of matchboxes. They had also made a cardboard cooker—the rings and door put on in felt tip—and a table and two chairs with seat covers made from tiny scraps of material. The girls glued the curtains up at the window, and Lucy finished them off with a little strip of cloth for a valance. She then had Kasey paint the floor a muddy red, and Lucy herself painted black squares across it to resemble a quarry-tiled floor.

"Well I never . . ." exclaimed Hilda at last. "Whoever would have thought it would look so pretty!" The girls arranged and rearranged the furniture, while Lucy made herself and Hilda a nice cup of hot tea for their hard work!

During the week, Hilda shared bits of her life with Lucy—telling her all about her beloved Wilfred and of Vicar Todd's Betty. It

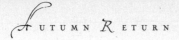

seemed to Lucy these people had come through their difficulties un-scathed, and it confused her. Eventually, she got up the nerve to broach the subject with Hilda.

"I was very bitter, my dear. Please don't think me perfect. I couldn't understand why God hadn't allowed me even a *few* years as a married woman. I told Him I wanted children many a time. It was several years before I accepted the fact that I was here, and Wil was not—and there was work to be done. God helped me see how I could show love to others. . . ." She trailed off, looking out to sea through the kitchen window. The girls were busy at the table. "*His* love," she added. "That's the only love we can depend upon."

Nothing more was said, and Lucy kept her sadness locked in tight, though she was very moved by what the old woman had shared with her. She felt strangely privileged. Perhaps one day she would feel ready to share with Hilda. She certainly felt comfortable with the sweet energetic woman and felt great admiration for her. Lucy found it hard to believe someone could give and give and not complain. Her selfless concern for others was enviable.

By Friday the doll's house was finished. Lucy pulled the four rooms together with the help of masking tape and painted over it in white. They painted a red-tiled roof on some cardboard. The front of the house was also made of cardboard. It had four small windows and a black front door, cut so it would open. Lucy painted the letter box and doorknocker in gold and taped the front of the house on one side of the boxes so it could be opened. When Jack came to retrieve them, the girls proudly walked their doll's house across the drive to the car, watched from the doorway by two rather tired ladies. Jack smiled his thanks and took his little ones home.

———

The following day, as the early dawn stole slowly across the bow of the horizon, Lucy made for the studio. The orange-red sky framed the golden edges of the low, long, hazy blue clouds. Inspired,

Lucy began to paint as she reacquainted herself with the story she had written, titled *The Little Boat*. She had been so busy lately, she hadn't had much time to work on her illustrations, but she was eager to start again.

As she painted, her mind wandered here, there, and eventually to Africa. She remembered the trip she and Tom had made to Victoria Falls. Water had seemed to be cascading from everywhere, and the white mist, which rose over fifty feet from the falls, could be seen from many miles away. Because of the cloud of mist, the falls were known in Africa as *The Smoke That Thunders*. They both had gotten soaked in the mist but loved it.

The waterfalls had reminded Lucy of huge sheets hanging on the washing line, flowing in the breeze, movement everywhere. The roaring sound and the spectacular greenery, with its strange, twisting, curling roots reaching for the sky, made for a rather surreal scene—like something from another planet. It was all so incredibly beautiful. They had walked hand in hand along the long snakelike path opposite the falls, enjoying the cool mist on their skin. Their hearts raced as they peered over the entwined-twig fence that prevented hikers from falling down the deep ravine.

Lucy remembered holding her slightly swollen stomach as she wondered whether God would give her a boy or a girl. She secretly hoped for a girl. But God was in control. He would give her what was right for her. Well, that was what Tom had insisted, and she had trusted him. After Danny was born, she and Tom had continued to try for a little girl, but Lucy did not become pregnant. Eventually, she resigned herself to not having more children and was very happy with her two boys. But when Rose was born, Lucy was filled with joy. It was nice to have a little girl for whom she could buy pretty clothes and dolls!

Lucy was jarred from her thoughts by the shrill ring of her phone.

"Oh, Luke, how lovely. How are things?"

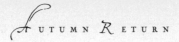

"Mum, sit down a minute."

Lucy's mind raced. She could tell something was wrong. Was it Karen—or perhaps Rose?

"Mum, we heard this morning that Ruth Lange has died. I'm so sorry, Mum."

Lucy sat down on the chair by the table in the hall, staring at the beautiful grain in the wooden front door. She noticed a tiny spider making her cobweb. *I'll have to remove that later.* She was devastated. Ruth had always been there for the children of the orphanage, doing good, caring. . . . *What will happen now?* The little spider did another circle on its web as Lucy tried to focus on Luke's clear soft voice on the other end of the line.

"Mum, are you there? Are you all right? Mum—Mum!"

"Oh yes—yes, I'm okay . . . shocked. When did it happen?" She stroked the hair at the nape of her neck, fiddled with a strand of it, curling and twisting it through her fingers. A strange numbness crept into her stomach.

"Last week. She had a heart attack. The strange thing is, Mum, I have a letter here for you from her. It's dated the twenty-second of last month. She sent it to Robert Hemmings, as she didn't know your new address. I'll send it on. Sorry to just call you like this and blurt it out. But I knew there would never be a right time to tell you." Luke cleared his throat. "I have to go, though, Mum. I'm helping to run an Alpha Course tonight. I'm so sorry."

"I know, Luke. Don't worry. I had to be told. Where did you say you were going off to?"

"An Alpha Course. It's where people who are interested in finding out about God can come and ask all the questions they never felt they could ask anyone before."

"That sounds good." Lucy absolutely did not want to talk about God right then, so she did not ask any more questions. "Bye, son. Speak to you soon."

"Bye, Mum. Love you."

Lucy replaced the receiver very slowly, still clutching at her hair and staring at the cobweb. Round and round went the little spider, enlarging its web. That was life, a circle. Ruth had come full circle, or had she? Was the circle only completed in heaven—in eternity? Lucy truly hoped so. But this life was so hard. How was she to survive without Tom by her side. And now Ruth was dead! She couldn't believe it. Even though Ruth was in her late seventies, it just didn't seem fair. *Lord, why?* The familiar questioning prayer passed her lips.

Painting no longer held Lucy's interest. Instead, she wandered downstairs and took a photograph album from the bookcase in the dining room. They were both there—Tom and Ruth—so real and alive and wonderfully used by God. Now they were gone! When she was on the phone with Luke, Lucy had managed to hold back the cry that swelled in her throat. But now the dam broke, and sobs came up from deep within her being, erupting eventually in a torrent of anger, bitterness, and hurt. No one was there for her, no one to help her face the maelstrom of emotions she felt. She felt as alone as the orphans in Africa! Even Ruth was gone. She would soon be just another sweet but distant memory.

She wanted to talk to someone—to tell it all. She was sure the vicar would understand. But she was also sure, like so many in his position, he would be busy, and she didn't want to take up his time. She thought of Hilda. No, she had come down to Cornwall to be alone. She had been convinced she didn't need people. Was God showing her she *did?* Lucy quickly pushed the thought—like so many others—to the back of her mind.

Though it was getting colder, Lucy decided to take a walk across the cliffs. She put on a deep red sweater with a polo neck and the new walking boots she had bought in the outdoor shop in Redruth. After putting her keys in her pocket, she locked the door behind her. The wind was strong, but her warm clothes and brisk walking speed kept her from feeling particularly cold. She went up the cliff on the

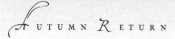

left side of the beach to the highest point and made her way across the winding single-track path, close to the edge. It took Lucy toward Godrevy Lighthouse, where she sat on the rocks, watching the sea crash with a great vengeance against the high rock that formed the base for the beautiful white octagonal lighthouse. It had stood there for over a hundred and fifty years, safe and dependable, guarding the boats from the danger of the reef, shining its brilliant light for miles around for all to see.

Lucy thought about God. He was, and always would be, her refuge, but she couldn't run into His arms just yet. As she gazed out at the lighthouse, Lucy remembered a line from a chorus—*You are my rock, in times of trouble.* No, she just wasn't ready. She got up and turned wearily homeward.

For the first time since she had moved to Cornwall, Lucy slept fitfully. Even the long walk across her beloved cliffs hadn't tired her. She was grateful when dawn came at last, and though the clouds were as heavy and gray as her thoughts, she managed to get out of bed. As she washed and dressed, Lucy tried to think about what to do with two little girls. They were her only reason to rise at all. But did she have the energy to entertain them? What was she thinking when she said she would watch them for Sue and Jack? Well, she had made the commitment. There was nothing she could do about it now—except push through it.

Before collecting the girls, Lucy went shopping at the super-market and ran into the vicar, who kindly broached the subject of her church attendance. Lucy assumed he thought it strange she would spend so much time with Hilda and him during the week, and yet be so reticent about attending church. She tried to explain, which was difficult in the middle of the large store full of bustling people, that she was unsure about her faith. She did not feel church was the place for her—maybe in the future, but she just wasn't sure at the moment. He smiled kindly and gently took her arm.

"Don't worry, my dear—it's our heart God is interested in, not whether we go to church. We're all so grateful for your help with the twins. They can be a handful for me and Hilda, and all the other mums at church are out at work."

Lucy couldn't help wondering if it wasn't her heart that was the problem. But she wasn't ready to discuss that with the vicar in the middle of the store. So she assured him she was enjoying the children and told him she had to rush because she was picking the girls up from school. Before she left, the vicar patted her arm gently and smiled.

"I care, my dear."

Suddenly, Lucy felt an overwhelming desire to open her heart to this dear man, but she quickly turned and walked away. *I mustn't allow it. I'll just get hurt again.*

As she left the store, though, Lucy couldn't help thinking how good it would have been to be able to tell him about her heartache over the loss of Tom and Ruth, and maybe even the incredible loss she felt when she left Africa. But she quickly dismissed it from her mind and headed out to pick up the girls.

———————

The next few weeks were spent in a hive of activity, and though the pain of Tom's and Ruth's deaths was still acute, Lucy began to love the gentle people of Tarran Bay. As the days of autumn passed pleasantly by, Lucy worked with Hilda and Vicar Todd to help the Trents and she began to feel very close to them. She was warmed by their love, not only for the twins and Jack and Sue but also for her. Lucy was surprised to realize she was also establishing a relationship with Sue, who, to everyone's relief, was making an excellent recovery.

One day Lucy decided to pop in to see how Sue was coping, and Sue invited her in for coffee.

"I came by to see how you are getting on," Lucy said as she followed Sue to the kitchen.

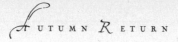

"Thanks, Lucy. I'm doing very well. Having the twins in school during the day makes it easier, and Jack is so good about doing the housework. I'm beginning to feel much stronger."

"Good. It shows!"

"One sugar?"

"Yes, thanks, but not heaped! I keep trying to cut it out, but it's hard!"

Sue grinned and wrinkled her nose as she sat opposite Lucy at the kitchen table and handed her the steaming coffee. It smelled so good to Lucy, who was rather chilled from her walk across the harbor to Sue's home.

"How's the treatment going?"

"It isn't as bad as I thought it would be. To be honest with you, Lucy, my biggest fear was of losing my hair with the radiotherapy— aren't I conceited!"

"No, not at all. I'm sure I'd have felt the same under the circumstances. How are you coping with the change in your body?" Lucy leaned over and touched Sue's hand. "You don't mind me asking, do you, dear?"

"No, it's good to be able to talk freely. I . . . I'm . . . coping very well. It's not so bad. It would have been much worse to lose an arm or leg—more debilitating."

"I hadn't thought of that. Do you ever wonder why it happened to you?"

"Yes, I questioned God every day I was in the hospital. But he showed me that He was with me through everything and that He can work everything out for good. I was able to befriend my roommate, Gail. She drove me mad at first, but eventually I saw her as God sees her and realized that she needs Him. I'm seeing her regularly now and have invited her to come to church. If she finds God, it will have made all this worthwhile—and if she doesn't, I will still have done my part and made a good friend."

"I don't know how you managed to hang on to your faith through all of this, Sue."

"Oh, I sometimes feel like throwing in the towel. Believe me, I thought about it many times. But often when I was at my lowest, God would speak to me through His Word. He gave me two verses that kept me going while I was in the hospital—'May the God of hope fill you with all joy and peace as you trust in Him.' And, 'Stand fast then, and do not submit again to a yoke of slavery, which you have once put off.' You see, I was full of fear, Lucy. I was afraid of cancer and the damage it did to my body, and I was afraid to die. But God strengthened me. If He could see me through a mastectomy, He can see me through any situation. I am no longer fearful of the future. I have learned a good lesson—I can put my trust in God!"

After a few moments Lucy spoke very softly. She didn't look up from her cup.

"I wish I had that kind of faith, Sue. I felt so lost and angry after Tom died. I don't see why God had to take him from me. Why does God do the things He does? I had a friend, Ruth, who—" Lucy's voice broke, and she couldn't continue.

Sue reached across the table and patted Lucy's free hand. When Lucy looked up she saw Sue was biting at her bottom lip rather nervously. *She doesn't know what to say*, thought Lucy sadly.

But then Sue spoke. "God knows best and He knows His plans. He has something very special for you, Lucy, and plenty for you to learn along the way. Talk to Him. Ask Him questions."

"I do—sometimes. He just doesn't seem to answer me like He does you. But I will try to do as you suggest." She removed her hand from the warmth of Sue's and fiddled with her necklace. Sue's words were beginning to make her think. As she looked at her new friend, Lucy wondered at the wisdom of someone so much younger than herself.

"Thanks so much for the coffee, Sue." Lucy stood and picked

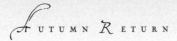

up her handbag, which was hanging from the back of her chair. "And for the good advice."

"You're very welcome Lucy. And thank *you* for everything you've done for the girls. They talk about you all the time!"

"They're delightful. You should be proud of them."

"Thank you—I am."

———

Lucy found excitement rising in her at the thought of her family arriving at her cottage for Christmas. When she was not with the girls, she spent most of her time stenciling the bathroom with pink briar roses, painting pictures of the views from her windows, and gardening. She gathered the leaves and made a compost heap. She cut back and made ready for spring. She lit at least three more bonfires and helped Hilda with hers.

Once, they invited the twins over to help. Afterward, they buried foil-wrapped potatoes deep in the fire and later ate them with lots of real butter. The girls loved it. Somehow, through the sharing of the chores, Hilda and Lucy became closer, and Lucy felt as though she had found a mother figure. She began to open up to Hilda and found her to be a wise confidante—someone she could trust with the deep concerns she had hid in her wounded heart. She felt a bit anxious that Christmas was quickly approaching, when the kitchen and dining room still had to be painted. But she knew she would finish in time. She even made it to church once or twice and unexpectedly enjoyed it.

Was God on the move? She tried hard to believe He was. As the weeks went by, her spirits seemed to be lifting. Contentment and comfort filled her as day after day she gave of her time, energy, and love to those she was growing to love and trust here in Tarran Bay. And once again she started to talk to God!

CHAPTER 12

The Dinner Party

Lucy stepped out of the bath and dried herself on a cream bath towel. It was hard to believe nearly three months had passed since her move to Tarran Bay. She was really beginning to feel she fit into the small village community. Lucy held back the white lace curtain and wiped away the steam to peer through the window. She couldn't see a thing! It was pitch black and unseasonably cold. She laughed when she thought of Dan's words to her all those months ago. *It'll be so cold there, Mum!* Sometimes her boys knew what they were talking about. *I believe I'll walk to Jack and Sue's anyway. It will be refreshing.* Jack and Sue had invited Lucy to dinner. They said it was to thank her for being so helpful with the twins. Surprisingly, she was excited. It had been a long time since she had looked forward to a social engagement.

While polishing her nails, Lucy thought about all that Sue had been through. She couldn't get the conversation she'd had with Sue a couple of weeks before out of her mind. Sue had been so strong and courageous. Jack too. Lucy was looking forward to being with them for a happier occasion. Sue was doing very well with her treatment, and the future was looking much brighter.

Lucy went to the wardrobe to find something a bit special to wear. She needed new clothes, but she could not bring herself to take on the shopping challenge. She had loved clothes once. . . . Opening the beautifully carved door, she took out a moss-green velvet shirt and a long black skirt and laid them on the bed. Black lace-up boots would finish off the outfit. She dressed and then dried her hair, spiking it up a little to make it more fashionable. She put on some silver drop earrings and lightly made up her face. As she looked in the mirror of her dressing table, her reflection pleased her. The soft water and sea air were doing her good. Lastly, she sprayed her neck and forearms with her favorite Miss Dior perfume and turned to take a last glance at her appearance in the long mirror on the wardrobe. She would do!

As she made her way down the winding staircase and into the kitchen, Lucy realized the Aga had come into its own since the weather had changed. It filled the kitchen with comforting warmth at all hours of the day. She took a bottle of sparkling apple juice from the fridge and gathered a plant wrapped in blue tissue that she'd bought for Sue. She placed her gifts on the hall table and put on her thick brown wool coat and lemon scarf.

The walk to the harbor took only a few minutes, and Lucy loved it. The moon was large and crescent-shaped and sat low in the sky—and so many stars were out tonight! It reminded her of the night sky of Africa.

Resting her drink and plant on the harbor wall, Lucy stopped a moment to look out at the crashing sea. A fine mist enveloped her. It would ruin her hair, but she didn't care. Her thoughts strayed to happier times on this very beach, to the times when Tom and the boys had played in the surf. Back they would go again and again, lifting their colored boards high above their heads, hoping that the next wave would take them farther than the last as they leapt over

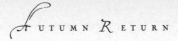

the oncoming surf. Sometimes she would join them, producing squeals of delight from her boys as she toppled time and again from the board. She never did get the hang of it. Tom had patiently tried to teach her, but to no avail. So she had spent most of her time on the beach near this very wall, reading in the sunshine on the blue tartan rug, propped up with cushions from the car. Such happy times. Her mind couldn't hold all the memories—good and bad. So many emotions, this way, that way, up and down, just like the choppy sea below her. Turning now with her gifts in her arms, she walked to the Trents'.

"Hello Lucy," Jack said with a beaming smile for his new friend as he opened the door. "Cold, isn't it?"

Lucy nodded, handing over the drink and plant. He took her coat, led her to the sitting room, and motioned for her to sit down near the roaring log fire. She loved this part of wintertime in Cornwall—everywhere she went fires burned brightly as the nights drew in.

"Glass of elderflower?"

"Oh yes, thanks. That would be lovely."

"You look rather cold. Would you prefer tea?"

"No, the elderflower will be nice. I was a bit early, so I stood at the harbor wall. I looked over the beach side and watched the sea. . . . I can't get used to the beauty. It's all so different. . . ." She trailed off, not wanting to talk about her past just yet.

Suddenly the twins appeared in the doorway.

"Tell us an Africa story," they shouted together. "Pleeeease!"

Jack looked down at Lucy and raised his eyebrows as if questioning her.

"Would you mind? Your stories are legendary!"

Sue shouted from the kitchen that they could have twenty minutes and no longer. "Lucy is mine tonight!" she called from her cooking. The food smelled wonderful and gave Lucy an appetite.

Lucy said she didn't mind telling them a story and stood to follow the girls. As she placed her elderflower on the mantel, she saw the butterfly card had a place of pride in the center of it. The twins led her to their very pretty pink, girly bedroom. Lucy smiled. *This is a change.* The boys' rooms had always been blue at home in Gloucester Gardens. She was pleased to see the doll's house sitting on the white chest of drawers. Giggling with anticipation, the girls jumped onto the top bunk. They cuddled up and looked down at Lucy as she sat in the comfortable chair next to the bed.

She recalled her story about a little African boy who lived on a farm, and how when he heard the parable of the lost sheep, he couldn't sleep until he gave his life to Jesus. She was amazed she could remember the stories so well after such a long time. It was satisfying to see that the little twins really seemed to like them. Her idea, at the time she created them, was that she would send them to Ruth for African children to enjoy. She'd never sent them. Too late now.

When she finished, the girls asked her to pray with them.

Oh no, how could she pray? Yet how could she not pray?

"You pray . . . pray for me," she said softly, and they did.

"Dear God," Kasey said, "please bless Lucy." And Carly added in a loud voice, "Amen!"

Can you bless me, Lord? Lucy thought as she made her way downstairs with the girls, who insisted on kissing their parents goodnight once more. As they reached the door, Lucy heard an unfamiliar voice coming from the sitting room. Entering the room she saw, to her dismay, that Jack and Sue had invited another guest—a man!

"Lucy," Jack said. "this is Gordon Seymour."

"Hello," she said, moving toward the attractive, middle-aged man—late forties, maybe fifty, she guessed. He wore a pair of beige chinos and a denim shirt. She shook his hand. *Not a man. I don't want to do this. But I can't leave now.*

"Was it a good story?" Jack asked his daughters.

"Oh yes, very good," they cried in unison. "You know,

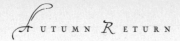

Daddy—she sings too," Carly said, looking up at Lucy and smiling.

Not innocently! Lucy thought, her face coloring. She hated that she blushed, but she simply couldn't control it.

"Do you sing?" Gordon asked.

"Not anymore."

Luckily, no one continued the subject, and after bringing the twins in to kiss their mother, Jack left to put the children to bed for the second time.

There were a few moments of awkward silence once Lucy and Gordon were alone.

"How are you settling in at Dawn Cottage?" Gordon seemed to know more about her than she did of him.

"Really well, thanks. I haven't done half the things I wanted to do. But I suppose I'll have more time now that I am not watching the girls so often."

"Yes, I hear you've been wonderful with them."

"They were fun, made me do young things, think young things."

Lucy sipped her drink, and Gordon smiled at her over his glass. His hair was brown, graying at the temples. He had dark brown eyes and was extremely fit and tanned. Lucy quickly looked away. She couldn't imagine why she was noticing his features.

"Dinner's ready," called Sue. "We're in the dining room—posh tonight!"

Jack returned and led the way. Lucy had only been in the sitting room and kitchen the times she had dropped off the girls. As she entered the dining room, she marveled at what you could learn about people from their homes. The sitting room was very *Laura Ashley*, but here in the dining room, it was more *Habitat*. The Trents obviously loved to read—books were everywhere, piled high on shelves that lined every wall. And from the titles, she could see their tastes were varied and interesting. The ceiling was low, with black painted beams, which she thought was rather a shame—probably done in the sixties. It was a lovely room, though. The fire burning in the fireplace filled the candle-lit room with a golden light, making everything warm and inviting.

Lucy sat next to Jack and opposite Gordon. She had been looking forward to the evening, but since Gordon had arrived she felt nervous. She didn't know why, except perhaps simply because he was a man. Men always made her uneasy—except for Tom. Her heart ached once more at the memory of him. She still found it hard to be with people without Tom to lean on. Lucy was rather shy by nature and had used him to hide behind. She didn't know why she lacked confidence around people. She had been a good teacher and had stood in front of thirty children on a daily basis. But it was much easier to deal with children. They were far more accepting than adults.

Sue brought in a tray of roast lamb cooked with rosemary and garlic. It looked absolutely delicious. The abundant supply of food made the huge oak table rather crowded, and as Sue tried to place the tray next to a blue glass bowl, which was filled with water and seashells and had little blue candles floating on top, Lucy reached across and moved her glass to give her some extra room.

"There you are," she said softly.

"Thank you, Lucy. I always prepare too much food."

"It looks wonderful."

Sue looked very sweet in a little black dress with a round neck and capped short sleeves. She wore a thin gold chain around her neck and some gold studs in her ears. Sue asked Jack to cut the meat and went back into the kitchen. When she returned she was carrying two tureens heaped with vegetables and roasted potatoes. Lucy could not imagine how they would fit on the already overladen table, but they found a place for everything. Once Sue was seated Jack said grace, and everyone began to help themselves to the food.

As Lucy filled her plate she listened to the others.

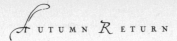

"Did you hear about the accident with the coach on the road to Bodmin?"

"So many died. Ice on the roads they supposed. So sad."

"The weather's cold. I think we're in for some snow."

"It never snows here!"

On and on they went, and she began to relax. Perhaps they wouldn't pry after all. But it came.

"So what made you write African stories?" Gordon asked.

"I spent some time in Mozambique. It was long ago. We . . . my husband and I went before the boys were born. We worked in an orphanage, and I used to think up stories that I thought would interest the children. They had nothing, you see. . . ."

Lucy noticed Sue and Jack glance at each other across the table. They were probably surprised to find out more about her in five minutes through Gordon than they had in the three months they had known her! They listened quietly, no doubt anticipating more information. Lucy was surprised she had shared so much but was not inclined to say more.

"I . . . I find it hard to talk about," Lucy said. "My husband died two years ago." She looked down at her food and cut into the meat carefully. She did not want to appear rude, but she couldn't say more.

Gordon seemed to understand, and he changed the subject.

"I never told you about Janey's news," he said, looking over to Sue. "She's pregnant."

Oh good, Lucy thought, *he has a wife!*

Gordon turned once more to Lucy. "My sister lives in Kenya, as do my parents. They all want me to go out there again, but I'm not sure."

Oh dear, it's a sister.

"When is the baby due?" Sue asked as she took a sip of her drink.

"In the spring. April, I think. I got the letter the day I had your results and forgot to mention it to you."

"What do your parents do?" Lucy asked, making an effort at some meaningful conversation.

"My father was a surgeon, and my mother a nurse. They started up a much-needed hospital out there almost twenty-five years ago. They helped young mothers, mostly—the ones who have a difficult time giving birth. Without Mum and Dad's help, most of them would have died in childbirth. The babies would be left as orphans, as the fathers usually don't want to have anything to do with them. It has been quite a revolutionary work. They are well respected, and I am very proud of them."

"You didn't want to go with them?"

"No, I felt it right to stay in England."

"What do you do?"

Jack laughed. "He's our doctor!"

"I was wondering when you would register at my surgery. You must be very healthy!"

He was smiling, teasing her—it was very annoying. She tilted her chin and looked him straight in the eye and said rather indignantly, "I don't like male doctors!"

Everyone roared with laughter. And though she hadn't meant it as a joke, her statement seemed to break the ice.

Over dessert Lucy learned more about the doctor, as well as Sue and Jack. She had wondered what Jack did at home all day long and learned that he was a computer expert, doing much of his work from home. He produced magazines—a regular one was for the health food industry.

"Now I'll know where to come if my computer acts up. I was scared to turn it on when I moved in. I know so little about how they work. Not that I'll need it much." She was relaxing, joining in.

"You know how to use one, though?" Jack inquired.

"Oh yes, I took some courses when I was teaching."

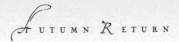

"A teacher!" Jack exclaimed. "I thought you had that look about you."

"What look?"

"Well, you know, that organized look, and there were all the ideas you had with the girls."

"Most of the teachers I know are quite disorganized. As for the crafts, I just enjoy them. I made a doll's house out of shoeboxes with my mother when I was little."

Dessert was simple, blackberry and apple crumble, custard, and cream. It was a delicious feast. The meal ended with cheese, water biscuits, and coffee. They were enjoying their conversation so much, the gathering didn't even leave the dining room. Finally, when she noticed the candles were sputtering, Lucy glanced at her wristwatch and was shocked to see it was nearly midnight.

"I must go. I need to paint my kitchen tomorrow. I should have finished all the painting by now. Never mind, I've lots of time." She added this quickly because she didn't want Jack or Sue to think her time with the twins had upset her plans. "I'd like it done before Christmas, though. My boys and their wives and my two grandchildren are coming to stay for a week."

"That'll be nice for you, Lucy. Perhaps we could meet them?"

"Oh yes, I'd love that."

"How old are your grandchildren?" Jack asked.

"Rose is two, and Jamey is a little more than a year and a half."

"How nice."

"Very tiring, actually, but fun. I was sad Tom never got to see them. He died two months before Rose was born. He was so looking forward to being a granddad." Lucy closed her eyes briefly. "These things happen." The thought made her sad. It was time to leave, so she rose to her feet and offered to help wash up. She was thankful when Sue told her there was no need—they had a dishwasher. Jack took her coat from the rack in the hallway and helped her into it. She took the pale lemon angora scarf from the sleeve and wrapped it around her neck to protect her from the cold. Gordon took his jacket from the coat rack, too, making Lucy slightly uncomfortable. Though she had enjoyed the evening very much, she expected he would ask to walk her home, and it worried her.

She turned to Sue. "Thanks for a lovely evening, Sue. The food was wonderful, as well as the company."

The hostess smiled and said, "You're most welcome. Thanks for all your help with the girls." She spontaneously hugged her new-found friend.

"I was just being practical," Lucy said softly, then added, "I really did enjoy it." Lucy was surprised by the love she felt for this dear young woman.

Turning now, she stepped out into the cold night. Jack held the door for her, kissed her cheek, and gave her a warm hug. She couldn't dislike these special people. They obviously loved God, yet they didn't go on about it. They were just very kind.

"Let me walk you home," Gordon said.

There—it had come, as she knew it would.

"I'm fine, really." Lucy hurried down the path, desperate to get away, but he shouted good-bye to his friends, caught up with her at the gate, and opened it for her.

"Don't be silly," he said cheerfully. "It's no problem."

"Thank you." She resigned herself to his care for the short walk and decided to make the best of it. They walked past the harbor and across the beach. Her cottage was on the other side of the bay, and though she often walked this way during the day, at night the rocks seemed daunting, dark, and overpowering, with their black, shadowy caves and hidden crevices. In the light of the moon, the empty upturned rowing boats looked like huge tortoise shells resting on the sand. They talked about the evening, about how well Sue was looking in such a short space of time, and they were still talking when they reached Lucy's gate.

"I know where I've seen you," he said as they stood together

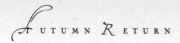

outside her front garden gates. "You're the lady on the beach."

"You make me sound like a woman of mystery—from an Agatha Christie novel!"

Gordon smiled down at her. He was so tall.

"St. Ives. I noticed you there. It was late, and I saw you alone on the beach. It was a beautiful evening—an amazing sunset. I was watching you from my board."

"The windsurfer!" She remembered. It had been one of the most amazing sunsets she had ever seen! And Lucy had seen quite a few amazing sunsets in her time. "I nearly painted you!" she said with a laugh. Now she hesitated, not wanting to ask him in for coffee, but not knowing how to play the situation. She guessed he was much younger than she. Lucy didn't want him to think her aloof—but at the same time, she didn't want him to think that she saw anything in his walking her home. He saved the day.

"Lovely to have met you at last. Hope I'll see you soon." He began to walk away but turned quickly. "Oh yes, I'll drop in the number of a very good female doctor in Redruth for you!"

Lucy thought Gordon was being a bit cheeky but knew she deserved his jesting. She smiled weakly and said, "Thank you. Good night."

After she shut the front door, Lucy peeked through the window to watch Gordon as he walked up the lane. It was nearly half past twelve.

———

Lucy didn't go straight to bed. Her mind was full of the evening's conversation. The talk about Gordon's family in Africa had started her thinking, and she didn't feel tired in the least. Instead, she made herself some cocoa and went to the little study at the end of the hall. Opening the door and switching on the light, she walked to the corner of the room and picked up Tom's guitar from its stand. Sitting down near the desk, her fingers strummed its strings. It was very out of tune. She cringed at the sound, which reminded her of a strangling cat. Taking the guitar by its neck, she opened the desk drawer to find the tuner. She remembered seeing it the day she was looking for the African stories for the girls. Yes, there it was. She also saw Tom's Leatherman, a present she'd given him when he and Luke had gone back to Africa eleven years before. They'd gone for a month to help build a little clinic on Ruth's compound. When they returned he said he had used the multipurpose tool countless times, and he continued to use it through the years that followed.

Seeing it, Lucy remembered the radiator in the hall was full of air—the heat just wasn't getting to it properly. The Leatherman was just what she needed to release the valve. She hurried to the hall and within minutes had accomplished her task. *Dan would be proud of me*, she thought with a wry smile as the radiator began to heat up again. *And he said I couldn't even change a fuse!* She returned the tool to its worn brown leather pouch and laid it on the desk as she picked up the tuner.

After tuning the guitar, Lucy began to sing the song she had written so long ago when she learned an old school friend had died of a drug overdose.

Have your illusions of life been shattered,
Your trust in mankind been betrayed?
Has the love of your own life been costly?
For it will lead you to an early grave.

Just look to Jesus. He's the answer.
Look to Him. He will give you life anew, life anew.

I know my Savior can heal hurts.
Put your trust in Him. He's the Rock.
Die to your old life and let Him reign there,
And He will lead you to eternal life.

Just look to Jesus. He's the . . .

Her voice trailed off, her eyes stinging with yet more tears. So many tears! *You are the only answer, I know. I just can't feel you.*

The song had another verse, but Lucy couldn't sing it. Yet somehow she felt stronger, ready to take on another difficult task. She placed the old guitar back in its rest, switched on her computer, and sat in front of it—something she hadn't done for more than two years. The first file she found was a story called *The Naughty Boys*, which she had written many years before. It needed a little work, but maybe the twins would enjoy it. She sat there for some time revising her work, when a thought crossed her mind. She remembered seeing the book *My Naughty Little Sister* on the twins' bedside cabinet—perhaps she could illustrate her story and give it to them as a Christmas present.

The idea increased Lucy's enthusiasm, and she didn't give a thought to the passing time until she looked out the window in front of her and noticed the arrival of dawn. The mist of the previous day had cleared, and Lucy could just make out the heaving gray-green sea. The waves chopped in huge triangles, not seeming to know which way to go. The sky was filled with quickly moving dark gray clouds. *Oh no. I'll never get the kitchen painted now.* Skipping her normal bedtime ritual, Lucy hurried to bed for a few hours sleep before her day of painting began.

CHAPTER 13

Friendship

Lucy awoke to the wind rushing around the cottage, leaving eerie sounds in its wake. It reminded her of the bungalow in Mozambique with the wind whistling in the huge nearby trees. Considering the hour she went to bed, Lucy had slept well and felt refreshed. Her mind wandered back to the previous night's wonderful dinner. She was beginning to feel like a substitute for the mother she could tell Sue so greatly missed. Lucy had always wanted a daughter, though in truth she was pleased to know she was too young to be Sue's mother—but only just! She glanced at her tiny blue enamel alarm clock and saw that the time was ten o'clock. *I must get cracking!*

Slipping off the bedclothes, Lucy pushed her feet into her beige suede slippers and made for the bathroom. *That kitchen will get painted today, even if I have to stay up until dawn a second night.* After a snatched breakfast of toast and her favorite Marmite savory spread, Lucy covered the whole area with dust sheets. After slipping into her painting outfit, she carried the creamy yellow paint from the utility room and started right in. She took special care around the beautiful multicolored tiles placed above the sink and behind the Aga.

As she worked, Lucy found herself singing occasionally. It surprised her. Years ago, she had always accompanied her work with a song. But she had somehow lost the joy of music when Tom died. *Maybe it's returning. Can it be that my life is on its way back?* The thought made Lucy a little nervous, but she also felt a glimmer of excitement about the change—and her future. Lucy wondered what the boys would make of her home and her newfound friends. She hoped they would finally understand she was in the right place.

She took a break around noon, grabbing a sandwich to stave off her hunger. As she ate, she studied her cozy kitchen.

Even with dust sheets, the room was wonderful. Brass saucepans in ranging sizes hung from the beams on large hooks. Utensils hung from a small steel frame above the Aga, along with garlic bunches and onion strings. Though covered by a cloth, the one-hundred-year-old school clock that was once her mother's ticked away the time. She loved the sound of the clock, so peaceful and calming.

Since she was eager to finish, Lucy picked up her roller after only a short rest. As she worked, Lucy contemplated her life. She had been given so much—marriage to a good man, wonderful children, and the sweetest grandchildren. But other than her family, life seemed futile. Was she just passing through? Was there really a heaven? Did all of her efforts really make any difference? Why did it all seem so hard? It had always been hard—trying to solve people's problems was difficult work. And caring for others had seemed almost impossible since Tom had died. But it was possible—she saw it in the life of Jesus, and others throughout history. What was she missing? She remembered an interview she had heard with Mother Teresa of Calcutta on the radio. "I never see numbers," she had said, "I just see one . . . one . . . one."

In spite of the paint fumes, Lucy's mind began to clear. Maybe her problem had been that she always tried to help too many people

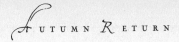

at once. Tom had always said she should point people to God and not attempt to solve the world's problems on her own. *"That's pride,"* he had said. *"You are putting yourself in the place of God. You must seek His power."*

So she needed to pace herself—which she was learning—and somehow she needed to tap into God's power. How was she going to do that? Lucy feared she had no idea where to start.

A knock startled her from her thoughts. "Just a minute!" Lucy called to the unknown visitor. She quickly rolled one last spot beside the window before going to open the door, roller in hand. She forgot to worry about what she looked like until she caught a glimpse of herself in the hall mirror. *Oh no!* She was covered with paint, but it was too late to do anything about it now. The visitor knew she was home.

It was Gordon.

"Well, well, the painted lady!"

"Don't mock!" Lucy was horrified to think of what a sight she was.

"Have I taken you from your painting?"

"No, just finished." Lucy could not imagine why she had admitted that—it was the perfect excuse to get him to leave.

"I've brought you the number of the doctor in Redruth," he said, walking straight past her uninvited and placing a little card on the telephone table. Lucy held the roller up out of his way as he passed her, abashed at his entrance. She needed time to think!

"Got time for a cuppa?"

The shame of it! "Yes," she said meekly.

Gordon said he liked the changes she'd made to the cottage. He had been in to visit "Old Parsons" many a time, and things had been a little dark.

"It's so warm and bright now," he said.

"Yes, even on a day like this." She motioned with the sticky yellow roller to the window. "I'll just clean up. Perhaps you

149

wouldn't mind putting the kettle on—since you invited yourself!" She walked toward the utility room to wash up. "And would you mind opening the window for me, Gordon? The smell of paint is giving me a headache."

"My pleasure." He grinned.

Lucy was furious he hadn't rung first. What a mess she looked. Then she realized he probably didn't have her telephone number. Well, that was not much of an excuse for his presumptuousness. She peered in Tom's old shaving mirror, which hung on the catch of the small window that looked out onto the garden, and scratched paint from her nose.

"Don't bother with that." The sound of Gordon's voice made Lucy jump. He was leaning in the doorway. "It suits you!"

Flustered, she washed her brushes and roller and wiped her hands on a towel. At last she returned to the kitchen, trying desperately to push a smile to her pursed lips. They sat opposite each other at the kitchen table, and try as she might, Lucy just couldn't dislike him. He was trying to be fun and kind. As she was cleaning up, he had even removed the dust sheets for her and folded them neatly on the back of her granddad chair.

"I was wondering if you were busy on Wednesday evening?"

He couldn't be serious. Perhaps he was going to ask her to baby-sit the twins so he could take Jack and Sue out. She couldn't think what to say, so she weakly said, "No."

"Well, then come to the pub with me. It's quite nice. They do a good bar meal, so don't eat. I'll pick you up at seven." And without waiting for an answer, he stood up, walked to the front door, and was gone, leaving her standing in the doorway staring at his departing back in total disbelief. He hadn't even drunk his tea!

It would serve him right if I don't go—that would show him! But she knew she would be there. It sounded like fun.

On Wednesday afternoon, after making some finishing touches to the kitchen, Lucy found the letter from Ruth on the front door mat. Luke had certainly taken his time sending it to her. Lucy held the letter to her breast, as though it were Ruth herself. She made for the refuge of the sofa and put her feet up on a cushion that she had placed on the coffee table. She was very anxious to know her friend's thoughts so close to her death. Crossing her feet she began to read.

My Dear Lucy,

How are you? You seemed so sad in your last letter, my dear. Are you adjusting to Tom's death yet? Would you like to come and stay for a while? You would be most welcome. There's always lots to do here. Perhaps it's too soon, but do think about it, dear.

I'm feeling so weary these days. I have lots of help, though, so please don't worry. I only want you to come if you think it would be good for you. Most of my help comes from the children who've grown up here. They help with the teaching, cooking, and cleaning. We seem to be getting more and more children who have lost parents to AIDS these days. The war is over, but another enemy comes!

I feel God is preparing me for something new. . . .

Lucy put the letter down in her lap and wept. After a bit, she wiped her misted eyes on her shirt sleeves—Tom's shirt sleeves. She loved to wear Tom's old shirts to decorate in. Strange how the wearing of them made her feel comforted—safe. She read on.

I feel He is preparing someone younger to take over. It needs to be someone strong—strong in spirit and in health. Do you understand? Pray about it for me, won't you, Lucy? I'm praying it will happen soon.

Lucy shivered. She couldn't forget how certain Tom had been that they should return. They might have been there now. . . . The timing would have been perfect.

We see so many babies with AIDS, Lucy. It's heartbreaking. I

151

keep them for a day or two, and then Matthew takes them to the hospital in Maputo. They have some drugs there, but never enough. Do you remember?

Lucy remembered it all as though it were yesterday.

Matthew is fine. He has gray hair now but is still teaching and is as strong as an ox. At one time I thought he might take over, but I'm sure God wants a younger man, a man of the world who can negotiate with the authorities and try to get a better education for the children.

Matthew sends his love. He never did forget that night with the brier. Well, my dear, write to me. Tell me your thoughts. I pray for your faith to return. Never forget the song "God Is So Good—O Mwari Waka Naka."

You sang it so beautifully, Lucy. Sing it again. God bless you, dear.

Love in Him,
Ruth

Lucy left the letter on the sofa, but the thought of it stayed with her for the rest of the afternoon.

At six o'clock a knock at the door aroused Lucy from a short nap. When she opened the door no one was there, but she found yet another envelope on the mat. Though the envelope was nondescript, the notelet had tiny daisies on it. It was from Vicar Todd. She smiled. What a precious man.

Dear Lucy,

You are cordially invited to a thanksgiving tea at the vicarage at five o'clock on Sunday. Hilda and I hope you can make it.

God bless you,
Vicar Todd

Lucy thought it most strange. It was already December, the harvest long since brought in. . . . But she would go. It was sure to be

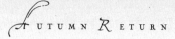

eventful—the vicar was always up to something. She put the little card on the kitchen table and went to ring the boys. Arrangements had to be made for Christmas. She hadn't bought a single present and wanted some ideas for gifts. Luke answered after the first ring.

"Hello, Luke. It's Mum."

"Hi, Mum. How are you? How is Sue . . . is it Sue?"

"Sue is fine, and the twins can't wait to meet you all, especially Rose and Jamey. Luke, I'd like a few ideas for Christmas gifts."

Luke told her Karen's favorite perfume and mentioned she might like a pretty nightgown. He wanted a book. And Rose would like anything suitable for an under-three-year-old from the Early Learning Shop. She thanked him, saying she hoped Danny would be as easy as he was.

"Did you get the letter, Mum? I'm so sorry. I forgot all about it. I found it under some bills in the hallway on Wednesday and sent it immediately."

153

"Yes, I got it this morning. Don't worry about it being late. So much has been going on here, I sometimes forgot about it myself. I did enjoy reading it, though. Actually, I guess I was a little sad and happy at the same time. Do you know what I mean?"

"Yes, Mum, I do. That's still the way I feel when I look at some of Dad's things you gave me."

Lucy continued. "I think Ruth knew that she was dying."

"That's what Robert Hemmings said. He said she'd written to him just before she died, and he got the same feeling. Well, Mum, must go. We're off to Dan's for supper."

"How nice. Give them my love, won't you, and ask him to ring me with gift ideas for his family."

She was so pleased that her sons were close. It had always saddened Lucy that she had no siblings of her own. It would have been so nice to share her feelings with a brother or sister. It gave her a warm feeling to think of her sons and their wives having supper together. They all got on so well. Perhaps she had done some things right.

———————

Gordon knocked on Lucy's door at a quarter to seven. She wasn't quite ready, so she invited him in and told him to take a seat in the sitting room while she went upstairs to finish getting ready. She looked at herself in the dressing table mirror—the very mirror that Tom had chosen for her in a London antique shop. *What am I doing? What on earth would Tom think of me?* Lucy wanted to run down the winding kitchen staircase and explain she couldn't possibly go out with him. It was far too soon.

Taking a deep breath, Lucy moved to the window and looked out onto the moonlit waters. *This is not a romantic date.* She was just having dinner with a new friend. Why read anything more into it? Lucy had told her boys all about her new friends, but she decided not to tell them about Gordon. It wasn't serious. She didn't want them making a mountain out of a molehill. She had only loved one man, and that was truly how she wanted it to stay—for the moment.

Lucy knew she shouldn't keep Gordon waiting any longer, so with a last glance at her reflection in the mirror, she made her way downstairs. Gordon was looking out at the same view of the moon through the French doors.

"Isn't it beautiful, Lucy? You can see the bay so much better from your cottage than I can from mine."

Lucy thought about where his cottage was situated, which was near Jack and Sue's.

"You must only see the harbor and the pub—still a very nice view."

"Yes, but I do love the open sea."

"Me too. I never thought I'd have such a view. I looked at the same boring house for over thirty years back in London!"

154

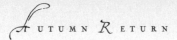

"Yes, London has its good points, but I'll take Cornwall any day. Well, shall we go?"

Gordon led Lucy across the beach. They stood and watched the night fishermen chugging out to sea.

"They are so brave!" Lucy wrapped her coat more tightly about her. "I'm afraid of the sea."

"Then you must conquer that fear, my dear! The sea isn't to be feared—revered maybe—but not feared. I love the sea."

"Well, it frightens me," she said softly. They wandered slowly on toward the pub, which sat opposite Gordon's home.

When they entered, Lucy was drawn to the cozy, old-fashioned character of the pub. A huge log fire blazed in the red stone hearth. Gleaming brass pots and pans hung from the beams, and antique china plates lined the walls. Gordon led Lucy to a table near a window with a delightful view of the harbor. The lighted boats looked so charming. Gordon drew some attention as he crossed the room to get Perriers and menus. Lucy chuckled. In reality, she was probably the one causing the stir—the doctor and the new lady!

When Gordon returned he sat opposite Lucy and handed her a menu. She was actually quite relieved the large oak table was between them. She was having a good time, but Lucy wasn't sure she would make it through the meal if he had sat down next to her. She ordered chili con carne with rice and tortilla chips. Gordon chose fish and chips. The meal was enjoyable, the conversation light and gentle. As they talked of music, plays, and books, they discovered they had a number of things in common.

"What brought you to Tarran Bay, Lucy?" Gordon asked at last.

"My family spent many a holiday here, and I just felt it right to come. My boys didn't agree with me, I'm afraid. But they'll get used to it. I needed a change."

"I agree. It's a great place to live."

"Are the winters bad?"

"Not particularly—a bit wet and windy. But I'd rather be here in the bad weather than in London any day of the week!"

"Do you come from London, too?"

"Yep, 'fraid so!"

"Whereabouts?"

"Surrey."

"Very nice. I came from the north side of London—Oakthorpe."

"I've heard of it, but I've never been there."

Lucy smiled. "No, I don't suppose you have. It's small but pretty. It has been a market town for over a thousand years. It boasts many interesting old churches, too. The town was in one direction from our home, and farmland, rolling green hills, and woodland were in the other direction. I loved to walk there with Tom and the boys. My boys did love to climb trees!" She smiled at the memory. "It was a nice place to bring up the children, but now I like it here."

"I'm sure you do," Gordon said. "We may be prejudiced, but how could anything compare with Cornwall!"

Lucy was amazed at the variety of topics they found to talk about, and she was surprised when the pub landlord called for last orders.

Gordon glanced at his watch. "It's eleven o'clock, Lucy. Time flies. I'll walk you home."

As they rose from the table and left the pub, Lucy felt all eyes were turned toward them. She wondered if Gordon had any idea of the gossip that would fly after they'd gone. People from small villages loved to gossip, and this particular story would probably keep them going for months!

On the way back to Lucy's cottage, they walked by way of the beach once more, their feet crunching on the tiny pebbles close to the shoreline. Gordon stooped, picked up one of the larger stones, and threw it high toward the stars. It fell with a mighty splash into the icy seawater.

"Look at those stars," Lucy said, gazing skyward. "It's such a

beautiful, clear night, but so cold. I can't get used to this weather,"
she said with a shudder. "One minute it rains, then it gets misty,
then the sun shines. I never know what to wear!"

"You'll get used to it," he answered as they walked on past the
huge cave on the main beach.

They walked in silence for a while, and Lucy admitted to herself
that she really liked spending time with Gordon. Even the silences
were companionable. However, as they neared her cottage, Lucy
began to feel agitated once more. *How would the evening end? Would
Gordon get the wrong idea if she invited him in?*

But once again, she was saved from having to make the decision.
Before they reached her gate, Gordon brought up the subject.

"Can I come in for coffee?"

"Sure, that would be nice." She was relieved. Once again she
avoided making a decision about their relationship.

They sat in the sitting room, Lucy on the chair and Gordon on
the sofa opposite her. She put the tray on the coffee table in front of
the fire, which Gordon had lit for her, and poured the coffee from
the glass jug into pottery mugs.

From the cushion next to him, he picked up the envelope she
had discarded earlier. "A letter from Africa?" As if he suddenly realized he might be prying, he replaced it immediately and seemed a
little flustered.

"Yes, I should have had it over a month ago. It was sent to London, as she didn't know my address in Cornwall. It was delivered
this morning."

"She?" he inquired, taking the mug from her. Lucy leaned back
in her chair.

"Oh yes, sorry. Ruth—Ruth Lange. We stayed with her in Africa. She died just after she sent the letter. I found it very difficult to
read."

"Yes, I'm sure you did."

Only a few days ago she hadn't wanted to talk. Somehow the

letter and her friendship with Gordon seemed to change everything.

"Ruth was a missionary we went to help in Mozambique."

Gordon just sipped his coffee. She could tell he wanted to hear more. Would she simply open the memories to some stranger? She hadn't even unlocked all of them to herself. Lucy felt tears welling in her eyes.

Gordon set his mug down on the table, placed his elbows on his knees, rested his face in his hands, and looked at her thoughtfully. Lucy couldn't help noticing how handsome he looked when he was serious.

"Lucy . . . ." He hesitated at first but soon continued. "You only find peace through the truth."

Lucy looked into her mug. Somehow he had known exactly what she needed to hear. But she wasn't ready.

"It's too soon."

"Two years is not too soon, Lucy. You must talk about it, or you'll never be free."

That was the truth. She certainly wasn't free.

"I hate to talk about it. I was a failure—to Ruth—to Tom—to Africa." She paused momentarily, but what weighed on her heart had to be said. "And I was a failure to God!" It was the first time she had admitted that thought out loud.

Gordon picked up his mug again and leaned back on the sofa.

"There are no failures in God's kingdom, Lucy."

She found his words hard to believe, but she knew it was what she needed to hear. Tears were flowing down her cheeks as Lucy struggled to compose herself. *Just to talk to him—anything would do.* She was all locked up, and she felt as though Gordon had known it from the moment he'd met her. He stayed silent, politely looking around the room while she composed herself. Lucy was grateful. She didn't want him fussing over her.

Gordon leaned his elbows on his knees once again and drank

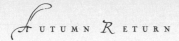

some more coffee. "Where did you get these African paintings?" he asked, breaking the silence.

"I painted them," she replied as she got up and went into the kitchen to fetch a tissue. She also splashed some cold water on her face, and after taking a couple of sips of water, Lucy returned feeling much better. When she reentered the room, Gordon was looking more closely at her paintings.

"I'm impressed!" Gordon turned to grin at her. "The colors are so vibrant—they're so alive!"

Lucy was a bit uncomfortable accepting his compliments, so she ignored his comments.

"Would you like more coffee, Gordon?"

"Yes, please. But . . . am I in the way?"

"No. . . . Well, I don't think so," she answered truthfully as she poured him another coffee. "I must confess that it's been good to talk to someone, you know, not connected with my past."

Gordon smiled, encouraging her to go on. Lucy relaxed into the comfort of the chair, snuggling into the deep feather cushions. She slipped off her shoes and tucked her legs up on the chair. She was finally ready to share about her time in Africa.

"There was so much need in Mozambique, you see—what with the civil war raging all around us."

Lucy looked to Gordon for encouragement. He didn't say anything—he seemed content to listen. Lucy was finally ready—she trusted him.

"When we arrived in Mozambique, the country was in the midst of a horrible uprising. We were in an area that was fairly insulated from the fighting, but we had frightening outbreaks from time to time, and we received a constant flow of children who had suffered the consequences of the senseless fighting—either by the loss of parents or physical harm.

"I don't claim to understand the reasons for the fighting. I have never been very interested in politics. So I couldn't tell you if there was a 'right' side and a 'wrong' side—all I know is that I saw horrible things done by *both* sides." Lucy started crying again. "The cruelty—those poor children—those awful men." She glanced sheepishly at him. "I'm sorry, it *was* the men, though. The women and children suffered the consequences of their hate."

"You don't have a very high opinion of men, do you, Lucy?"

"I loved my husband—he was wonderful—and I loved my father and my boys. But . . ." She trailed off. The tears came once again. "It was those warmongers and the soldiers. They laughed, you know—laughed at our fear. It was dreadful." She shook her head and looked down into her lap. She hated these memories.

"You helped, though—with the children."

"Yes. But that's the point, Gordon. I abandoned them. I let God down."

"Explain," he said patiently.

"I got pregnant."

"So?"

"It ruined everything. I was a coward. If I didn't miscarry first, I couldn't face giving birth in that primitive hospital with such unskilled doctors. And I couldn't bear the thought of bringing the baby up there. There was hardly any water. What little we had was barely enough for our drinking needs. It is hard to imagine water shortages if you haven't experienced it."

"I remember the water shortages in Kenya."

"Of course." She'd forgotten. He would also understand the hold Africa had on her. The amazing colors, the smell, the red earth, the people, the incredible sunsets. He would understand. How cathartic it was to talk to someone who seemed to instinctively know how she felt. Lucy took another log from the basket and placed it on the open fire. She and Gordon sat in silence. Life seemed to stand still. But there was more to be said. Lucy didn't look up but spoke into the fire.

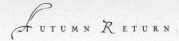

"I saw so many babies die . . . one too many! I just couldn't take it anymore."

"I understand. It is the most difficult thing about my practice. Yes, babies are the hardest to lose." Gordon's voice seemed to take on a strange tone. Lucy turned to face him. For a moment it seemed he was the one struggling with his words. Within moments he seemed back to his old self. "Go on, Lucy."

She was finding it easier to speak as she went deeper. "So when I found out I was pregnant, I insisted we come home. And I've felt like such a failure ever since. I failed God. He had His plan, and I walked away. We always talked of going back once the children were grown. Tom took Luke there for a month when he was eighteen, and they helped build a clinic. Luke loved it there, too. But he came home and met Karen."

She told Gordon more about her family. Just a little more—then she felt she would be free. The wrappings would be off once and for all. Finally she told him of the plans she and Tom had made only months before he died.

"Why did God take him from me?" Lucy knew Gordon couldn't give her an answer. No answer he gave would be adequate.

She began to sob, and Gordon took a cotton handkerchief from his jeans pocket and leaned over to give it to her. She wiped her tears.

He spoke softly. "Have you forgotten who is in control of your life? It wasn't Tom, Lucy. It was God. Only He knows His plans. Only He gives and takes life. He knows the choices we will make before we do, and He uses them for His good purpose."

At Gordon's words Lucy abruptly stopped crying. She had never considered her failure in the light of God's plans for her life. Once back in England she and Tom had never discussed the reasons for their homecoming. In fact, they had avoided the subject, because they both were saddened at their failure to stay. Lucy pondered Gordon's words. *If God is in control of my life, surely I can trust Him in the giving and taking of lives—or in turning a bad decision I make into something good.* Yes, she could believe He was trustworthy, even if His ways were hard to comprehend at times.

Gordon continued. "God wanted you to give the best to your children, Lucy. It's possible your yearning to come home was God's direction. We make decisions based on what we feel is right, trusting Him to lead and guide." Gordon paused, as if considering his next words. "Do your boys love God, Lucy?"

"Oh yes, with all their hearts. He is the center of their lives. They're both kind and caring, very involved in their churches. That was part of the reason I needed to move away. I felt like such a hypocrite. It was hard for them to see their mother so obviously losing her faith. I couldn't hide it from anyone. I don't think I went to church more than five times after Tom's funeral. And two of those were for the dedication of my sons' babies.

"The funeral was so difficult for me. Everyone seemed happy that Tom was in heaven, but I couldn't relate to anyone. I know they didn't mean they wouldn't miss Tom. But I wanted him on earth—with me and the boys. I felt so selfish and confused. I know the boys are very worried about me, but after God took Tom from me, I simply lost confidence in Him."

"If you lose something, you can find it again," Gordon said. "God wants to use your sons, and He can do that in spite of, and because of, the decisions you make. Lucy, it will take time, but you will get over Tom's untimely death—and Ruth's. You must trust God. It is so much easier to cope with life if you trust Him in every-thing. Sometimes He only gives us half the picture. We wouldn't need faith if we could see it all. And another thing—I learned this from Vicar Todd—if God takes something dear from you, He often replaces it with something just as good, or better."

He smiled at her. "Will you be okay? I should be going because I have an early start in the morning."

Lucy looked at her watch. It was three in the morning—another

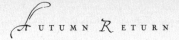

late night. For some reason Gordon bent and kissed her hair as he left. He thanked her for opening her heart to him and told her to stay where she was—he could see himself out.

"I think you'll sleep very well tonight," he called over his shoulder.

After Gordon left, Lucy sat peacefully for a while, watching the fire die. What a patient and kind man.

After turning off the two old brass lamps, she slowly made her way upstairs. Once in bed, she read from Tom's Bible—just a few verses, as it was so late. Where was the verse in Jeremiah that Tom quoted so often? Yes, there it was. *For I know the plans I have for you, declares the Lord, plans to prosper you and not to harm you, plans to give you hope and a future. Then you will call upon Me and come and pray to Me, and I will listen to you. You will seek Me and find Me, when you seek Me with all your heart. I will be found by you, says the Lord, and I will bring you back from captivity. . . .*

163

Lucy stopped abruptly and laid the Bible down on the bedside cabinet. She had tears in her eyes again, because she knew God was speaking to her. Was what Gordon had said about God's plan being worked out in spite of her decisions true? If so, it made all the years of regret so pointless and wasteful. She didn't know what to think. It was difficult to sleep with Gordon's words drifting in and out of her head—her mind wandering in all directions. She felt better though, as if the shelf that held her deepest sorrows was being dusted off and the problems lifted away by God. Only one sorrow was left sitting there for scrutiny—the one she hadn't yet confronted. Eventually she prayed. *Help me, Lord.* With that the sleep she longed for came.

CHAPTER 14

Thanksgiving

Lucy was up at her usual time on Sunday, and her thoughts turned to the day that lay ahead. Everything seemed different. She was changing—God was changing her. Lucy could barely contain her excitement. As she looked at her wristwatch, she decided it was time to return to church. After all her struggles, it was an easy decision. And she would certainly go to the thanksgiving tea.

She made some scrambled eggs and coffee, sat on the chair nearest to the kitchen window, and looked out over her front garden. It was rather devoid of color at this time of year, but Lucy still enjoyed it. She liked the peaceful combination of evergreens and the privet hedge that marked the boundary of her garden. The grass needed a final cut before winter really set in. She would do that later, once the sun had warmed it a little. Perhaps before she went to the thanksgiving tea. She ate her simple meal and, after washing up her dishes and placing them neatly on the old dresser, went to get ready for the day. Lucy couldn't see the sea as she looked out of her bedroom window, because an early-morning silver-white mist shrouded it. But a mist of that sort usually meant it would be sunny later! Her spirits rose again.

Lucy crossed the beach to go to church. She always loved the beach, whatever the weather. The mist was hanging low over the sea. But the sun was beginning to pierce through it, and the beach was clear and bright. The gentle inland breeze was rolling out across the surface of the water, taking the mist up toward the horizon in huge white plumes, leaving a sparkling, glittering sea with slow lapping waves turning silver on the shore. At first the cliffs could just be seen at the base, but gradually, as Lucy stood watching in wonder, she glimpsed the bluest of blue skies. Gulls called and swooped high above her head, hoping to catch a crab or two on the seashore. Lucy stood on the soft piles of seaweed that the tide had left behind the night before and smiled contentedly. But since there was still a chill in the air, she headed for the warmth and comfort of St Luke's.

The sermon was just what Lucy needed to hear. Vicar Todd spoke of the personal relationship with Christ that is open to everyone. He explained the freedom, power, and peace available through that relationship. Lucy listened and, to her great relief, found that she understood and believed. "Sing to the Lord a new song," he quoted from Psalms. She felt different. Was Gordon right about peace only coming when the truth was out? She looked at the beautiful stained-glass windows, all of them depicting the same thing, really—Jesus' love and kindness being demonstrated through His people. She could do it, but she needed God at the helm. She needed Him helping her through the hard times.

Lord, she prayed at the end of the service, *please forgive me for the wasted years. I want to know you. I need your power. Please forgive my sinful attitudes and come into my life afresh. Help me to forgive the African soldiers' cruelty to the innocent women and children of Mozambique. Help me work through the loss of loved ones and give me strength to live my life for you. I need your grace and power to do it. I want to make a difference in this world. I believe I'm ready now.*

At that moment Lucy felt a surge of peace—so real, so tangible—flooding her whole being. *"I will repay you for the years that the locusts have eaten."* God had spoken to her. As Lucy took a tissue from her coat pocket and blew her nose, Vicar Todd walked toward her pew, arms open wide, looking almost like an angel, though dressed in black. He had a huge smile on his face.

"Lucy, my dear. So good to see you." Bending down and looking into her eyes, he asked, "Are you well?"

"Oh yes, Vicar. Never better!"

"You've found the Lord!"

"Oh no. I already knew the Lord as my Savior. But today He spoke to me—or maybe I should say I finally understood how to listen to Him. I now know Him in a new way, a fuller way, a way that has eluded me for far too long. Jesus is now my Savior and *friend*. He is finally my source of strength and security."

"That is wonderful, Lucy." Vicar Todd sat down on the pew in front of Lucy, rested his arms on the backrest, and looked at her intently through his round glasses. "May I ask what He said to you?"

"Well, I think it was a verse from Joel. *'I will repay you for the years that the locusts have eaten.'* "

"Yes, Joel, chapter two, verse twenty-five! Wonderful verse, and very true!"

"Perhaps, if you have the time, Vicar, I could come and talk with you and Hilda about some things I need to get straight in my life. I'd like to tell you about my husband."

"Of course, my dear. Anytime. Perhaps we could make a date at the thanksgiving tea. You are coming, aren't you?"

"Wouldn't miss it!"

After he left, Lucy realized she had forgotten to ask the vicar the purpose of the thanksgiving tea. It didn't matter. She would know soon enough.

When Lucy arrived at the vicar's for the tea, she entered through the kitchen door so she could drop off her contributions—a layered chocolate cake and some flowers. As she entered the sitting room, she saw Gordon near the window watching the twins putting together a jigsaw puzzle. He looked up and smiled at her. She hadn't seen him at church and was glad he was at the tea. She wanted so much to tell him what had happened since they had last talked. But it would have to wait. Jack, Sue, and Hilda were there, as well as a few other people—some she knew, and some she hadn't yet met.

Vicar Todd greeted her with an extremely handsome young man in tow. He was very tall and thin, with long blond hair.

"Lucy, this is Mark Holding. He owns a gallery in St. Ives." As Vicar Todd made the introduction, Lucy shook Mark's hand. So this was the young man who had taken the girls to see *Babe* at the cinema in St. Ives! The twins had related the details of the outing to Lucy several times. Though she hadn't seen the film herself, Lucy now knew the story by heart!

She was also introduced to Mrs. Philips—there for tea, not work. Mr. and Mrs. Bryant from the bed-and-breakfast hugged her and asked how she was getting on in her renovation of Dawn Cottage and how she liked living in Tarran Bay. She was pleased to tell them that she was doing very well and had made lots of new friends since she had last seen them.

Sue came over to Lucy with a young lady beside her. "This is Gail, Lucy. Lucy—Gail."

"Hello, Gail, so pleased to meet you. Sue has told me so much about you."

"Sue is so kind to me, and Jack, too, of course. The girls are fun, aren't they?"

"They certainly are!"

"I hear you helped look after them while Sue was in the hospital and recovering."

"Yes, I thoroughly enjoyed it!" Lucy thought Gail looked quite

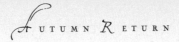

well considering what she had just been through.

After a time of chatting, Vicar Todd clapped his hands and asked for silence. Everyone turned to face him. He looked over at Hilda. "Thank you for coming, everyone. In case you haven't figured it out, Hilda and I decided to have a thanksgiving tea to celebrate Sue's wonderful recovery."

So *that* was what the tea was for! Lucy took Sue's hand and squeezed it.

"Almost everyone who helped her is here. And while we thank God for her recovery, we also thank you for your kind support. Well done. We love you, Sue." The vicar paused while everyone clapped. "And we have another special guest. Sue has brought a new friend with her today. She met her in the hospital when they were both recovering from surgery. Her friend's name is Gail." Vicar Todd smiled at the young woman, and she returned it. "Please, get to know her, won't you, and make her feel welcome. And now, it's time for tea!"

Gordon stood beside Lucy as they waited beside the kitchen table to fill their plates.

"How are you?" he whispered.

"I'm much better." She was able to look him in the eye. "Really, much better. You were right, though I hate to admit it. I've found my peace with God—only this morning actually. He spoke to me. I'll be all right now." Even though she was only whispering to Gordon, it drew some attention, and Lucy suddenly felt very self-conscious.

"I can see you are well on the way to recovery." Gordon bent down and took some salmon and cucumber sandwiches and then continued. "I'm very pleased. We must get together again. Are you free next weekend?" He looked at her sideways, quizzically.

Lucy looked down at the food on the table, trying to be inconspicuous. Enjoying a man's attention again was all very new for her—and *very* embarrassing. When she finally turned to him, it seemed the kitchen had gone quiet. Lucy couldn't imagine what to do. She was mortified, but she didn't want to simply cut Gordon off.

Thankfully, Vicar Todd came to the rescue when he suggested that everyone make their way back to the sitting room and that he would bring the tea and coffee on a tray.

"What day? What did you have in mind?" she asked him.

Vicar Todd was the only one in the room, and he was trying to make as much noise as possible with his cups and saucers.

"How about Saturday? I'll pick you up in the morning. We'll make a day of it."

"The whole day?" Lucy was not sure about spending an entire day with him. "What will we do?"

"You'll see. I'll pick you up at nine. Don't worry—it will be fun."

With an uncertain shrug, Lucy followed Vicar Todd into the sitting room, trying to put the thought of a whole day spent in Gordon's company out of her mind.

The little gathering was lovely. Mark spoke to her for some time about her African paintings. He said Gordon had told him all about them before she arrived, and he was eager to see them.

"Come any time." She gave him her number. Surely he would think them totally naïve. "They're very simple—and only fair. I never trained . . ."

Mark smiled, "Perhaps I should be the judge of that. I taught Gordon all he knows about art, and he has a good eye."

Before she left, Vicar Todd once again mentioned having Lucy for dinner during the week, and she accepted gratefully. He said he would call her soon to set up an evening.

———

At six-thirty Todd and Hilda were still in the large kitchen washing up the dishes. They were on the last things now, and Vicar

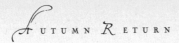

Todd was pleased, as he had to be at the church at seven-thirty for Evensong.

"It went well, didn't it, David."

"Smashing. It was wonderful that Gail came with Sue. We need to put in some prayer there."

"Yes, she seems troubled."

"I suppose having a mastectomy did that for her. It was bad enough for Sue, with a husband who loved her. Apparently, Gail's husband is a bit of a waster."

"We can pray about that, too," Hilda said.

Vicar Todd placed the last plate in the cupboard, wiped his hands on a cloth, and sat down next to Hilda. "I think Gordon and Lucy are becoming an item."

"I thought as much. I saw him call on her last Wednesday." Hilda got a bit flustered, as if she suddenly realized how what she had said might sound. "I couldn't help it. I was in the garden at the time."

Vicar Todd laughed. He knew Hilda wouldn't want to be thought of as a nosy neighbor.

"We need to pray for them. I always thought Gordon needed a good woman!"

Hilda smiled. "You're such a romantic old fool. But you're right—Gordon and Lucy seem right for each other."

"Gordon has never allowed himself to think of marrying, though. He told me once that being a doctor was the most important thing in his life—his only focus."

"Yes, he told me that, too. But that was his idea. Perhaps God has other plans!"

Gordon had once told Vicar Todd that he could never marry because of a pact he'd made with God. The vicar had privately questioned Gordon's decision. He believed one should never make pacts with Almighty God, but at the time he felt it was not his place to comment. However, as he and Hilda talked, he couldn't help wondering whether Gordon would let Lucy slip out of his hands, just as he had let Hilda slip from his. It was at times like these that Vicar Todd wondered why he had never declared his love to Hilda.

Suddenly, he knew—without a shadow of a doubt—that this was the time. *Even if she thinks me an old fool and leaves the room laughing—or crying—I must tell her how I feel.*

Vicar Todd realized he had been quiet for quite some time, and Hilda had a puzzled look on her face. *Well, there's no time like the present.* He took her hand. *Just say it. It's the best way.*

"Hilda, I have something to tell you—something I should have told you many years ago." He took a deep swallow but proceeded without delay. "I love you."

There, it was done—out in the open and painless. But he was a bit hesitant as he waited for Hilda's response. Her lovely face turned bright red!

"David—*really!* I don't know what to say."

"Did you not know?"

Hilda smiled and answered softly. "Yes, David, I suppose I knew. But I assumed you had a reason for not bringing it up."

"Nothing but timidity—and circumstances. But I suppose it is too late."

"Not too late to know the truth, but we are a little old for all that now." She gently released his hand and clasped her hands in her lap.

"Yes, I suppose you are right, but it will make life easier." Now it was Vicar Todd's turn for his face to go red. He could feel the heat. "Hilda? Do you feel the same about me?"

For the longest time, Hilda just stared down at her clasped hands. At last she looked over to where he sat.

"Yes, I love you, David. I have loved you for more years than I can count. And every year my love for you has grown." Her gaze returned once more to her hands resting in her lap. "For the longest time, I hoped that we would marry. . . ."

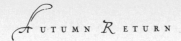

Vicar Todd felt a lump growing in his throat.

Hilda unclasped her hands and rested them on his. "But we have had good lives, filled with God's blessings, and we must not question our choices." She smiled and looked into Vicar Todd's kind face. "Wil was my first love—but you, my dear David, are my true love."

They sat for a moment. Vicar Todd couldn't help but think of what might have been. But soon Hilda straightened up and brought him back to the present.

"Shall we pray, David? Otherwise we'll be late for Evensong."

"Of course!" exclaimed Vicar Todd. He would have sat there all evening, leaving a church full of confused worshipers.

They bowed their heads, and Vicar Todd prayed first.

"Father, thank you for today. I think it was a special time for everyone. Thank you for bringing Gail into our midst. Help her to find you, Lord. We also pray for Gordon and Lucy, asking that if this relationship is right, it will grow and develop, and that they will seek your face in all their plans. Amen."

Hilda's voice was clear and strong as she prayed. "Bless Sue and Jack. Help them come to terms with all the changes Sue's operation has brought into their lives. Bless those dear girls, Lord. Thank you for them. And, Lord, bless David as he leads us this evening." With a little squeeze of his hand, she continued. "And thank you for his friendship *and love*. Amen."

CHAPTER 15

Dinner With the Vicar

Lucy enjoyed her first Evensong. It felt wonderful to sing again. She was so alive and vibrant. Afterward, she walked home with Gordon, who left her at her gate.

"See you at nine on Saturday. We'll be gone all day! And wear warm clothes."

"I'll be ready! Good night, Gordon."

"Good night. Sleep well."

"I always sleep well in Cornwall!"

"Of course you do. It's the air!"

As Lucy turned the key in the door and entered the warmth of the hallway, she realized—more than she cared to admit—that she was looking forward to going out with Gordon. She wasn't certain how much she liked the mystery destination idea, but she was determined to go with the flow. She made some cocoa and sat in the sitting room, staring at the empty grate. No point in lighting the fire. The heating was on, and everything was warm and cozy. She picked up her Bible and searched for the verse in Joel the vicar had mentioned to her.

Yes, there it was in chapter two. She read on and found

the words leaping out at her as if for the first time. Verse twenty-eight said, *And it shall come to pass afterward that I will pour out my spirit on all flesh; your sons and your daughters shall prophecy, your old men shall dream dreams. Your young men shall see visions. And also on My men-servants and on My maidservants I will pour out My Spirit in those days.*

Lucy put down the Bible. She couldn't read anymore. Her eyes were moist with tears. God wanted to speak to her. And even more important—she was finally listening to His still small voice. With tears running down her cheeks she prayed, then got into bed and slept deeply once again.

———————

Tuesday morning the ringing phone broke Lucy's slumber rather abruptly. She was still half-asleep as she pulled her robe around her and fumbled her feet into her slippers. She slipped downstairs. It was Vicar Todd.

"My dear," he began cheerily. "I hope it's not too early for you?"

Lucy wasn't aware of the time but thought it must be early, as she felt so tired and a little tense. "I've been having too many late nights, Vicar. It's my own fault."

"Oh, I am sorry. I'll be brief, then. Hilda and I wondered if it would be too soon for you to come over for dinner this evening. I have a bit of a full week."

Lucy smiled. She couldn't think of anything nicer, and she relaxed. "I'd love to come. What time?"

"Seven?"

"Perfect. I must cut the lawns and the privet today. Everything looks so untidy. I should have done it weeks ago. It's not too late, is it?"

"No. We had some chilly spots, but the warmer weather lasted much longer this year. Don't tire yourself out, though. If you'd like, perhaps Hilda and I could lend a hand."

"Oh no. You have far too much to do!"

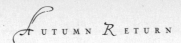

"Please let us help you, dear. We love to work in gardens. And it won't take long with three hands on deck!"

Lucy gave in with grateful thanks and replaced the receiver. They would be over at ten. The clock said eight. No time for going back to bed. She had washing and ironing to catch up on. All this gallivanting about was seriously damaging her normal routine. She didn't care—she'd lived by a routine all her life. She needed this wonderful change. She sang in the shower and then started the housework with a vengeance.

Hilda and Vicar Todd arrived within ten minutes of each other—first Hilda, then the vicar. After a short visit, Lucy asked if they would give her a minute to put the ironing in the airing cupboard, so she left them sitting together at the kitchen table admiring her newly painted kitchen.

"I do like all this warm yellow, Lucy!" Vicar Todd said.

"It brightens up a dull day," Lucy agreed as she descended the staircase. "Are you two ready for some hard work?"

"Yes, it's our only chance for exercise!"

They worked well as a team. Lucy mowed the two large lawns with the electric mower while Vicar Todd and Hilda tackled the privet hedge. Everything looked neat and tidy by one o'clock. Lucy invited them in for lunch, but they declined.

"We both like an afternoon nap, and then we want to prepare a nice dinner for you."

"Oh, please don't go to any trouble. I eat anything!"

"It's no trouble, my dear," Vicar Todd said, kissing her cold, rosy cheek.

"Thanks for the help. I appreciate it!"

After eating a hasty lunch, Lucy cleaned the inside of the windows. She had hired a window cleaner to do the outside, but she hadn't touched the inside since she put up the curtains. It was a happy job, and she did it while listening to classical music on the radio. By late afternoon she stopped, satisfied with her progress. It felt good to finally be getting her home in order.

Lucy arrived at the vicarage promptly at seven. Vicar Todd was at the door immediately to greet her.

"Welcome, Lucy. Do come in. May I take your coat?"

Lucy handed him her coat, as well as some flowers and a box of Belgian chocolates. "It's a small thank-you for all the help in the garden."

"How very kind. Come through to the kitchen, Lucy." She followed the vicar down the wide hallway with its beautiful black-and-white Victorian tiles. "Hilda is waiting for us."

Hilda stood as Lucy entered the kitchen. "Hello, dear. How are you?"

"Very hungry. Whatever you've cooked for dinner smells wonderful!"

Hilda placed the flowers Lucy had brought in a vase and put them in the center of the table, then began to dish up the steak and kidney pudding. After the vicar said grace, they started to eat. Lucy hadn't had a dinner such as this since she was a child in her grandmother's home, and sweet memories flooded her thoughts.

"Hilda, you're a marvel. I haven't eaten this for years. It's delicious!"

"Have you never cooked a steamed pudding?"

Lucy was embarrassed to say she had not.

"It's so easy, dear. I'll come over and teach you one day."

"I would really like that. I'm sure my boys would love it. I once told the vicar that I only cook because I have to. But I'm trying to improve."

When Lucy thought back to that earlier conversation, she was amazed. Time had certainly flown. She felt as though she'd known these dear people for years.

"Tell us about Tom, Lucy," Vicar Todd said at last.

He said it so matter-of-factly, Lucy found it easy to share every-

thing with them. Oh, the incredible freedom of opening up with trusted friends. She explained about their time in Africa and why they returned home when she became pregnant with Luke. She also told them that helping needy people in London had almost become an obsession with her as she tried to relieve the guilt she felt at leaving all the needy children in Africa.

At that point, Vicar Todd laughed and said, "Then we gave you more needy people to care for!"

Lucy smiled. "It has been different here. At first I tried to help out in my own power, but I am slowly learning to rely on God's power. I've found that's the key." She then explained about her meeting with God on Sunday morning and how wonderful she'd felt ever since.

Hilda's eyes filled with tears. She jumped up from her chair like a child, took Lucy's cheeks in her hands, kissed her, and then hugged her.

"You've found the Helper!" she said, smiling down at her.

"The helper?"

"The Holy Spirit. He has been with you since you accepted Jesus as your Savior, but you were living your life without His power. You can't make a difference without His help."

Yes, she understood. For years she'd done everything in her own strength.

Although it was difficult for her, Lucy also wanted to talk to them about her relationship with Gordon. "I have spent time with Gordon Seymour lately, and I've shared more with him than any man since Tom died." Lucy hesitated. "Sorry, Vicar—I know you're a man, too. But I don't think of you as a man. I mean— you're my vicar!"

Vicar Todd smiled kindly at her, indicating he understood, and Lucy continued, still a little bit flustered. "Anyway, he has been wonderful for me. I can't tell you how much that has meant to me. He seems to draw me out of myself."

Vicar Todd agreed with her assessment. "Gordon has been a small group leader in our church for several years now. He is a very good counselor. I know, because I trained him myself!"

Both Hilda and Lucy laughed.

"David isn't one for hiding his light!" mocked Hilda.

"We're told to shine our light brightly, my dear!" retorted Vicar Todd as he put the last bite of the delicious pudding into his mouth.

"A little out of context, but you do—and I'm glad!" said Hilda.

Lucy placed her knife and fork neatly onto her empty plate. "What's for dessert?"

"Apple pie and custard!" Vicar Todd announced proudly from where he stood near the oven. "I cooked it myself!" Once again, laughter filled the room.

Lucy was happier than she'd been for years. Most of her sadness just seemed to flow away like a river into the sea, where it was swallowed up and dealt with at last. The future looked so much brighter.

As they finished their dessert, Vicar Todd leaned across to Lucy and asked, "Do you truly think your life has been a waste, my dear?"

"To be honest, yes, I have sometimes felt that way—throughout my life. But since Tom died, I have thought it all the time."

"Read the story of Joseph, Lucy. Nothing is wasted in God's plans for us. He uses all of us, in spite of our imperfections. He used you, and the best is yet to come!"

"Oh, I do hope so!" Lucy replied.

"You can be sure of it," Hilda said gently.

Always the perfect host, the vicar offered his guests another large slice of pie.

Lucy looked down at her stomach and patted it. *I must watch my weight!* But tonight she was celebrating and decided to throw caution to the wind. "Perhaps just a little more would be all right!"

They had a lovely time and ended the evening in the sitting room with a cup of coffee in front of the fire. Vicar Todd asked Lucy

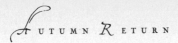

if he could pray for her, and she gave her grateful approval. He prayed that God would guide Lucy in the way she should go, that He would help her make wise decisions concerning the future, and that she would be abundantly blessed in all she did for Him!

Lucy left the vicarage at ten o'clock, feeling as though she were walking on a cloud. Because her way was so brightly lit by the moon, she decided to climb up the path along the cliff. It was a strange thing to do, but she was warm from the food and the fire, and she wanted to talk to God in the open air. It was a bright night and Lucy had her boots on, so she had no problem negotiating the well-trod cliff path.

When Lucy reached her favorite spot, she stood and watched the view in wonder. The moon was full and hung like a brilliant white orb in the night. The stars were out and clear as could be. She watched a shooting star, marveling at God's incredible handiwork. The moon was reflected beautifully in the inklike waters below. Occasionally a white-tipped wave glimmered in the moonlight, and the silhouette of Gull Island stood strong and alone in the center of everything.

"What a wonderful world I live in," Lucy exclaimed as she wrapped her coat around herself, sat down on the soft turf, and began to pray.

"Dear Lord, I love you so much. It overwhelms me to know you sent your Son to die for me, and to be my friend, too. It is difficult not to regret all the years I spent trying to love you and live for you without understanding I needed to rely on your power. Help me to stay focused on the present and the future. I look forward to living for you with your direction and in your strength. Thank you for my dear boys. Bless them, Lord, and their families." She paused. "Guide them into your will. Help them to continue to serve you, wherever that may be. And please protect and bless little Rose and Jamey. May they grow up to love you, Lord. And please bless these wonderful people of Tarran Bay."

She gazed down at her new home. It looked like a miniature village, with just a few lights shining from the tiny windows.

"And bless Gordon. Thank you for his kindness to me. It scares me to even pray this, but bless our relationship. Help us to seek your will."

As she ended her prayer, Lucy took a hanky from her handbag and blew her nose. "I'm so happy!" She began to laugh aloud. She softly sang the song she'd learned at a Billy Graham crusade—"O Happy Day." She sang it all the way home, her legs almost running away from her as she picked up momentum down the steep path. She felt like a little girl again and knew the only explanation for her joy was that she had finally opened the door for the Holy Spirit to comfort her and to work in her life!

As she made her way down the cliff homeward, Lucy resolved she must get over her last hurdle. A still small voice said, "All in good time."

At last she was back in Dawn Cottage and went to find her Bible. She opened to the book of Acts. *And He said to them, "It is not for you to know times or seasons which the Father has put in His own authority. But you shall receive power when the Holy Spirit has come upon you: and you shall be witnesses to Me in Jerusalem, and in all Judea and Samaria, and to the end of the earth!"* Lucy laid her Bible down on the sofa. *And I shall be a witness for you, Lord, in Tarran Bay!*

———

During the week Lucy made endless lists of all that she would need for Christmas. She also cleaned the house and did some baking. In the midst of it all, she found time to visit with both Hilda and Sue and felt more at peace with herself than she had in years.

CHAPTER 16

Gordon's Surprise

On Saturday morning, Lucy was up before six o'clock. It was one of those increasingly familiar Cornish days where the sea and the sky molded into one gray mass and the eye could see no horizon. Lucy didn't mind. At least it wasn't raining. She had started painting a picture for Hilda and wanted to finish it. So she went to the studio and applied the finishing touches as she sang her favorite choruses. Soon she was satisfied with her work, so she put away her supplies, took a long hot shower, and got dressed. Knowing a long day lay ahead of her, she enjoyed a full breakfast of bacon and fried eggs.

Gordon was at the cottage promptly at nine, and Lucy was ready for him. As they drove down the now familiar lanes to St. Ives, Lucy reveled in the scenery, still looking magnificent, even though the trees were bare. Gordon refused to tell Lucy what they were going to do, so she decided she might as well just sit back and enjoy being driven around for a change. Because Gordon had warned her to wear something warm, Lucy had chosen to wear washed-out Levis, a chunky bright-red sweater over a cotton shirt,

brown leather boots, and a green waxed-cotton coat that had be-
longed to Tom. As she got out of the car, she pulled the brown
corduroy collar up over her ears and put on a red wool beret and a
matching scarf and gloves. Gordon parked on the quayside right in
front of the shops, seeming not to worry about getting a ticket.

"It's Mark's gallery. He lets me use his parking space." He
smiled at Lucy over the roof of his little blue Morris, and she smiled
back. "We'll pop in for a coffee, and then we're going out in my
boat!"

"No, I'm frightened of the sea!"

"You'll be safe with me."

Lucy almost began to argue with him. Imagine Gordon making
that decision for her, after she told him of her fears! He could be so
maddening! But then she remembered she was trying to learn to
trust God—and others—more than she had in the past. She would
be safe with Gordon. She was certain he wouldn't do anything to
hurt her. With a fair amount of trepidation, she decided his surprise
boat trip would be a good chance to try her wings.

Gordon took Lucy's arm and led her into Mark's gallery. She
lingered over the many different styles of paintings. There were oils,
watercolors, and acrylics—all so beautiful. She couldn't compete
with these.

"Hi, Lucy." Mark came toward her, handsome as ever, wearing
jeans and a blue sweat shirt, his hair tied back in a ponytail. "Do
you like them?" he asked, putting his hands behind his back. He
leaned forward to look at the oil that Lucy had spotted of the sea at
night on St. Michael's Mount. A huge moon was silvering the crest-
ing waves as they broke on the shore.

"They're wonderful, really, quite breathtaking. I have never
been able to paint waves. I've tried many times. How do they ever
get that translucency? I should have gone to classes. I just paint what
I see. I hope Gordon hasn't led you to believe mine are worth selling. You will be horribly disappointed if he has."

"Rubbish," Gordon said from behind them. "She's too modest! Coffee's ready."

He had made it for them in the little back room Mark used for his office. Gordon always seemed to make himself at home, wherever he happened to be. She liked his self-confidence.

"We're going fishing!" he told Mark.

Lucy shook her head in disbelief once more. She cupped the coffee mug in her gloved hands in an attempt to warm them up for the journey ahead. This man was exasperating.

"He didn't tell you, did he?" Mark smiled. "Same old Gordon. I expect you'll enjoy yourself, though."

After the coffee they said good-bye to Mark and went out into the chilly winter weather. They took the life jackets, picnic basket, and fishing gear from the back of the Morris and walked to the harbor.

"The tide will be in at eight, so we can have the whole day in the boat." He helped her down the stone stairway to the dock. Before she was within ten feet of the boat, Lucy took a life jacket and strapped it tightly about her. She was willing to step out in faith, but she wasn't going to take any foolish chances. She nervously stepped into the boat and took the picnic basket from him.

"Tuck it in the wheelhouse, Lucy. It will keep a little drier there."

Lucy surveyed the boat. It was painted navy blue with white trimming, and the roof of the tiny wheelhouse was painted red. She tucked the hamper in the corner as requested and turned back to Gordon.

"Are you expecting rain?" she asked, looking up at the rather cloudy sky.

"Not especially. The waves get high sometimes, and the spray comes in the boat."

Now Lucy was *really* nervous. She was a land lover! Soon, however, Gordon had the engine started, and Lucy closed her eyes tightly as they began their journey out of the harbor enclosure and into the deep, gray, choppy sea.

After half an hour, Lucy had to admit that it was wonderfully exhilarating to be out in the boat in Gordon's safe hands. She loved the coastline, and as he told her which landmarks to look for, she was able to work out where they were. They went past Carbis Bay, Lelant, and Godrevy Beach—with its beautiful lighthouse perched on the black rocks. Soon they were approaching Tarran Bay. It was marvelous to see Gull Island up close, with all the wonderful birds nesting in the many rocky nooks and crannies.

Lucy loved everything about the village of Tarran Bay. She could see her little cottage nestled up on the hillside. It seemed to beckon her—safe, secure, at last full of God's sweet presence.

During the last week, Lucy had felt God's love in a way she had never known it before. In the past she had leaned on Tom's faith, and when God took him home, the cracks in her spiritual life began to appear.

All those wasted years. But she clung to God's words to her from only a week ago, that He would restore the years the locusts had eaten. And Vicar Todd had said that in God's plans, nothing is wasted. Would He be able to redeem the years and bring something new and good to her life? Lucy knew she had one more thing she needed to talk to God about. No rush now, she thought, with a calm recognition of God's love for her. There was plenty of time for her healing.

Gordon stopped the motor, and they ate lunch on the scrubbed wooden seat of the fishing boat, sitting either side of the huge wicker hamper and gazing out to sea. The lunch included thickly buttered buns of crusty bread, cheese, and pickles. Gordon had also provided two flasks—one contained hearty vegetable soup and the other steaming tea. They finished the meal off with huge chunks of fruit-cake and apples.

"How long have you had your boat, Gordon?" Lucy asked as

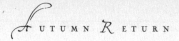

she nervously sipped her drink. She was trying desperately to take her mind from the fact that the boat was rising and falling on the swell of a rather high sea!

"I've owned a boat ever since I came down here. This one is just four years old, though. I love the sea, Lucy. Sometimes when I feel drained after a day in the surgery I come out to the boat. Even if I don't go out in her, I enjoy cleaning her up or giving her a fresh lick of paint. Then there are all the other fishermen and folks who own boats to chat with. They're a rather extraordinary crowd, all from different walks of life, but with a common link—a love of the sea."

"That's hard for me to imagine. I'm having a good time, but I'm still not really keen on the churning waves."

"I understand that everyone doesn't love the sea the way I do, but there is no reason to fear it. Respect, yes. Fear, no." Gordon gave Lucy a reassuring smile. "I only went out in bad weather once, and I had to pray hard to fight the fear. Now I never go out without checking the shipping forecast. It's foolish not to. The sea can be dangerous if you don't respect it."

"Tom used to take the boys fishing whenever we came down for holidays. I usually stayed on dry land and painted away the time!"

"I expect your life was busy and you needed the time to yourself."

"That's why Tom let me stay behind. He knew I needed a break. Oh, Gordon, I am sorry. I seem to talk about Tom all the time."

"I don't mind in the least. You can't just cut out the past. I want to know all about you—and your family."

"Thanks, Gordon. It's so nice to be free to talk about Tom. It's amazing, really—it just doesn't seem to hurt so much anymore."

"Wounds take time to heal. But in a healthy situation, they will heal eventually. The memory is still there, in the form of a scar, but the pain is gone."

"Doctor's talk!"

"Well, that's where *I* have to apologize. I use medical metaphors all the time, I'm afraid."

"Well, don't stop on my account. I like them!" Lucy turned to face Gordon and asked, "Why do you keep your boat in St. Ives harbor rather than Tarran Bay?" She looked out over the beautiful bay and harbor.

"Tarran Bay's harbor is a renowned danger spot. It sits at a very strange angle, and I am not as good as Jack is at negotiating the boat so close to the rocks."

Lucy took a closer look. "Oh, really?"

"You may not believe it, but we have pulled in on a fairly calm day, so we are perfectly safe. But St. Ives is a better port for me. Most of my boating friends live there, and there's *always* something going on."

"Yes, I know what you mean. I think that's what I love about it, too. It's so picturesque, with all the tiny cottages piling up the hill-side, and the little shops and restaurants. It's a cosmopolitan sort of place, isn't it?"

"Oh yes. People come to St. Ives from all over the world."

"Even with the lack of parking spaces, I just can't stay away. But I need a peaceful home right now, and Tarran Bay is perfect." Lucy sat rather thoughtfully for a moment. "Even in summer," she added, a little breathlessly as spray from the foaming ocean brushed her face.

"I know what you mean. But even Tarran Bay is a bustling place in the summer months."

"Ah, but because you've rested over the winter, you don't mind sharing it with others, do you?"

"No, I guess not. Most folks make their living from the tourists. We need them as much as they need the scenery!"

"Very true. I wouldn't be here now if I hadn't been a tourist once."

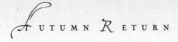

They smiled at each other and sat quietly, contentedly finishing their feast.

"I'll take you up to Padstow now, and then we'll head back for some fishing," Gordon said.

Lucy was very pleased, for she liked the bustling town of Padstow. She stood in the tiny wheelhouse at the helm of the boat and watched the waves and the beautiful, bubbling clouds. The high-flying gulls swooped and fell, calling to one another in their raucous manner. Lucy had been to Padstow before, but just like everywhere else, it looked so different from the sea. She admired the prettily painted houses, all pale blues, pinks, and lemons, set in a square around the harbor, in which many yachts and smaller sailboats took shelter.

"This certainly is the place for the rich and famous, Lucy. Look at the beautiful yachts. I'd love one myself."

"I suppose they're rather expensive."

"A bit out of my reach, sadly!"

"Well, I like this boat. Why the name *Escapade?*"

"Well, that's what we menfolk do. We go on escapades in her!"

Lucy smiled. She could imagine the sort of adventures he and Jack might get up to!

"Well, Lucy, time for catching some supper, I think. Are you ready?"

"Ready as I'll ever be!" Now that she had adjusted somewhat to the sway of the boat, she was enjoying her day out immensely.

They journeyed slowly back to St. Ives, where Gordon anchored and taught Lucy to fish.

"You don't need any bait, Lucy. You just put these feathers on the hook, and the fish are attracted to them as they move in the water." Gordon took out a small tin and showed her the contents. It was full of different hooks and feathers.

Lucy was pleased that she didn't need live bait, because the thought of putting a wriggling fish or worm on the end of the hook rather repulsed her. She let down the line and stood patiently, enjoying the wind in her hair and the smell of the sea, even though it was getting colder.

Suddenly, she felt a pull on the line and panicked.

"Gordon, help me. I think I've got a bite."

Gordon didn't rush to her aid.

"Don't worry. Just hang in there and draw it in slowly."

Lucy was annoyed. She wanted his help. Glancing at him sideways, she realized he was reeling in his own fish. So she did as he said and soon caught sight of the beautiful turquoise and gray stripe of her fish flash on the surface of the water. Lucy found she was eager to reel in her first catch. But as she began to lift it out of the water, a larger fish leapt to the surface and whipped her fish clean off the line. Lucy screamed and let go of her rod. Thankfully Gordon was there immediately, catching the rod before it fell into the sea.

"What on earth was that?" she exclaimed, clutching her cheeks with both of her gloved hands. The experience had shaken her up.

"I haven't seen that happen in years. It was only a dogfish pinching your catch. Nothing to worry over. Let's try again." He put a freshly feathered hook on the line, handed it to her, and walked back to his own rod. Lucy pursed her lips but didn't show him her annoyance. She would show him. She would catch a fish if it killed her!

Soon Lucy caught her first fish and quickly returned her line to the water, eager to beat Gordon at his own fishing game—and she did! Gordon laughed as she pointed out her higher tally.

"See. I knew you could do it. You just need a push now and then."

Soon it was time to head home. They kept enough mackerel for supper and threw the others back.

"I'm cooking tonight," Gordon said as they finally docked and made their way back to the car.

"That sounds wonderful," Lucy said as she helped Gordon pack the equipment into the Morris.

They drove home in silence. It had been a wonderful day. Lucy felt a deep contentment. She loved the way she could be silent with him, and it didn't matter. Gordon dropped her off outside her cottage so she could shower and change into fresh clothes. She stank of fish!

"I'll pick you up in an hour."

"No need. I like the walk." She smiled, and he nodded. And once she was safely inside the front door he drove away.

———

Supper was delicious. Gordon's kitchen was very basic, but his cooking was not! He fried the fish in garlic and olive oil, and they enjoyed them with cheesy cauliflower and baked potatoes filled with butter. After the meal, Lucy insisted she help him do the washing up. As they stood together to do the simple domestic task, it brought back memories of Tom once again. But she was not sad. Her life had changed—for the better. As Gordon placed a saucepan on the rack, he brushed Lucy's hand with his soapy forearm. Her heart missed a beat. It shocked Lucy that such an innocent movement had affected her that way. Gordon glanced at her momentarily and wrinkled his nose as a grin crossed his face. Did he feel something, too? Lucy dried the saucepan and placed it on the work surface. Not knowing how to react, Lucy tried to avoid eye contact.

While she wiped the last of the knives and forks, Gordon made some fresh coffee and suggested they take it into the sitting room. Lucy liked his home. It was solid and warm. The fireplace was larger than the one in Dawn Cottage. It was very impressive, with an old bread oven on the right-hand side.

As she studied the paintings that covered the walls, she understood why he was drawn to her paintings. Though his collection was much more skillfully done, there were similarities—he really liked bright colors. "Your paintings are lovely, Gordon. Your house almost looks like Mark's gallery."

"It's my hobby. I've collected for several years. Mark taught me the ins and outs."

"I like them, Gordon. They are all very good. Are any of them yours?"

"Unfortunately, no. Oh, I've tried, believe me. Finally, even Mark had to concede that I was rubbish. He told me not to give up my day job!"

As he laughed at his own joke, Gordon leaned forward to look into Lucy's eyes. "So the day wasn't as bad as you expected, was it?"

Lucy smiled. "No, it wasn't. But I was worried for a while. That dogfish took me by surprise. I thought it was a shark!"

"Yes, I guessed that. I know I was a bit hard on you, Lucy. But I knew if I let you off, you'd never fish again!"

"Yes, you're probably right. I don't think I've ever caught my own supper before."

"Fun, isn't it."

"It was great fun. Thank you for taking me. I really enjoyed myself."

"I enjoyed myself, too. It's nice to have someone to share experiences with."

As the evening wore on, they began to talk about God. Lucy told him all her new feelings, and most of the time, he sat grinning like a Cheshire cat. She watched him as she shared her personal struggles since Tom's death. And the gentle sparkle in his eyes and his sincere interest in her as a person made it easy for her to like him very much. But she was sure it wasn't love—and that was okay. She was in no hurry. Tom was still so close, and she couldn't let him go—not yet. It was lovely for her to have a friend, though, and to her surprise, a male friend. Perhaps she had been too hard on men all these years.

192

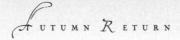

When they reached a lull in the conversation, Gordon went into the kitchen to make some more coffee. When he returned, he asked Lucy if he could tell her something. He seemed so solemn all of a sudden. Lucy did not speak, but she leaned forward and nodded.

"Lucy, you know how you had locked things up deep inside you?"

"Yes."

"Well, I have things locked up, too—things I've not told many people. But I want to tell you. I want to be honest with you, Lucy." He hesitated a moment, as if he were gathering the courage to continue.

Lucy sat silently, not really knowing whether to speak or not. She couldn't imagine what he was trying to say, but it was obviously very distressing to him. So to be on the safe side she kept silent.

"I have loved God for as long as I can remember, but at university . . . well, I set aside my faith for drink, women, and parties. I became completely involved in the seedy side of campus life, and I didn't even care. I met a girl there—her name was Jean. She was very beautiful. All the boys liked her, but she liked me—and I was so proud. I thought I'd gotten myself quite a catch. We made foolish choices. I knew better, but I didn't . . . I got her pregnant. We were horrified." Suddenly his face screwed up and Gordon put his head in his hands.

He almost choked as he finally spoke again. "I made her have an abortion."

Lucy could not prevent an involuntary intake of breath.

Gordon closed his eyes, as if willing himself to continue. "She cried for days afterward, and I couldn't comfort her. We couldn't even bear to *look* at each other. Within weeks we drifted apart. I have never seen her since, but I have thought of her often. I hope she is okay." Gordon sat for a moment.

Lucy was in shock and couldn't think of anything to say to console him.

"I knew abortion was wrong—as a Christian *and* as a medical student. But I felt we had no other choice. I wanted to be a doctor like my father before me. I couldn't let anything get in the way. My parents would have been devastated to find out their wonderful Christian son got his girlfriend pregnant. They worked hard to put me through university. They waited to go to Kenya until I passed my exams. After spending their savings and money from the sale of the house on my education and the hospital, they lived on almost nothing in Kenya. They were paid no salary. They gave up so much for me. I couldn't let them down . . . do you see?"

He looked into Lucy's eyes, as if waiting for encouragement from her. But she *didn't* see. Well, she did, but she couldn't believe it. She smiled weakly.

"It has been a difficult mistake to live with. I asked God to forgive my selfishness and vowed I would sacrifice marriage and children as penance for what I'd done. I have purposely steered myself away from romance. I promised to be a good and faithful doctor—one who would save life, not take it away. You see, Lucy, I was the coward, not you. Do you understand? Do you think I am a terrible person?"

Lucy didn't know what to say. He was so sincere, so very sorry, and he seemed to be looking for something from her. God had forgiven him. How could she cast a stone? Lucy knew she should offer words of consolation, but she would need God's grace to do it. She knew all she needed to do was ask. But a baby—he had chosen to kill a baby! He knew how precious life is, and yet he—

It had been a long, exhilarating day, and suddenly Lucy felt very weary. She couldn't deal with this information now. "I must go. I've had too many late nights recently, what with getting ready for Christmas and gallivanting with you." Her attempts at lightheartedness sounded so hollow. "Thank you for a wonderful day. It has been a long time since I have enjoyed myself so much."

They both stood and Gordon said he would walk her home.

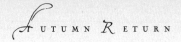

Lucy insisted she would be fine on her own. In truth, she needed to be alone to gather her thoughts together. Struggling to hold back the tears, she picked up her handbag from the floor beside the chair. The thought of babies being aborted by the very people who should love them the most had always angered her—and now it had become personal. At the door he held her shoulders and kissed her forehead. He seemed nervous. Lucy knew she should say something to re-assure him, but she couldn't say more than a few token words.

"Thank you for telling me more about yourself, Gordon. I had wondered why a nice-looking man like you wasn't married. It must have been difficult for you to tell me."

On the way home Lucy's heart felt unusually heavy. Why didn't things ever go the way one planned? As she turned the key in the front door of Dawn Cottage, Lucy knew she would never be able to share her deepest sorrow with Gordon. Though she was honored by the trust he had placed in her, it had not brought them closer. His words only tore at her wound and made it go deeper.

CHAPTER 17

Mark Holding

Over the next few days—partially in an attempt to put her struggles with Gordon's revelation out of her mind— Lucy worked on her illustrating. She wanted the paintings finished by the end of the week so that she could put them together with her story and make a little book of it for Carly and Kasey. She needed to complete it quickly, because she simply had to get going on her Christmas preparations. There was so little time left and so much to be done. She needed to clean and arrange the guest bedrooms and move more chairs into the sitting room. She also wanted to get as much cooking as she could out of the way and into the freezer, which would enable her to give more time to her family while they were visiting. Then there were the presents to choose and wrap, a tree . . .

One thing at a time, she thought. *No sense getting myself all bound up in knots.* She had just returned to her painting when a knock at the door took her thoughts swiftly to more immediate things. *Who could it be?* she wondered, leaving her easel and paints. Perhaps it would be Gordon. Lucy hoped not. She wasn't ready to cross that bridge yet.

When she opened the door Lucy was amazed to see Mark Holding.

"Hello, Mark. What a nice surprise. Do come in."

He stepped through the door and into the bright hallway.

"I was passing through on my way to Redruth and thought I'd pop in and see your paintings. At it now, are you?" he asked, looking at the long slim brush in her hand.

"I am, actually. Would you like some coffee or tea?"

"Coffee, please." He had already stopped at the paintings in the sitting room, so she left him, slightly worried at what his reaction might be, and started on the coffee.

"They're very good," Mark said, taking a seat at the table in the kitchen. "Have you any more?"

"Yes, lots—somewhere. Probably in a box in the study. I can't remember. They're very old and not in frames."

"I'd like to see them."

"Have your coffee first."

"Thanks, but I'll wait. Lead the way."

Lucy was surprised. It appeared Mark was not one to wait when he decided to do something. So she led the way up the kitchen staircase to the study. It was a low, winding staircase, and Mark had to bend down so as not to bump his head on the beams. She made for the study, but he stopped at the open door of her studio and stepped inside, uninvited, to see what she was painting. She left him there and went to see what she could find in the cupboard in the alcove. She was sure she'd put her paintings in a box there, shoved on the top shelf, never to see the light of day.

At last she stood in the doorway with a bundle of paintings in her arms and the paintbrush between her teeth. "What are you doing?" she asked, trying to speak through the wooden handle of the brush.

"Sorry, I can't understand you!"

"What a serious young man you are," she said after putting the

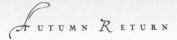

paintings on the table under the window and placing the brush on top of them.

"I'm just impressed, that's all. What's this you're working on?" He waved at the pictures that she'd tacked in a line along the wall in sequence with her story.

"Oh, I'm trying to illustrate a little story I wrote some years ago. I thought it would make a nice present for the twins."

"Well, I like them. I think you should photocopy them for the twins. I'll do it for you. And then I'll put these in frames, and we'll see if they sell."

Lucy was amazed he thought them worth selling. Her work was very simple, nothing special. The colors were vibrant, though. Perhaps that's what he liked. She showed him twenty more paintings of varying sizes she'd painted while in Africa. Then there were a dozen or more that she'd painted in Cornwall on holidays. Mark wanted them all. He said he would frame them for her and would take the money off with his percentage at sale.

"But what if they don't sell?"

"Well, then you'll have them professionally framed, won't you."

He had picked them up and put them under his arm when Lucy had a sudden thought.

"Leave them there for a moment, Mark. I could do with a hand getting two chairs from my spare rooms and putting them in the sitting room." She explained about her family coming for Christmas and how much she was looking forward to it.

They laughed together as they struggled down the winding staircase. At a difficult turn, Lucy stopped for a break. "The movers got them up here somehow. This has to work."

They got both chairs down eventually, and while Mark went back to get the paintings, Lucy made him more coffee, as his first cup had gone stone cold.

"So how did you come to live here, Lucy?" Mark asked as he sat down at the kitchen table once again.

"It's a long story."

"I've got bags of time!"

Lucy began to tell Mark how she had lost her faith when Tom died. As she talked, Lucy thought again of how much he reminded her of Danny, a little older perhaps, but he had the same easy manner. He stopped her before she had really started.

"Lucy, I think I should tell you that I'm not a Christian."

"Oh, I see. I—"

"I know, you assumed. Well, I'm not offended. I can see how you might have thought that I was, because Gordon and I are so close. Do carry on. I'm interested."

"Do you really want to know?"

"I love to hear about people. I find their stories fascinating."

So she continued, amazed at herself. She hardly knew the young man and yet felt completely at ease with him. She told him about Africa, about Tom, about Ruth's letter, and about the way Gordon had helped her face some issues she had shelved for far too long. She finished, as she had to be honest, with her experience in church and her prayer asking for forgiveness.

"I hope this doesn't make you uncomfortable, but you wanted the truth. I feel wonderful. I know there is work for me to do for God. I suppose I lived in Tom's shadow a bit. I'm sad to say I liked it that way—hiding behind him. I didn't really realize it until recently. I can't lean on him any longer—because he's not here to lean on! I have to live my own life."

"And are you learning to do that?"

"Yes, I think I finally am, Mark. I'm finally on track. With God's help, I'm starting to enjoy life again. Great, isn't it?"

"Yes, it is. Say, speaking of enjoying life, how did you enjoy your fishing trip?"

Lucy was certain Mark had changed the subject because he was growing uncomfortable with all the God talk. But she was glad she'd taken the opportunity—she liked Mark immensely.

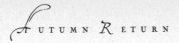

"Oh, it was wonderful. I caught fish and made them for supper!" When she told him about the "shark" experience, he slapped the table and laughed loudly.

"Trust that to happen on your first fishing trip! Well, Lucy, much as I'd love to stay, I'm afraid I have work to do. I'm glad you had a good time. Somehow I knew you would." More softly he added, "You're good medicine for the doctor."

His statement brought the final minutes of her last conversation with Gordon back to Lucy's mind. Sadly, she couldn't help thinking that her reaction to his painful revelation was more like *bad* medicine. What was she to do?

Mark rose to his feet, thanking her for everything. As he left with her paintings under his arm, Lucy wondered if she should have said so much to a virtual stranger. What had happened to her?

As she went back upstairs to finish her work, she thought again of Gordon. Was it true that she was good for him? When he told her about the abortion, she had found it incredibly difficult to understand his part in it. She knew that she shouldn't judge him. He had suffered through the pain of that mistake for a long time. But how could he have forced his girlfriend to abort his baby? Lucy knew she would have to work out her feelings—with God's help. She would call him, but she didn't feel ready just yet. Later, perhaps.

Lucy finished her final picture, cleaned up, had lunch, and went for a walk across the cliffs. It was sunny, but surprisingly cold. The sky was blue with wispy swirling clouds that looked just like a paisley eiderdown made from the strong wind. The walk took over two hours, up through dead heather and bracken, higher and higher, until she reached the top of the cliff, where she lay down to look over the top to the sea. She didn't dare stand on the edge for fear of the wind blowing her over.

She loved this view of Gull Island—so majestic and alone in the middle of the bay. She and Tom had often stood at this point. Her thoughts saddened slightly. She realized with some surprise that she didn't feel so alone anymore. She began to wonder at all the years she had lived not fully understanding what it meant to live the Christian life. Now she knew Jesus as her friend, as well as her Savior. She felt His love continuously. She knew that she could go to Him with anything, no matter how difficult. And she understood the Holy Spirit was meant to be her helper. It was amazing to feel so loved and cared for at last. She lay there quietly for some time, watching the gulls swoop and turn, calling to one another as they looped in the wind. Delighted, she also watched two seals as they played near the rocks below her, just as Gordon had told her they would.

Suddenly, such joy infused her entire being that she wanted to stay there for hours. But reluctantly, she rose to her feet and made her way downward. As she passed Hilda's cottage, Lucy couldn't resist popping in to see her dear old friend, in spite of the work waiting for her at home. Hilda was delighted to see Lucy and welcomed her into the warmth of her homey kitchen with its ancient reminders of a more genteel time. *It will all be lost with this generation*, Lucy thought sadly.

As Hilda prepared tea, she asked Lucy about her plans for Christmas.

"My family is coming to stay with me, Hilda. I'm so looking forward to showing them the cottage and introducing them to all my new friends."

"I am pleased, dear. I thought you might go to London for the festivities."

"Oh no, this is to be a very different Christmas—all part of my new beginning!"

"Will I be able to meet them?"

"Of course you will." Lucy took Hilda's frail hand into her own. "I've told them all about you, Hilda. They're eager to meet you."

Hilda smiled.

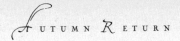

"Where will you put everyone?"

"Well, it will be a squash, but Sue has offered two cots that will go into the bedrooms. Thankfully, the rooms are quite big. It'll be fun." Lucy stopped and glanced at the clock. "Speaking of fun, I must fly. Too much to do, you know." She put her teacup in the sink and headed to the door. "By the way, where can I get a Christmas tree?"

"I'd go to the forest shop if I were you. They sell such nice ones."

"You'll have to tell me how to get there—I don't suppose I could coax you into coming in the car with me?"

"I'm afraid not, my dear. I'm too old to change now. It's difficult to turn around the habits of a lifetime!"

Lucy laughed. "I didn't think you would. I must admit I was wondering how I would fit both of us and a tree in that Mini of mine! Thanks for the tea. See you soon."

When she returned home, Lucy tried calling Gordon several times, but he never answered. She hoped he was okay but didn't feel right about popping in on him unannounced. Maybe he was avoiding her. Was it possible he was feeling awkward, too? Or was he angry with her? Well, there was nothing she could do about it now, so she decided to worry about it later.

The following day, Lucy walked over to the Trents' to ask about the cots.

Sue answered the door. "Hello, Lucy. Do come in. Have you got time for coffee?"

"I hoped you'd ask me that, Sue. But I'm actually here to find out if it will still work for me to borrow the cots and children's things we talked about."

"Absolutely—no problem at all."

"I hate to impose, but do you think Jack could help me get them over?"

"Of course I can!" Jack said, coming out of his study rubbing his eyes with the back of his hands. He gave Lucy a hug and followed the women into the kitchen.

"I'm glad you stopped by, Lucy. I need a coffee myself!"

They all sat at the huge table drinking coffee and eating Hilda's homemade cookies.

"Are you nearly ready for your family's visit, Lucy?" Sue asked.

"Nearly—Mark got some chairs downstairs for me. I just need to arrange the cots and all the other supplies you are lending me, and then it's mostly cooking and decorating the house. I would like to buy a real tree."

"So would I," Sue said, looking at Jack with a grin.

Jack grimaced. "I get fed up with all the needles on the carpet. It's a bit of a bone of contention! I do like real trees—but only if we can get one that doesn't drop too soon."

"I always get mine the week before Christmas, and it seems to last out the festivities. I would like a big one, but the Mini is just too small."

"Oh that's no problem. We'll take you when we go to get ours. The estate car is big enough to fit two nice big trees!" Sue said enthusiastically. Jack just groaned and stood up from the table.

"Women!"

"The girls will want a big tree, too, Jack. I'm afraid you're outnumbered three to one!"

"Won't the girls want to come with us to choose a tree?" Lucy asked, remembering the pleasure she and Tom had when taking the boys to choose theirs.

"Of course. Don't worry. Jack can put the roof rack on the car, can't you, Jack?" Jack just made an even louder mock groan and went back to the sanctuary of his study. From the study, he called

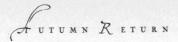

to say he would bring the cots and things over to Lucy at five o'clock.

After lunch Lucy went into Redruth to buy Christmas presents and groceries. She found the Early Learning Toy Shop first and got all the toys she wanted for the children there. Then she went into Peacock's, the only large department store in town, and found all the other gifts she needed. She had already ordered some of Denise's and Karen's presents from a catalog, since the shop was in London and she couldn't get there before Christmas. As she had expected, the supermarket was packed, but she didn't mind. She'd allowed herself the whole afternoon for shopping. It was fun, but as she couldn't carry everything in one go, she needed two trips to the car park.

Jack came over with the cots and all the rest promptly at five. It took them several trips from his car to get it all unloaded. During that time Lucy thanked him several times for their generosity. She had no idea how to set up the cots, so she was grateful when Jack did it in no time. She thought of what Danny had said to her and had to agree that there were some skills she just wasn't any good at. She thanked God for good friends!

When they finished she invited him in for tea. He thanked her but declined, as he had much to do that evening. After he left, Lucy put on a CD of Christmas carols from Kings College Oxford to get her in the mood of the season and spent the rest of the evening wrapping parcels and writing out her Christmas cards. She was eagerly anticipating her family's arrival. They would certainly be surprised to see how she had changed in such a short space of time.

Lucy spent the next day baking. She cooked a rich fruitcake, which she should have done much earlier in the year, but it didn't really matter. She would ice it in a few days—plenty of time before Christmas Day. She had decided to paint a simple Christmas story theme with edible paints to put on top of the cake. Once the cake was in the oven, she made three-dozen mince tarts and put them in the freezer. After lunch she made lasagna and a shepherd's pie. She didn't want to be stuck in the kitchen when there were grand-children to play with. Lucy always cooked the turkey on Christmas Day, so she ordered a fresh one from the local butcher shop. It would be delivered to her door on Christmas Eve morning. Every-thing was coming together nicely. She couldn't believe it. She sup-posed it was because she wasn't distracted by anything, or anybody.

A couple of days later Lucy got a call from Mark asking her to come to the gallery. He said he would treat her to lunch. How could she refuse?

"Bring me that last picture, will you? The one on the easel. Is it finished?"

"Yes, I'll bring it."

"Oh, Lucy, forgive me. I was supposed to give you a message from Gordon. He had to go to London for a course on tropical dis-eases. He hadn't planned to go until January, but someone dropped out, so he took his place. He will be gone until Christmas Eve. I'm so sorry I forgot to tell you."

"Don't worry, Mark. I know how busy you are, traipsing up and down Cornwall for finds!" Lucy was quite relieved by Mark's mes-sage. She still didn't know what Gordon was thinking. She didn't even know exactly what *she* was thinking, but she had been worried when she hadn't heard from him. At least she knew he had tried to get a message to her. As she got into the Mini and made for St. Ives with her last painting in a brown envelope on the seat next to her, Lucy wondered why Gordon would want to take a course on tropical diseases.

As she entered the gallery door, Lucy noted it was tastefully dec-orated for Christmas—not a sign of tinsel! Mark had set out a

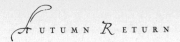

warmed spicy drink, which filled the whole place with a wonderful Christmassy smell! Sprigs of red-berried holly and ivy and large glass bowls of oranges, spiked with cloves in differing diagonal and swirling patterns, were placed throughout the gallery. There were also huge handmade wooden bowls overflowing with nuts. Lucy made a mental note to put nuts on her list. She was surprised to see how busy the gallery was. She had expected it to be dead at this time of year, with all the holidaymakers long since gone. She was impressed when she realized Mark's clientele base was broader than just St. Ives.

Lucy was astonished when she saw her paintings hanging with all the others she had admired only two weeks ago. When her gaze drifted to a price tag, her hands went to her mouth to stop a gasp. She quickly checked another tag—they couldn't possibly be correct!

"You're surprised. Well, don't be," Mark said, walking up behind her and handing her a beverage. "I've already sold four of your African paintings to an American, and with my expenses taken off, I still have three hundred pounds for you. You'd better get yourself an accountant."

"My son Danny is an accountant," she whispered, looking at the remaining pictures in total disbelief. "He looks like you," she added vacantly.

Mark laughed.

"Well, won't he be surprised."

Mark took Lucy to a little café on the harbor front. It had a pleasant ambiance, with terra-cotta walls and painted pictures of Italian scenery in six-foot panels on three walls. Lucy decided on leek and potato soup, followed by a pasta dish, and Mark picked the same soup and a vegetable curry. He told her he'd been a vegetarian for a few years but missed bacon and eggs so much that he was now back to eating meat and fish occasionally.

"I'm afraid I do like my meat," Lucy said as she put down the menu. After the young waitress took the order, Mark handed her the copied pictures.

"Take a look at these, Lucy. What do you think?" He went on to suggest that since he had a new computer, she should let him finish the book for her. "You could send me the story through the post. I'd enjoy doing it for you."

Lucy took the copies and studied them carefully. It was amazing what computers could do these days. "You can't tell the copies from the real thing!" She looked at Mark intently. "Are you sure you want to take this on? You seem so busy. I wouldn't want it to be a nuisance."

"Lucy, you should know me by now. I wouldn't have offered if I didn't have the time. I like the challenge of doing something different. Please say yes."

"Well, of course, I'd be delighted. It probably would be hard for me to finish it. I have so much to do at home, what with the family all coming at Christmas."

At that moment the soup arrived and they started to eat.

"Good, isn't it?" Mark said enthusiastically. "I like it here—everything is homemade and delicious!"

"It is," agreed Lucy, who was enjoying her trip to St. Ives immensely. She glanced from the window. Large, smoky-white clouds billowed around the bay. It was all so wonderful. *The boys will love it here in winter.* She would bring them for lunch during their visit.

Mark broke the comfortable silence as the soup dishes were removed and the second course arrived. He began to tell her about his own family, who over the years had all moved to New Zealand.

"I think I might go out there next year. It's been years since I've been there. Mum and Dad aren't getting any younger."

"So why have you left it so long?"

"Time, money, getting the gallery up and running. I didn't always agree with my father either, and it caused problems between

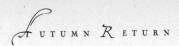

my parents. I think it's time, though. I'll be thirty soon. Time flies, and soon I'll be too old."

Lucy smiled at his statement that thirty was creeping up on too old.

"You have all the time in the world, Mark. Thirty is nothing. But you should go—see it as an adventure! I'm sure your mother and father would be delighted to see you."

Lucy ate her food silently, thinking how strange it all was—her new beginning helping in some small way to pay for his trip to a faraway place!

"Why did your parents decide to go to New Zealand?" Lucy asked as she cut into the pasta.

"Business. My dad is a bit of an entrepreneur. He enjoys new challenges. Actually, in spite of our differences, he set me up in the gallery. That's why I want it to work so badly." Mark became thoughtful for a moment. "I had to make it work."

209

Lucy sensed the struggle between Mark and his father was great and didn't push him. If he wanted to tell her, he would in his own time.

"Do you have any brothers and sisters?"

"One sister—Mary. She's sweet. She made me an uncle! Derek, her husband, is a nice guy. We write and send photos and suchlike. Maybe I should go, or young Sam will be grown up and married before I know it!"

"As you said, Mark, time does fly. I still find it hard to believe I'm a grandmother!"

"I find it hard to believe, too." He smiled at her. "I'm afraid the gallery is calling, Lucy. John needs his lunch break."

"And who is John?" she asked politely.

"Just my number one man. He works very hard for me. When I have to go away on an occasional buying trip he runs the shop, and he also keeps the accountant and tax man happy. He's a great bloke."

"I'm sure I saw him in the gallery, but he was busy with a customer. I imagine it is a comfort to have someone you can trust working for you. Well, off you go then. And thanks, Mark—about the book. I really appreciate it."

"No problem." As Mark stood he grabbed the bill, insisting on paying. "You won't forget to send me the story, will you?"

"I won't forget."

"Bye, Lucy. Take care!"

When they separated, Lucy wasn't quite ready to leave St. Ives, so she decided to take a walk to "her spot." She snuggled her thick cream wool coat about her to block the chilly air and stood in wonder watching the boats. She'd never seen St. Ives' harbor in the winter. In many ways it was the same, but at the same time different. She sat on the rocks—her and Tom's rocks. Strangely, she suddenly felt so close to him—more certain of, and content in, the love he had for her than ever before. It seemed a bit silly, but though she knew Tom wasn't there and did not believe for one minute that he could hear her, she said to the air, "I've sold a painting, Tom. I've sold four paintings!" And she knew without a shadow of a doubt, he would have been very proud of her—for the paintings *and* for her personal and spiritual growth.

She sat there for some time watching the boats coming and going out on the high, choppy sea, wondering at the courage of the sailors. People were about on dry land, too, cleaning or repairing their boats in the harbor. She forgot about the cold and just enjoyed watching the incoming tide, as she had on her earlier visit in September. At last she hiked up to her car and drove home with joy in her heart and singing a song she'd written many years ago before going to Africa.

I love you, Lord.
I love you, Lord.
You're the joy of my heart.

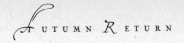

I love you, Lord,
For the life you impart.
I only want to serve you.
I just want to give.
I only want to worship you.
You're my reason to live.

She really meant it. At last she really did want to give and serve and live. How could she have ever doubted Him? She sang it again and again all the way home.

She prayed for Mark. She prayed that he would go and visit his parents. She could only imagine how badly they would want him to go to New Zealand. Whatever the reason for his delay, she prayed God would work it out at the right time. She asked God to bring the dear young man to faith in Him. She wouldn't push, but she *would* pray.

211

CHAPTER 18

Christmas

After picking the girls up from school on Thursday, Jack and Sue called for Lucy. It was very cold, so everyone was wrapped up in warm coats, scarves, and gloves. Lucy sat between the girls in the backseat, and off they set for the thirty-minute drive to the forest.

"How are my girls?" she asked.

"Fine, thank you, Lucy," Kasey said.

"And you, Carly?" Lucy turned to the quieter twin.

"I'm tired. I had lots of sums to do at school today."

"Oh, I am sorry to hear that. Did you get them all right?"

"No!" was the grumpy reply.

Lucy decided on a different tack. "What are you going to have for Christmas? Have you written a list yet?"

"Yes, I have!" Kasey said very precisely. "I want a baby girl doll that drinks real water and wets her nappy!"

Lucy smiled and turned. With the side-to-side glances at the twins she felt as though she were at a tennis match! "And you, Carly?"

"I want a doll that drinks water, wets her nappy, and

cries!" She looked around Lucy to see what her sister would say.

"Oh," Kasey said, "I forgot that bit."

Lucy tried to avoid an argument by moving to a new subject. "Aren't you going to ask me what's on my list?"

"Grown-ups don't write lists!"

"Oh yes we do!" said all three adults together. Carly perked up after that, and the journey was all chatter about the school nativity play. The girls were going to be angels. Lucy laughed! What else could they possibly be!

At the forest garden center, Carly chose a tree for her mummy and daddy, and Kasey was allowed to choose Lucy's. Once Jack had put the trees onto the roof rack, the party decided to go for tea and cakes in the coffee shop. It was toasty warm in the shop, and every-one shed their coats and settled down to hot mince pies, with a dol-lop of fresh cream on top—such wonderful treats.

The following day Jack came over and helped Lucy put up her tree. At Lucy's request, he placed it next to the fireplace. She knew the fire would probably hasten the needles dropping off the tree, but it looked wonderful in that spot, and she couldn't resist.

"Thanks so much, Jack. I couldn't have managed it on my own. Would you like a coffee?"

"It's no trouble, Lucy. I could never repay the kindness you've shown my family. But I can't stop for coffee, as the girls are champ-ing at the bit to decorate the tree."

"I understand. Would you ask the girls if they would like to come for tea on Saturday? I thought they could help me decorate mine!"

"They'd love it, Lucy. Thanks."

Jack left by the back door, and Lucy stood looking at the tree. *Now, where did I put the decorations?* She was sure she had put them in the study when she moved in. If not, they would be in the garage. As she expected, the basket was in the study under the desk. Lucy carefully took it downstairs. It was bulky and rather heavy, but she

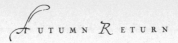

managed without mishap. Once in the sitting room, she set it next to the tree. For many years now she had stored the decorations in one of Tom's old fishing baskets. When she opened the lid, Lucy was dismayed to find she began to feel sad—so she quickly shut it. She decided it would be better to do it with the twins. Their joyful mayhem would take her mind from the past.

Danny called early that evening to check on last-minute arrangements. He said everyone was fine, and they were looking forward to spending Christmas with her. Lucy's spirits lifted after the phone call, and she spent the rest of the evening wrapping up the pictures she'd painted for her neighbors. By ten o'clock, she was very tired and went to bed with a cup of cocoa. It had been a good day.

Carly and Kasey arrived on Saturday promptly at three o'clock. Sue dropped them off and whispered her thanks to Lucy, saying they were grateful for the time to get some last-minute gifts for the girls. As she made her way up the hall, Lucy had no question where she'd find the girls. They were in the sitting room, enraptured by the tree.

"So are we ready for decorating the tree—or would you like a milk shake first?"

"Can we do the tree first?" Carly asked in whispered tones.

"Of course we can." Lucy moved over to the basket and lifted the lid. The girls crowded around her to peep inside at the glittering treasures. Out came the candlelights, which Lucy placed on the tree first. Then there were the baubles—some from Lucy's own childhood. They found red-and-green checked ribbons, which they tied on the ends of some of the branches, and tiny novelty wooden toys, which they hung all over the tree. As they progressed, Lucy realized the tree was looking rather full at the bottom, so she lifted the girls onto a stool to reach the higher branches.

"Doesn't it look lovely, Lucy?" Carly said, standing back to get a better look. Kasey joined her.

"I think it's missing something," Lucy said seriously.

"What is missing?" Kasey asked, staring up at Lucy in surprise, as if she couldn't think what could be missing from the wonderful tree they had created.

"I know," Lucy said at last. "It's sugar mice, lollipops, and chocolate treats!"

"Oh yes," Carly said. "I forgot about sweets!"

"Have you got some, Lucy?" Kasey asked.

"Yes. They are on the dresser in the kitchen. Would you like to fetch them for me? They're on the tin tray." Both girls ran to the dresser and were back in no time to finish off the tree with edible treats.

"Now it looks finished!" Kasey said, hands on hips.

"No—there's still something missing," Lucy teased. "Can't you guess?"

"No! Tell us, Lucy."

"A big star for the top of the tree! We must have a star to remind us of the star over Bethlehem when Jesus was born."

"Oh yes, we forgot. A star is very important, isn't it? Where is it, then?" Kasey was so serious.

"I don't have one, I'm afraid."

"Oh, what a shame," cried Carly.

"We could make one," suggested Lucy. She had got the anticipated reply.

"Yes!" said the girls as they ran to the kitchen, where they usually did crafts with Lucy. All the equipment was ready. "You knew we would make you one, didn't you, Lucy?" They knew Lucy well.

"I knew you would make me the best one ever!"

They all sat together around the table while Lucy cut the star out of cardboard and the girls spread glue all over it. Then they sprinkled on gold and silver glitter with a relief of red on the edges.

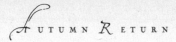

"It's beautiful." Carly's eyes were wide with wonder.

"And we made it!" Kasey said proudly.

"Yes, you did. We need to let it dry for a bit. Let's have our tea now. Then we can put the star on the tree and switch on the lights."

"Okay, what's for tea?"

"Under the tea towel by the sink."

The girls lifted the towel and cheered with delight when they found chicken nuggets, sausage rolls, pizza, crisps, and nibbles. They eagerly helped Lucy clear the table and, after washing their hands, began their feast. For dessert, they had a chocolate and orange trifle.

At last it was time to finish the tree. Lucy suggested Kasey put the star on top of the tree and Carly switch on the lights. The girls ran to the sitting room. Lucy helped Kasey with the star, then went to turn the main lamps off. When Carly switched on the Christmas lights, everyone was speechless—but not for long.

"It's so pretty," Carly said, in her sweet, calm way.

"It's nearly as good as ours!" Kasey added.

"Well, that's praise indeed. Now, choose a sweet from the tree, and I'll take you home. Thank you for all your help, girls. I could never have managed on my own."

"You're very welcome!" Kasey said. Carly just smiled and asked if she could have a white sugar mouse.

Lucy bundled the girls up to take them home. It was a very dark night, so they took a large black torch to illuminate the way as they negotiated the short walk down the lane to the harbor.

Sue invited Lucy in and tried to understand her excited offspring explain their afternoon. They threw their coats on the chair in the hallway and made for the sitting room—chattering all the way—to check out their tree.

"Come see our tree, Lucy," they called to her.

Sue laughed at her girls' enthusiasm. "Go and see the tree. They are so proud of it. Then come and have a cup of tea in the kitchen. I'm making mince pies!"

"I knew you were baking something." Lucy laughed. "You're covered in flour!"

Lucy joined the girls and agreed their tree was very pretty indeed. She then went into the kitchen where the most delicious smells filled the air. Sue handed her a cup of refreshing tea. They chatted about Christmas, and Sue asked Lucy if she had everything she needed for her family's arrival.

"You've seen to everything. I don't have to worry about anything for the little ones. Thanks so much."

"No problem."

Lucy popped her head in the girls' bedroom before leaving. They were tucked up in bed, and Jack was reading them their bedtime story.

"Good night girls. Sleep tight!"

"Good night, Lucy."

Back downstairs in the hallway Lucy said, "Good night, Sue. Thank you for the tea."

"You're very welcome. And thank you for everything you have done for us."

"My pleasure. Your family is a delight."

As Lucy walked home, she thought about returning to her empty cottage. Since Tom's death, spending so much time alone had been hard for her. It had become easier when she moved to Tarran Bay, and her outlook had improved dramatically in recent days. Though she often had visitors for coffee these days, she realized that she quite enjoyed her own company. It was comforting to know God was with her always. She stood at the gate of Dawn Cottage and smiled at the sight of the lighted Christmas tree through the window. It was such a welcoming sight. And the best thing was her cottage would soon be filled with her loving family.

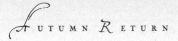

The night before Christmas Eve, Lucy stood at her front door peering out the little window. Luke had said they hoped to leave London by five o'clock—they should have arrived long ago. She was beginning to worry. Lucy was very relieved when a set of headlights pierced the darkness and flooded her front yard as it came to a halt in her drive. She flung open the door to rush out to greet her family. She hugged Karen first and then Luke. She couldn't help the tears of joy.

"Oh, Mum!" Luke's eyes were also filled with tears.

"I know, I know. It's been so long. Come on in. I'm all ready for you."

"It's gorgeous!" Karen exclaimed as she entered the front hall.

"Just wait until you see the views—and the back garden!"

Luke carried his sleeping child into the cottage. Lucy led him to their room, where she and Jack had set up the cot for Rose. Luke laid Rose down and covered her with the little pink duvet. Lucy was pleased by how prepared she was. Jack had brought two of everything, even two potties! As they walked down the hall, she explained how handy it was to have friends who had two of everything because of the twins.

Luke laughed. "Well, I guess we could have packed a little less." He gave Lucy a hug and kissed her cheek. "You look great, Mum."

"I *am* great, Luke. I'll tell you all about it when Danny and Denise arrive."

Downstairs, Karen was studying every nook and cranny.

"Nothing you told us about this place prepared me," she exclaimed as Luke and his mother entered the sitting room.

"Do you like it?"

"Oh, Lucy, it's a wonderful cottage. I never imagined it could be so lovely, and look at the tree!"

"The twins helped me with it on Saturday."

"Rose will have it over tomorrow," Luke said dryly.

"No, she won't. I never had any problems when you were little.

We'll just show her all the things on it and tell her that if she doesn't touch them, she can choose a chocolate from it every day!"

"Still thinking of everything." Luke gave his mother another hug. "I love you, Mum. It is wonderful to see the light back in your eyes."

Lucy made them some Marmite on toast and hot chocolate and showed them the whole cottage.

"I can't wait for you to see the view. Leave your curtains open, and it will be a surprise in the morning."

The following morning certainly brought a surprise even for Lucy, for it had snowed during the night. In fact, it was still snowing gently. Lucy opened her window. Everything was so quiet—just the gentle roll of the waves against the rocks in the distance to be heard. Lucy was sitting on her window seat reveling in God's creation when a timid knock disturbed her thoughts.

She smiled as she saw her gorgeous little grandchild peeping round the doorway. "Come in, Rose." Lucy held her arms open wide so that the little girl could jump on her lap. Lucy could not imagine how she had found her room, but she was glad she had. Rose felt so warm and soft in her lemon cotton jump suit, and her hair smelled of flowers. Lucy buried her nose in her granddaughter's dark curls. They sat cuddling and looking out at the fine, gently falling snow. The garden was enchanting. Suddenly Lucy remembered Dan, Denise, and little Jamey.

"Oh no!"

"What's wrong, Nanna?" Rose asked. She seemed unsettled by Lucy's concern.

"I'm worried about Uncle Dan and the roads, Rose. Let's wake Mummy and Daddy and see what they think."

They knocked on the door and found Luke and Karen peering out the window.

"I didn't think it ever snowed down here," Luke said as he bent his tall frame down to gaze through the low window.

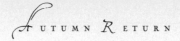

"Nor did I. I guess there's a first time for everything."

"Isn't it beautiful, though," Karen said.

"Yes," Lucy replied, "but what about Dan and Denise!"

"Oh, I never thought of that," Karen said.

"They'll be okay in that new Jeep thing of Dan's. It's got four-wheel drive," Luke said with a laugh. "You'd better ring him, though, tell him what to expect."

Lucy slipped downstairs and picked up the phone, but it was dead. The cottage was cold, too. "Oh no!" The heating hadn't come on. She hadn't noticed with all the excitement.

"What's wrong, Nanna?" Rose stood on the middle stairs and peeped through the rails at Lucy.

Lucy smiled. That's all she'd said so far!

"Nothing, darling. We just don't have any electricity. We'll have to get cracking. I must tell Daddy we need to get some logs from the shed. He'll have to light fires everywhere." At least the kitchen had stayed wonderfully warm thanks to the ever-faithful Aga. So Lucy began to make bacon and eggs while Luke lit fires in the sitting and dining rooms, leaving the doors between rooms open so the warmth could move all over the cottage. Finally, they sat around the table in chunky sweaters and ate a hearty breakfast.

The two women were rabbiting on and on, catching up with news from home, when they were all startled by a knock at the door. Luke took Rose to investigate and returned seconds later with a beaming smile. Behind him came Dan, Denise, and Jamey. It was only ten-thirty. They'd left at five A.M. to miss the traffic, and it had paid off. Excitement was everywhere—chatter, bustle, and laughter filled the cottage.

"It's like something from a chocolate box!" Dan said, on inspection of his mother's beautiful home.

"I don't care!" laughed Lucy. "I love it!"

"I love it too, Mum." Daniel gave his mother a hug with one arm, as Jamey was in the other.

Out came the frying pan. And once more the kitchen filled with the sweet smell of bacon. Karen showed Denise around while the boys brought in the endless luggage and baby gear. Karen and Denise were two of a kind!

"You won't need half of that," Karen said as they passed the men on the stairway. "Lucy's thought of everything." She winked at Denise.

Both families were staying only five days because their commitments at work could not be left any longer, so Lucy wanted to pack in as many activities as possible. She told them she wanted them to meet her new friends. They were eager to do so and had many questions to ask. The boys and their families spent the rest of the morning settling in, then after lunch, with a crisp, thin layer of snow underfoot, they walked to the beach. Though it was cold they trundled across the beach happily. The clouds were high in the sky, looking like flesh goose-bumped with cold. The awesome waves crashed hard against the shore. Daniel and Luke threw stones into the depths of the sea. Rose toddled after them and tossed a few pebbles, attempting to imitate her daddy and uncle. Huddled in their coats, the women stood against the harbor, looking out in wonder towards Gull Island.

When everyone was ready for afternoon tea, Lucy led them home by way of the harbor and pub, showing them where the Trents lived and acquainting the girls with Tarran Bay. The boys, of course, were very familiar with it and enjoyed sentimental memories along the way. They walked up the lane and past the bungalows. As they approached her cottage gates, Lucy was startled to see the back of Gordon's Morris Traveller.

Her heart leapt, then fell. She wasn't ready for an impromptu visit. The children might get the wrong impression. They would think she had a boyfriend, which simply wasn't true. As they neared the car Gordon got out of the driver's door. He turned to smile at Lucy and her family.

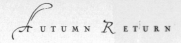
"Hi, Lucy. Your family—how lovely!"

Lucy thought he seemed a bit uncomfortable, too. How was she going to explain this? Well, maybe she could try part of the truth. "This is Gordon Seymour. He's our local doctor." She figured she had no choice but to invite Gordon in for tea, and he eagerly accepted.

Lucy had never entertained such a large number of guests at Dawn Cottage, so she was happy to find the big brown teapot she had always used for such occasions at their home in Gloucester Gardens. She placed it ceremoniously in the center of the table with the nonmatching jug and sugar bowl. She slipped the old knitted cozy with the bobble her mother had made over the teapot. Lucy was certain her sons were experiencing the same sweet nostalgia that had swept over her. It was a friendly melancholy, filled with contentment.

"How did your course go, Gordon?" Lucy asked.

"It went very well. I was scheduled to take it in January, but someone backed out and I was able to go early. I was lucky to find someone to take over the surgery for a couple of weeks."

"I think you were missed," Lucy said matter-of-factly.

"Are you our mother's doctor, Gordon?" Luke suddenly asked.

Gordon looked at Lucy.

Her mind whirled. *He doesn't know what to say. How on earth do I get out of this one?* Lucy turned to Luke and calmly said, "Now, Luke, you know I don't like men doctors. Gordon is Sue's doctor, and that's how we met." Lucy was quite pleased with her answer. She was really learning to think on her feet. She thought Danny and Luke looked at each other rather strangely, but she was certain she had avoided a difficult situation.

Gordon seemed to enjoy Rose and Jamey's chatter. He knelt down with them to play and spoke to them at their level. Lucy smiled. He would have made a good father. Gordon did not stay long, and when Lucy walked him to the door, he handed her a gift from his pocket.

"Open it in the morning, Lucy, and have a merry Christmas. I do hope I haven't caused you any problems with your family."

"Of course not!" she said. What could she say? They were probably whispering now.

Gordon turned to leave, but Lucy knew she needed to say something about their last time together. "Gordon." She kept her voice low to avoid attracting any attention from her family.

Gordon turned and stepped toward her. "Yes?"

"About our last conversation . . ." She hesitated. "I'm afraid I handled it badly. Your words struck a nerve, and I didn't know how to react. Thank you for telling me. Let's talk about it again . . ." Lucy glanced toward the kitchen. ". . . sometime."

Gordon brushed her cheek and smiled. "Thank you, Lucy." He turned to leave once again. "We'll talk soon."

Lucy watched Gordon drive slowly up the hill. She was so glad he was back—and very pleased she had had the courage to apologize to him. She tried not to worry about what the boys might think. After all, she and Gordon weren't really an item.

Suddenly Karen called from the kitchen. "Mum, where's a rag? Rose has spilled her drink!"

Lucy slipped the little parcel into her trouser pocket and headed for the disaster zone.

———

Squeals of delight drifting from the ground floor woke Lucy on Christmas Day. She'd slept like a log, so she roused herself slowly, thanking God for her family and for the special day that lay before her. She glanced at Gordon's little parcel on her bedside table and reached for it. As she undid the red ribbon, peeled off the gold paper, and lifted the lid of the box, she felt her heart begin to beat a little faster. It was a silver brooch in a modern style—just the sort

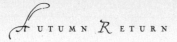

of gift Lucy loved. It was expensive. It said so much, too much. As Lucy took the brooch from the box and held it in her hand, she was shocked by her feelings. He had chosen it especially for her. She wanted to cry. He wasn't looking for romance—he'd told her so. What did Gordon Seymour want?

She didn't dress immediately, as she wanted to join the fun around the tree. So she put on her robe, brushed her hair, and headed downstairs. As she passed the radiator in the hall, Lucy was relieved to discover the electricity was back on.

As she expected, her family was gathered around the tree beside the fireplace. They all looked up as she entered the doorway. Surrounded by wrapping paper and wearing huge smiles, they welcomed her with a *Merry Christmas*. They had decided to let the children open a few of their parcels, saving some until after lunch, when it was the tradition in Lucy's home to open the gifts. She kissed each member of her family, took great interest in the children's new toys, and then went to make a light breakfast of toast, marmalade, and hot tea.

Church was early—nine-thirty—to give everyone plenty of time to prepare lunch. The family followed the sound of a single church bell that called the people of Tarran Bay to worship. They trudged through the melting snow toward the vicar, who stood in welcome in the archway of St. Luke's.

"The snow is quickly melting," Lucy said to the vicar as he kissed her cheek and gave his Christmas greetings.

"It doesn't last long here, I'm afraid. I've only seen it snow a handful of times."

Lucy introduced her entourage to him, and they entered the warmth in silent awe. A line of locals joined them as they walked into the holy place, where a sort of glowing tranquillity filled the stone walls on this Christmas morning. Huge arrangements of spruce, ivy, and holly, with red berries and twisted sticks of hazel branches, sat on the stone window ledges. Hilda and Sue, along with some other church ladies, had been very busy making the sanctuary festive. Cream candles flickered everywhere as the congregation moved slowly up the aisle.

Some of the local children presented a Nativity play that brought tears to Lucy's eyes. She remembered the many Christmas plays she'd been to in the past. She'd helped with so many over the years—encouraging the tiny ones with their lines and moves on stage. It was so rewarding to see their parents almost busting at the seams with pride. Those days were getting easier to remember now.

After the reading, which was given by Jack, Vicar Todd gave a rousing sermon about the light coming into the world at Christmas. "Coming down," he said, with his eyes heavenward and his hands lifted up toward the high wood-beamed roof of the church. "It was the best present our heavenly Father could ever give to the world." Even the children seemed mesmerized by his words.

Lucy smiled. What a wonderful contrast to last Christmas, when she knew she had made everyone so miserable. She had wanted to be alone, so her sadness wouldn't touch them. No, they had insisted that she spend the day with them in Luke's home, where everyone had gathered. She had wanted so badly to be at home, alone with her memory of Tom, alone and heartbroken—at home, where she couldn't hurt anybody. She silently thanked God for the wonderful turnaround. At last she had joy.

At the close of his sermon, Vicar Todd said loudly, "Happy birthday, Jesus!" And everyone spontaneously clapped! What a wonderful end to the service.

Tea was served afterward in the adjoining hall, and Lucy was able to introduce her family to everyone, including, to her delight, Mark Holding.

"What are you doing here?" she asked expectantly.

"I like to be with my friends during the holidays. Merry Christmas, Lucy." He stooped and kissed her cheek.

"Well, I am very glad you are here. There is no better way to

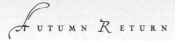

spend Christmas." Although she knew Mark thought she meant with friends, Lucy meant with the body of Christ, in church. And as Mark walked off to greet Sue and Jack, Lucy said a quick prayer and rushed over to greet Gordon.

"Thank you for the brooch. It's beautiful."

Gordon bent down and whispered to her, his breath close to her ear. "I got it in London. I'm glad you like it." He kissed her cheek, which pleased Lucy, though she hoped her children hadn't seen it.

"I have something for you, too," she said gently, "I'll pop it over sometime." Lucy wondered if her painting for Gordon was enough. She had painted pictures for everyone. Should she have given him something more special? No, it was too soon. The picture was fine.

Before leaving the church, Jack and Sue invited everyone for tea on Boxing Day. Only Mark couldn't make it, because he was off to Scotland to stay with relatives through New Year's Day.

Lunch was wonderful, and Lucy was amazed to find how well she had conquered the Aga. It had been a lingering feast in the cozy atmosphere of the holly-clad dining room. The fire as well as the red candles on the table and mantel illuminated the small gathering. The room sparkled, as did the conversation.

At last the family gathered in the sitting room to open gifts. There were Victorian-style nightdresses for Karen and Denise. Lucy had worried they wouldn't arrive on time, but they had come the week before. She also got a Chinese cookbook for Karen and a Delia Smith cookbook for Denise. Lucy suggested they could swap at some time. For Luke, she had chosen the book he had asked for and a sweater. And for Danny, a book and a new leather wallet, for which Denise had told her he was desperate. The children played with their Playmobil sets all afternoon, which blessed Lucy. She received perfume and a professionally framed photograph of their small family from Luke and Karen, and a novel and a sweater from

Dan and Denise. They all thanked and hugged one another and enjoyed the rest of the day playing with the children.

Once the young ones were safely tucked away in bed, the grown-ups ended the day with a rousing video by candlelight. Lucy bid her family good-night at eleven but could hear their muffled talk until after midnight. When the house at last became quiet, she lay back on the pillows and thanked God with all her heart for a wonderful family and a perfect Christmas Day!

After breakfast on Boxing Day, Luke asked Lucy to bring her tea into the sitting room where Dan was lighting a fire. She sat down in the granddad chair, which she'd brought from the kitchen the day before, and anxiously scanned her family's serious faces.

Luke broke the silence. "Mum, Karen and I have something to tell you. We thought it best to wait until after Christmas to bring it up."

Lucy felt a tightening in her stomach. "Go on, dear." She braced herself for his news. He seemed so serious all of a sudden.

"Karen and I are off to Mozambique." He paused briefly. "We are going to take over Ruth's work."

Lucy's throat contorted, and she couldn't hold back the stinging tears. But they weren't tears of sadness—they were tears of immense joy, of pride in her son.

Suddenly everything fell into place. Her mind cleared and the past all made incredible sense. She had felt such a failure when she left Africa. But she had truly believed she needed to come home to England to give birth to Luke and, right or wrong, God used her decision for good. Luke, who had been conceived in that wonderful place, was now returning there to be used of God. AIDS was the killer in Africa now, and Luke and Karen were young enough to take on the challenge.

For my thoughts are not your thoughts, nor are your ways my ways.

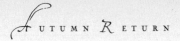

Why hadn't she believed in God's perfect plan and timing sooner? If only she could have grasped it years ago. Life would have been so much easier if she'd abandoned herself into His loving care sooner. All the years of secret regret now paled into insignificance. And the thought of what God was about to achieve through her eldest son finally began to fill the void.

"Oh, Luke, it's perfect. I'm so happy," she managed to say at last.

"Are you really happy?" Luke inquired.

"Yes, Luke. Your dad would have been so proud!" She stood and hugged her son.

Luke's arms went quickly around her shoulders. He held her close and whispered in her ear. "Thanks, Mum. It means so much to know you are happy about it."

"It's the best news I've had since my grandchildren were born."

She then went over to Karen. She had sat taut during the conversation, but she relaxed as Lucy hugged her, too. Dan gave his mother a tissue from the box. They all took tissues!

"God is going to use you to carry on where we left off."

Luke went on to explain that God had placed a burden for Mozambique on his heart from the time he had visited Ruth's orphanage with his father. But about six months ago he began to feel a sense of urgency. When he finally got up the nerve to bring it up to Karen, she was a little taken aback, though not surprised. She knew of his burden and was willing to take it on for herself. As he spoke, Lucy could see the love Luke and Karen had for each other—and for God—and she rejoiced in their future.

Luke said when they heard of Ruth's death, he and Karen knew their time to make a decision had come, and they went to see their pastor, Robert Hemmings. He was enthusiastic when he heard their plans—said it was an answer to many people's prayers. He assured them that the church would support them financially, as well as in prayer.

"We'll be leaving mid-January." He was still apologetic. "I know it's soon, but there is so much to do."

Lucy patted his hand to assure him that everything was all right. "It's fine, dear. I understand. But I will miss you all. Maybe I'll come up to London for a visit so we can spend a little more time together before you leave."

Luke's eyes brightened. "That would be great, Mum." And the whole family joined in with their agreement.

Lucy truly was thrilled for them, but she couldn't help worrying a bit about her sweet granddaughter. "Are you at all concerned about how Rose will settle there?"

"No," Karen answered slowly. "We've thought everything through and believe that she's young enough to easily adapt."

"Yes, you're probably right," Lucy said. She was certain Luke and Karen were making thoughtful decisions, based on God's direction. He would be with them.

At that moment Lucy knew that now was the time for the last parcel of her past to come off the shelf. "I need to tell you all something. You will probably wonder why I haven't told you about this before. I can't answer that. I just know I need to tell you now." Lucy took a deep breath. "When your father and I went to Africa, I became pregnant almost immediately."

Lucy noticed her family looking at each other with varying degrees of confusion on their faces. They were trying to understand what she was saying.

"I was very ill, but I desperately wanted the baby. I had a doctor whose advice I questioned. But there was no one else to go to at the time. He gave me some medicine, and because I felt so terrible, I took it without questioning what it was. I lost my little girl five months into the pregnancy. I never knew if it was the medicine that caused the miscarriage, but I blamed the doctor. I was devastated. We buried her there!"

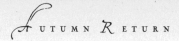

Luke handed her a bunch of tissues. She mopped her eyes. "I'm so sorry."

"Mum, don't." Danny was anxious.

"Is that why you don't like men doctors, Mum?" Denise asked.

"I suppose I associate all male doctors with that experience. He was not a good doctor. That's why I felt I had to leave when I became pregnant again. I couldn't risk losing another baby. The doctors who work with the orphanage are far superior now. Things change.

"I'm sorry I never told you before. I thought the best way to get over the loss of my baby was to never mention her or the miscarriage again. I don't know why God never gave me a little girl to replace Grace. We tried to have another baby after Danny, but it never happened. I was happy with my healthy boys, though. And now I have Rose—and Jamey. I know I'll be with Grace in heaven some day, and Dad is with her now." She made a ball of the damp tissues in her hand and smiled. "Some things we just don't understand here on earth. I am finally learning to leave some things with Jesus."

"That's the best place for the things we question," Dan said.

Dan looked at Denise, who sat next to him.

"Go on," she encouraged him.

"I also have some news. I hope you will be happy about it."

Lucy turned her attention to her second son. All this news. How would she handle it?

Danny took a deep breath. "We're going to have another baby. It's due in August." Lucy could not contain herself. The tears that had so recently ended began again—in full force. Rather than a tissue or two, Luke gave Lucy the whole box.

"I'm so happy," was all she could muster at first. Then the family spent the next minutes rejoicing in the new life that would soon be joining their family.

After a while, Lucy changed the subject. "I have something good to share with you, too. I've started to sell my paintings in a gallery in St. Ives. It belongs to Mark—you met him at church. He put incredible price tags on them, and they are selling. It's amazing! Anyway, he says I'll need an accountant." She looked over at Danny, who beamed a reassuring smile back at his mother.

"I'm not surprised, Mum. Dad always said you should put them in the art shop."

"I know. I just never thought they were good enough. But Mark thinks they're good, and I guess he should know."

———

Tea at the Trents' was marvelous, a spread typical of dear Sue. Hilda, Vicar Todd, and Gordon were all there, and the children enjoyed showing off their new games and toys. The twins were absolutely marvelous. They took care of the younger ones, giving Karen and Denise a chance to visit with the adults. After tea Lucy gave her presents to her friends. She had painted them all pictures of different views of Tarran Bay. They were delighted and wondered where on earth she had found the time to do them. Lastly, she gave Gordon an African scene, since she knew he liked bright colors. He was very moved as he unwrapped his gift, holding it up for everyone to see. As he smiled and gave her the little wink she was becoming accustomed to, Lucy realized she was blushing.

"Thank you so much, Lucy. It's perfect."

"My pleasure, Gordon. I'm glad you like it." Lucy felt very awkward. It seemed everyone in the room was certain she and Gordon were an item. So she was thankful when Sue announced it was time for Lucy to receive her presents.

Jack and Sue gave her some silver earrings. Vicar Todd gave her a new Bible with a verse in the front—*Come unto me, all you who are weary, and I will give you rest.*

"I'll treasure it," she said.

Hilda gave her a pretty blue-and-lemon-patterned chiffon scarf. Lastly, Lucy called Carly and Kasey into the room and gave

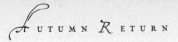

them each a Playmobil set and her completed storybook. Mark had made a wonderful job of it on his new computer. It had a glossy front cover and inside the script flowed around the illustrations. The book was very professionally done. The twins seemed delighted with it.

"*The Naughty Boys*," they read slowly. They kissed and thanked her so very politely.

Lucy asked Luke and Dan to tell her friends all their exciting news. As they spoke, Gordon nodded knowingly at Lucy and once again smiled his secret smile from the other side of the room. Because Sue and Jack had never heard the details of Lucy's time in Africa, they asked her to unfold it now. She eagerly told her story and though it was difficult, she included the story of her first pregnancy and miscarriage. Everyone was kind and encouraging. But when she looked to Gordon, she was surprised to see his face was white and drawn. *He understands my struggle and blames himself. I should have told him about it when we were alone.* Lucy knew she couldn't find the time until after her family left, but soon after it had to be done.

"We have a present for you, Lucy," the twins said, rushing toward her with excitement. Lucy opened the little parcel. It was one of their butterfly pictures in a wooden frame, its pink and gold wings edged with multicolored glitter.

"It's beautiful," Lucy exclaimed, delighted with the homemade gift.

"It reminded us of you," Sue said. "You're out of your chrysalis at last."

Lucy knew it was true. At last she was completely free, and this lovely painting would have a place of pride on her mantelpiece. She gave the girls a huge hug.

CHAPTER 19

New Year

Before her family left, Lucy took them to the beach for one last stroll. It was too cold to do much, but Lucy made one of her famous sand castles for the children and the twins. She started by constructing a tall column of sand. And then, with the aid of a bucket of water, she dripped wet sand down and around it, making what she called a fairy castle. It was finished off with patterns of pretty shells and looked like something from a children's storybook. Dan and Denise said they would certainly be back in the summer so Jamey could toddle around in a swimsuit instead of a snowsuit.

On the last evening of her family's visit, Lucy treated everyone to dinner at the Italian Café in St. Ives. Luke and Danny were intrigued by how different the resort town looked in winter. They spent several hours reliving years of summer memories.

Too soon a tearful Lucy, surrounded by all her new friends, waved a sad farewell to her family. As lonely as she felt, Lucy was encouraged to know she had such good friends to lessen the sting of separation and was touched that they all came out to say good-bye with her.

Within minutes of her family's departure, Lucy immediately began a campaign to get her cottage back to normal. As wonderful as her family was, and as careful and courteous as they had tried to be, she felt her house looked like a disaster area when they left.

Lucy had just put the kettle on the Aga to make a cup of tea when she saw Gordon coming down the path. When she opened the door, Lucy could tell Gordon was as eager to see her as she was to see him, but neither said a word. He followed her into the kitchen and sat at the table while Lucy finished preparing the tea.

As she handed him a cup of hot tea, he looked into her eyes. "Tired?"

"A bit. It was so good to have them here, though. I think they understand me at last."

"I think they were thrilled with your change. I got some time with Danny at Jack and Sue's. He said he'd never seen you so happy. Lovely boys, lovely family!"

"I know it was difficult for them before to understand how I felt. But sadly, everything I shared with them was true. Perhaps at last they can piece the puzzle together, just as I've been able to do."

"Now they realize it was the right time for you to make a new beginning and that it was God's leading."

"Yes, that's it all right—a new beginning. Everything's changed now."

He thanked her for the Christmas present once more. "It's hanging on the wall above the fireplace. It fits in perfectly."

"I think my painting is improving. I'm more confident perhaps."

"Good, it shows. Lucy, I need to talk. Do you have the time?"

She looked at his anxious face, his forehead pulled into creases above his eyes. Yes, it was time to talk. "I will always have time for you, Gordon."

He touched her hand gently across the table, patted, and then

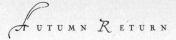

released it. "I hurt you very badly, didn't I—when I shared my past with you?"

"Well, to be honest, yes. But you didn't know about my miscarriage. Tom and Ruth—and God—were the only ones who shared my secret. I always react strongly when I hear of women who have felt pressured into having an abortion. I would have done anything to save my little daughter." Lucy dabbed her eyes to keep the tears from spilling onto her cheeks.

"Can you forgive me, Lucy? I need your friendship."

Lucy was touched by his plea. It was time for the final healing. She took his hand "Yes, Gordon, I do. We all make mistakes. I think it was a mistake for me to hold my sorrow and guilt inside. I should have told the boys about Grace sooner. I had my reasons, but they seem selfish now."

"I think they understand."

"I hope so."

"Are you really pleased that Luke and Karen are going to Mozambique?"

"Yes, I am thrilled. It gives new meaning and purpose to the choices Tom and I made all those years ago. I feel we've come full circle."

"That's good, then." Gordon stood to leave, and Lucy rose to take the cups from the table. He took her hand and gently kissed it. "Thank you."

"For what?"

"Your kindness."

Lucy was overwhelmed by his gesture. She didn't know what to say. She knew her feelings for him were growing, but she wasn't certain how she wanted their relationship to progress, and she absolutely did not want to play games. So she said nothing but squeezed his hand as she released it.

"Lucy, would you like to go to the pub for New Year's Eve?

Jack and Sue will be there, and I thought I'd try to persuade Vicar Todd and Hilda to join us.''

"I'd love to go. But I don't think you'll get Vicar Todd and Hilda to stay up until midnight!''

"Oh, there's a first time for everything!''

Gordon kissed her cheek as he bade her farewell. She watched him leave the gate and went back to work.

It was a windy day, good for drying the washing. Karen and Denise had taken all the linen off and piled it on the beds, as she'd asked. So she took it downstairs and put it into the washing machine. She took the Hoover upstairs and started on the bedrooms. Lucy enjoyed vacuuming. It was the most satisfying of household chores. Soon she was done with the bedrooms and went to the stairway. She stopped at the window on the landing and looked out toward the cliffs. The sea was out—her favorite time at the beach. So, as she put the Hoover away, she decided she would go for a walk after lunch. Soon Lucy had a clean house and three loads of wash flapping in the breeze on the clothesline. She grabbed a quick lunch and headed outdoors.

No one was on the beach, which pleased Lucy. Before moving to Tarran Bay, she had hardly ever had a whole beach to herself. There were always too many holidaymakers around. She made her way to the left side of the beach and went through the tunnel. Halfway through she stopped and looked at the scene through the rugged arched hole at the end. The pencil-thin line of deep sapphire blue rimmed the horizon. As white clouds drew in from the west—occasionally hiding the sun from view—the middle area turned a soft dove gray. Close to her, the soft, white, foamy waves rolled gently over the low smoothed-granite rocks. The view was breathtaking. And it never ceased to draw her, always holding some new magic with the flaming sunrises and sunsets and unpredictable weather. She thought this place the most wonderful spot in the world.

The first time they discovered Tarran Bay was an unexpected

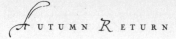

event. It was a miserable drizzly day. The boys were bored and boisterous. Out of desperation, Tom had decided on a touring day. Lucy knew the boys would hate being locked in the car all morning, but she was at her wits' end and needed a break, so she finally gave in. After taking the coast road from Tintagel, they had driven for three-quarters of an hour when they happened on the Tarran Bay road. The boys were fed up and fighting, so Tom said they would stop to find a café and have some lunch. When they finally found a parking spot, Tom saw a surf shop he wanted to check out, so Lucy took the boys to the beach to run off a little energy. The rain had ended, and what had started out as a rather miserable day suddenly swung around and turned into bright sunshine.

They walked down onto the beach beside the harbor wall and around the little bay. Lucy relished the boys' cries of delight as they explored a bit ahead of her. What a change from only moments before. Lucy marveled at the transformation. She felt such peace.

"Look here, Mummy—quickly. We've found a hidden tunnel!" the boys shouted together, waiting impatiently for their dawdling mother to join them. She was taking in the sights and looking for interesting pebbles to take back home with her and didn't want to be rushed. Her artistic heart was noting all the incredible colors of her surroundings.

"Hurry! There's a secret beach on the other side!"

As they entered the tunnel, the boys shouted out their names, and their voices echoed off the high dark walls of the rock face. Through the tunnel, they pursued their adventure, on and around the new stretch of sand, littered with lovely rocks and hidden rock pools and treasures.

Then they found the baths in the rocks. The boys begged Lucy to let them take off their jeans and sweatshirts and jump into the baths with just their underwear on. Lucy thought they were mad and told them so. "You will freeze." But she said they could have five minutes if their dad said they could return to the beach after lunch.

After they ate, Lucy stopped in a shop to purchase swimming trunks for the boys. She sat on the beach while the boys ran off with Tom to show him their delightful discoveries, and of course the adventure included a five-minute dip in the secret baths. When they returned, they all walked into the village for some ice cream and then returned to the beach. By then it was warm enough to swim, so Lucy and Tom sat on a blanket on the beach and watched their two sons splash and jump in the waves.

"It's fabulous, isn't it, Tom? I mean—you think you have found the perfect place, and then you go and find another even more fantastic beach."

"Yes, I have to say it would take a lot to pip this one at the post! You know, I could settle here, Lucy."

Those times—when her family had all been together—seemed so long ago as Lucy now went on through the tunnel, snuggling her coat about her. She went out onto the white sand to climb the rocks and look in all the pools. She was thrilled to find herself able to relive those pleasant times without pain. In fact, she found the memories heartwarming.

Through the sparkling water in one of the pools she spotted a pure-white stone, the size of a tenpence coin and in the shape of a heart. She reached down and pulled it free from the other pebbles. It was a beautiful memento—a reminder of God's blessings in the past and His promises for the future. A part of her almost believed it had been placed there just for her. She carefully placed the smooth stone in her coat pocket. She felt like a bird, completely free. Never would a cage hold her again. Her shelf was finally empty of sorrows and regrets. She made her way back through the tunnel to her home feeling completely refreshed.

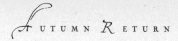

On New Year's Eve, Gordon picked Lucy up at eight. They walked down the lane arm in arm, so at peace with each other.

"Love the dress, Lucy!" Gordon said. "You look stunning!"

Lucy bent her head in embarrassment. She had searched high and low for the perfect dress, and she was pleased he had noticed. It was a long flowing gown of moss-green velvet, and it made her feel very elegant. It had been a long time since a man had commented on her looks.

The pub was packed this cold last night of December. An Irish folk band played at the far end of the large room, and heaping seafood platters, steaming soup tureens, and a variety of other dishes covered the long tables under the windows.

Sue and Lucy sat together and chatted while the men ordered beverages for them at the bar.

"Did you have a nice time with your family, Lucy?"

"Wonderful! We've never stayed together like that as a family since they married, because they all lived within walking distance of my home in London. It was lovely getting up with the children on Christmas morning. It took me back to all the Christmases when the boys were young." Lucy smiled at the memory. "I love Christmas."

"Me too. The girls had a ball!"

"Thank you for inviting my family on Boxing Day, Sue. It was so kind when you already had a full house."

"You know me, Lucy—I love to entertain." She leaned forward to speak over the band. "I have some wonderful news to share with you, Lucy. Gail came around for coffee on Friday, and though I knew she was close to giving her heart to the Lord, I didn't expect it so soon. She sat at the kitchen table and asked endless questions. I answered truthfully and as well as I could. I find it hard when I haven't got all the answers. Do you know what I mean?"

Lucy smiled and nodded knowingly.

"Well, suddenly she said, 'I'm ready now. I want to give my heart to Jesus!' It was so wonderful, Lucy. When she left the cottage, she looked absolutely radiant. The transformation in her in just a couple of months has been amazing."

"Lots of prayer went up, though. We shouldn't be surprised, should we?"

"No. But I was . . . very *pleasantly* surprised."

Sue twisted in her seat. "I'm thirsty. What has happened to those men?"

Since Lucy had a better view, she craned her neck and said, "It looks like there is a long line. We might still be sitting here by ourselves when the new year arrives."

They laughed for a moment, and then Sue returned to the subject of Gail. "I also found out Gail is very good with figures. I couldn't believe how quickly she was able to add everything up when we went Christmas shopping together. She said she had always enjoyed mathematics in school. I mentioned it to Jack, and we decided to suggest she enroll in a Woman Returner Course. She is so excited about making some positive changes. I think she can finally see a light at the end of her tunnel."

"That's absolutely wonderful, Sue. What is a Woman Returner Course? I've never heard of it!"

"It's a course run by the government for women who want to return to work after having stayed at home to raise their children. It trains them in computers and other skills, preparing them for a variety of jobs."

"Oh, I see. Everything changes so fast these days. Has she any ideas of what she would like to do?"

"Well, I suggested going for a bank clerk job once she's finished the course. She doesn't think she can do it, but I told her that with God's help, anything can happen!"

Lucy tilted her head to one side and smiled at Sue. *Isn't that the truth!* she thought. The men finally returned with the drinks and joined in the conversation. As the evening wore on, everyone joined the band in singing a number of old-time favorites. At half past

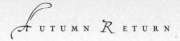

eleven, the pub door opened and, to everyone's surprise and delight, in walked Vicar Todd and Hilda!

"Over here, Vicar!" Gordon called. He went to find a couple of chairs, and as he placed them next to Lucy, he whispered in her ear, "Told you so!"

Lucy turned and looked up into his smiling face. She knew first-hand how good he was at getting people to do things. She liked his tenacity. With a little encouragement—sometimes, even a push— new experiences could be won.

"Hilda, what a lovely surprise." Lucy gave her friend a hug and a kiss as the elderly lady settled into the chair.

"To be honest, Lucy, I haven't done this for years. But David insisted we come. He said he didn't want our friends to think we are old fuddy-duddies."

"I think it's great!" Sue said from across the table.

At midnight they hugged and kissed one another, entering the new year on a joyful note. *This year*, thought Lucy, *is full of new hope!*

Todd and Hilda left the party immediately after midnight, proud of their accomplishment but tired. Jack and Sue left soon after so the baby-sitter could get home at a decent hour. But because neither was too eager for the evening to end, Lucy and Gordon stayed until one o'clock. As Gordon walked her home in the crisp, cold moonlight, Lucy was filled with a sense of well-being, a sense that all was right with the world. Though she knew she would be weary the next day, she invited Gordon in for coffee.

After a time of peaceful silence, with just the ticking of the clock from the kitchen and the cracking and resettling of the glowing logs in the grate, Gordon asked, "It's more than friendship now, isn't it, Lucy?"

Lucy looked into her cup. "I'm nervous, but yes, something is happening."

"Let's not rush," he said calmly, taking her free hand in his and squeezing it gently.

"I thought romance was out of the question for you, Gordon."

"I'm beginning to understand there are no strings to God's forgiveness. I think I made an impulsive decision that wasn't in my best interest, and it certainly wasn't God's choice for me. But that decision has brought me to where I am today. God has forgiven me, and I just need to start making right decisions from here on out—with His help."

"That sounds like a good idea. We can both work on that." It was early in their relationship, and Lucy didn't want to get serious too soon. Memories of Tom still filled her heart, so she wasn't ready to take a big step yet. But she *was* comfortable with letting things run their natural course.

"Did you enjoy the evening, Lucy?"

"It was wonderful. I must say, I haven't felt this good for a long time. I didn't think I would ever enjoy life again. God has been so patient with me."

"God is very patient with all His children, Lucy."

"I realize that now."

"So, Lucy, where do we go from here?"

"I guess we just take it a day at a time and see what happens." Lucy hesitated. She didn't want to sound silly, but she wanted everything out in the open. "I keep wondering what Tom would think."

"Do you mean of our relationship?"

"Well . . . yes—everything. I know he's gone, but I find myself worrying that he would be hurt."

Gordon turned to face her, not taking his hand from hers. "I understand, Lucy. I know you can't erase that part of your life—I wouldn't want you to. But enjoy this new life. I believe God has brought us together. We don't know what the end result will be, but let's trust God to guide us. And by the way, I think Tom would be

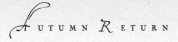

proud to see how you've grown and that you are getting on with your life."

"I hope so. He was a wonderful man. He was quieter than you, though his sense of humor was as good as yours!"

"Well, there you are then!"

After they finished their coffee, Gordon placed his arm around Lucy's shoulders, and they sat quietly for a while. Gordon broke the silence. "Lucy, I understand your connection to the past. You will have those memories forever. But it is also important to look forward. No use looking back. Live in the present. Live in what God is doing in your life now."

"I'm learning—bit by bit."

"So am I."

Lucy stood up to place a few more logs on the fire. "I have to go to London soon. Luke and Karen leave for Africa on the sixteenth. I need to spend some time with them, and I want to be there for their leaving service and party."

"I know. I'll miss you."

Lucy smiled. His attention for her was all so unexpected. It felt wonderful to have another person interested in her plans—and missing her!

She carried on. "I am nervous for them. I don't think they understand the hardships they will face. But I know God is in control. Unfortunately, it is hard for me to keep my hands off the situation. I keep thinking I need to fix the problems, to soften the blows."

"I understand. But they'll cope. It will make them strong, as it did you and Tom."

"I know it made Tom stronger, but I can't say the same for me. It's funny. I envy them a little. In a way I wish I were going with them."

"I know what you mean. You said it yourself—Africa gets in your blood!"

They parted with a gentle first kiss. Gordon was going to be very busy the next few days, so they didn't make plans to see each other before Lucy left, but she promised to phone him as soon as she was safely in London. It felt comforting to know he cared.

———————

A few days later, Lucy was on her way to London. She was to stay with Danny and Denise, since Luke's home was being made ready for renting out while they were away. Though she was looking forward to visiting her family, she found it difficult to leave Tarran Bay. It had become her home. Her thoughts seemed to stay more in the present these days, and she was happy about it. Sadness had receded at last.

As she drove into London, she decided to stop by her old home. She parked outside for a moment and thought about all that had happened in just a few months. Her life had completely changed. As she looked at the front garden, all bare and bland and cloaked in winter, she saw it as a symbol of what she had become before her move to Tarran Bay. If she hadn't gone with her idea to move to Cornwall, she might still be in wintertime! *Thank you, Lord*, she whispered and continued on, at peace with her past and full of confidence in her future.

When she reached Danny's house, he was at the door ready to take her travel bags. "Mum, lovely to see you! Was the journey okay?"

"Fine, it was good to travel on a Wednesday—not so much traffic on the roads."

Denise was there now, with Jamey toddling up behind her and calling, "Nanna, my Nanna!"

Lucy felt as though her heart would burst. She picked him up and kissed his cheek. "I have something for you in my bag, Jamey." She looked at Denise. "May he have a few jelly babies?"

"Just this once." Denise was strict about the kind of food Jamey ate, and Lucy respected her wishes.

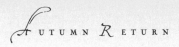
While Danny put Lucy's bags in the spare room, Denise made her a cup of refreshing tea, and they sat in the sitting room together. Lucy's heart swelled with joy at seeing her children in their own home. Denise had an artistic flair, which was reflected in her home. She could make wonderful treasures from very ordinary things, and often frequented the junk shops, coming home with some new find or another. Danny loved it, saying that he never knew what he would come home to next!

"So how is everyone?" Lucy asked.

"Very well. I was with Karen all week, helping with boxing up and packing. It's quite hard for her, because the agent who is renting the property for them said all their personal items had to go into the loft. She's nearly there. Luke is off tomorrow, so he'll be able to put all the boxes up for her. Danny will help after work. I asked my mum if she'd take Jamey and Rose tomorrow at lunchtime so we can go out for a girly lunch!"

"Wonderful, I'll pay!" Lucy said.

"No, Mum—I'm paying! It's my gift to you and Karen. Now, are you tired?" Denise asked.

Lucy confessed she was and went for a lie-down before dinner.

———

The following day, the girls went to lunch and chatted mostly about Africa. Karen wanted to know everything Lucy could remember about the people, the customs, and the culture of Mozambique. Lucy was careful to make sure any negative thoughts she might still harbor didn't come through. She tried to remember the good times, yet had to be honest and share some of the difficulties that Karen and Luke were sure to face. It was a precious time with her daughters-in-law that Lucy would treasure for a long while.

The next day the whole family went to the leaving party at the church hall. Lucy felt a slight trepidation at having to see old friends—some she had probably hurt. She was afraid they might have taken her leaving as a running away from them. She needn't have worried. Everyone welcomed her with open arms. As she reveled in their kindness, she decided it was likely that a lot of her struggles with people were self-inflicted. It saddened her to think of how different life might have been had she been different. But she had learned too much in the last months to linger in past regrets, so Lucy joined the party with gusto.

Everyone wanted to know all about her new home in Tarran Bay. Lucy even went so far as to extend a few invitations for visits to her cottage. They asked lot of questions about her new friends, but she didn't let on about Gordon. Their relationship was too new, too personal to discuss with anyone. She wasn't quite certain what she *thought* about it, let alone what she would *say* about it.

After everyone finished eating, Robert Hemmings tapped his glass and asked for quiet.

"I thought it would be helpful if Luke told us a little about the plans he and Karen have for their time in Africa." He looked over at Luke, who seemed eager to speak.

"Thanks, everyone—for everything. You have all been so very kind. Your generosity has overwhelmed Karen and me. We wouldn't be going to Africa without your support. Last Sunday I explained about the orphanage work, so I won't go over that again. What I will say is that we don't know *what* to expect.

"I felt God's calling to Africa after I went there with my dad nearly twelve years ago. I think that my work with children here will help Karen and me carry on where Ruth Lange left off. I don't plan to go in and change everything. I want to take time to understand the running of the place and the staff and the children. Karen, Rose, and I will need time to adapt to the climate and culture of Mozambique.

"But please don't think of us as anything special. We are *all* called to go out and preach the gospel. We can do that in many different ways. Just sharing our lives with others in the way God

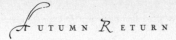

desires is sometimes as effective or even more effective than preaching to them. We have to put our faith into action. The fruit is ripe for the harvest, and we are ready. Please continue to pray for us. Once again, thank you all and God bless you."

As Luke sat down, a thunderous applause went up. Lucy was very proud and once again wished Tom could have been sitting beside her to share the joy of this moment. However, if Tom had been there, perhaps Luke would not be going to Africa. God's timing was perfect.

It was a fun, full day, and when Lucy finally collapsed into bed late that night, she felt more content than she remembered feeling in London for many years. One thing worried her though—she had invited so many people to visit her in Cornwall that if they all took her up on it, she would never have a minute to spare!

Finally, the day came for Luke, Karen, and Rose to leave. Lucy waved them off at Heathrow Airport, along with Robert Hemmings, Danny, Denise, and Jamey. The parting was tearful, the future unknown. Difficulties lay ahead of them, but they had God on their side. Lucy rested in that. She had finally put her life and the lives of her loved ones completely in His competent hands.

The next day Lucy went to visit Robert Hemmings at the vicarage.

"Lucy, my dear, welcome." Robert led the way to the sitting room, and they both sat down.

His wife, Mary, brought in some tea and cakes and joined them. "It's so good to see you looking so well, Lucy. It appears that Cornwall is doing you a world of good."

"Yes, it has been absolutely wonderful. I've made new friends, and I do love to be near the sea."

"Are you close enough to see it from your cottage?" Mary asked as she poured the tea.

"Yes, from most of the rooms. It is wonderful waking up to the sound of the seagulls. I look out the bedroom window every day and still can't get over the joy of being there. I needed a change after Tom died, but I was in such a muddle, I didn't know what to do. Fortunately, God knew what I needed, and I truly believe He directed me there."

"I understand, dear. It was incredibly difficult for you without Tom. I can't imagine how hard it would be to lose Robert. In addition, you had to cope with the horrible way in which he died. I'm glad you've found another part of the church to join, one where you feel at home."

What a gracious lady Mary was. Lucy felt so relaxed with her old friends.

"Oh, I *do* feel at home at St. Luke's. I don't understand why everything happened the way it did, but I am closer to God now than I've ever been."

Robert chuckled. "Sometimes the road is hard, but that's why God takes us on journeys, Lucy—to help us to see Him in everything. Even when the skies are gray, the sunshine is always just around the corner. We're happy for you, Lucy."

"You must come down to stay with me. You will love Tarran Bay." Here she went again! Her house was going to become a bed-and-breakfast. But the thought did not frighten her. Instead, it invigorated her. She was offering hospitality in God's power.

Mary looked over at Robert. "That would be wonderful, Lucy. We could use some time away."

"Just let me know. You will always be more than welcome!"

Lucy paused. She knew she needed to broach a difficult subject, so she quickly breathed a prayer for God's help to say the right words. "I'm sorry I was so negative before I left here. You must have despaired of me."

"I did feel a bit of a failure, Lucy," Robert said. "After all, I had known you for over thirty years, but I couldn't help you, and that

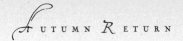

saddened me. But I'm glad your new vicar is kind and wise. Luke told me about him."

"It wasn't your fault at all, Robert. It was me."

Robert and Mary said they understood. They assured her there were no hard feelings on their part. She was grateful to them and thanked them for their support of Luke, Karen, and Rose.

———

A few days later, as Lucy sailed toward home, she was glad that London was a thing of the past. It had been a happy time—a putting-things-right time. Lucy was so pleased to have had the opportunity to restore old friendships, but now Tarran Bay was calling her home.

251

CHAPTER 20

The 30th Birthday

When Lucy opened her front door, she found an envelope sticking out from underneath the mat. The cottage was very cold, but she was eager to read the message, so without even shedding her coat she opened the note. She was invited to Mark's gallery for his thirtieth birthday—Friday at eight o'clock! *Tonight!* It would be good to see all her friends, but she would have to hurry to get ready. Lucy was glad she had purchased some clothes in London. At least she had something new to wear. She went through the clothes and chose a long donkey-brown linen skirt and a wine-colored chenille sweater.

Before dressing, Lucy quickly painted a small picture for Mark. It was the view of the sea in front of his gallery. She couldn't remember every detail but thought she had captured it fairly well. After placing it in a thick wooden frame, she wrapped the gift in gold paper left over from Christmas.

While she was dressing, the phone rang. It was Gordon calling to welcome her home. He asked if she wanted a lift to the party, and she gladly accepted. They didn't talk long, as Lucy felt she was a little behind in her preparations, but she was waiting at the door when Gordon arrived. The drive to St. Ives was pleasant, but she and Gordon did not talk of anything serious. It seemed to Lucy that Gordon was as uncertain as she was about how to go about picking up their relationship again. She was relieved when they reached Mark's gallery.

The party was a small gathering of Mark's friends, not more than twenty. Two of his relatives from Scotland were there—a cousin, Pete, and his wife, Jane. They were charming and Christians.

When Mark opened his gift, Lucy told him he could not sell it. "It's for you!" she laughed. She knew his mind! He gave her a big grin and promised he would put it in a place of pride in his flat.

As the evening progressed, Lucy got chatting with Pete and Jane.

"How long have you lived here, Lucy?" Jane asked.

"Less than five months. It seems longer because so much has happened to me since I arrived."

"Mark told me all about you and your paintings. I haven't seen any, but I know he likes your style. He is a good judge of art. I don't know anything about it, but I can tell he knows his stuff because the gallery is doing so well. He also said you shared your testimony with him, and it made him think."

"I'm pleased about that."

"Yes, Mark needs the Lord. I'm afraid he's a bit of a closed book."

"I think he's very kind," Lucy said softly.

Jane smiled. "So do we! And I think he's closer to wanting a relationship with God than he's ever been!"

"Oh, I do hope so. I'll step up the prayers!"

At nine o'clock, Mark announced that the food was ready, and everyone began to eat. The food was spread on a table in the corner and looked delicious. There was caviar and little water biscuits, fresh

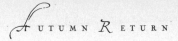

salmon, pâté, winter salads, beautiful cakes with fresh cream, and mousses whipped to perfection—a feast indeed. It was so typical of Mark to go all out!

Lucy thought it strange that none of her paintings hung on the wall. When she asked Mark about it, she was shocked to find that Mark had sold the lot. Amazingly, one man had bought all the African scenes in one fell swoop! He said he wanted them for his office in Johannesburg. Mark asked for more, and Lucy knew she would be busy for the rest of the winter. Once she selected her food, Lucy went and sat with Gordon. Jack and Sue came to join them, and they spent a few minutes updating each other on their lives. A little later Jack waved Mark over to their group, and he sat down beside Lucy.

With a gleam in his eye, Jack said, "I have some news."

His manner told her the news was not bad, and Lucy got the feeling the others knew his secret. She waited expectantly.

"I've found a publisher who's interested in your children's stories!"

Lucy's mouth fell open. At first she didn't understand what he was saying. "How . . . When?"

"I know a chap"—he swallowed the last of the pie—"through my work. I sent him the book you made for the twins, and he loved it. When I said there were more, he asked to see them all. He wants to talk to you about publishing them."

"Mark made up the book," she said.

Mark grinned. "But you wrote them, Lucy, and *you* painted the pictures!"

Lucy's hand moved to her throat. First the paintings, now the stories. *God, why? What for? Why now?* She couldn't believe it. She wanted to run out, stand on the harbor wall, lift her hands to heaven, and shout her thank-you to God. But she didn't. She just sat completely still, and not a soul would have guessed at the excitement inside her—except perhaps Gordon, who was watching her reaction from the corner of his eye!

Mark held his glass to Lucy. "Congratulations, Lucy."

She blushed!

Everyone then lifted their glasses to the host. "To Mark—happy birthday!"

Lucy was very quiet on the way home. Gordon also said little. Finally, though her thoughts were still reeling from the news about her book, Lucy knew she needed to break the silence and bring up the issue of their relationship. But she didn't know exactly how to start.

"I'm older than you!" she said at last, completely out of the blue.

Gordon didn't seem a bit phased by her strange statement.

"How old are you?"

"Fifty-five."

"Only three years! That's not a problem, is it? You look years younger than me, anyway."

She smiled and leaned back against the red leather seat. Surprisingly, that brief exchange made her feel comfortable and contented. Gordon stroked her hair, winked, and turned his attention back to the road. Lucy decided they had said enough for now. The rest would be said in its time.

Later that night, as she lay in her bed with the mustard-colored glass lamp illuminating the room, Lucy looked toward the window. The stenciled muslin curtains looked translucent in the bright light from the moon. It cast the shadow of the small paned window onto her bed. Her mind was too busy for sleep, and she began to weave a wonderful plan.

With the money from her paintings, and now from her stories, she could give more support to Luke and Karen for their work. Maybe she could even go to Mozambique to visit them! It would be

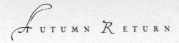

difficult for her to return there. The flight alone would be a fear to overcome, but going back after so long . . . without Tom—and no Ruth! How could she possibly do it? But it would be the perfect finale for her healing. And God was giving her the means. If He wanted her to do it, He would give her the strength. Soon she was making plans, and eventually she slept a truly peaceful sleep—the sounds and sights of the Africa she loved filling her dreams.

After church on Sunday, Hilda and Vicar Todd invited Lucy for dinner at the vicarage. During the meal, she began to unfold her plan to her wise friends, knowing they would counsel her well and tell her the truth.

"I think it's a wonderful plan," Vicar Todd said excitedly. "When will you go?"

"To be honest, I'm not sure. Denise and Danny's baby is due in August, and I'll want to be there to help them when it arrives. I think I should go this spring."

"That sounds perfect," Hilda said. "But it's not far off." She piled Lucy's plate with perfectly roasted potatoes and beef. The Yorkshire puddings were enormous.

"Do you think it's too soon for me to go? They've only been there a short time. They might not be properly adjusted yet."

"I think they'll be delighted to see you whenever you decide to go. We'll pray about it after dinner and ask God to reveal His perfect timing for you."

Hilda continued to dish food onto Lucy's plate as she spoke. Lucy thought she'd never get through it all—but she would try!

"Lucy, I know it is sometimes difficult to discern God's timing and plans for us, but I want to remind you of a verse with which I'm sure you're very familiar." The vicar closed his eyes as he spoke the Word of God. " 'Trust in the Lord with all your heart. And do not lean on your own understanding. In all your ways acknowledge

Him! And He will make your paths straight.' " He opened his eyes and looked intently at Lucy. "That's God's promise to you, Lucy. Never forget it!"

"I won't, Vicar. I don't want to do anything outside His will. I know it'll come to nothing if I do." Lucy leaned forward in her chair. "Do you think I am rushing in too soon with Gordon?" she asked quietly.

The vicar seemed pleased she had finally mentioned her relationship with Gordon. "No, dear, just let things happen. Gordon is a good man—a kind and caring man. He would be good for you, Lucy."

"And you will be good for him!" Hilda interjected.

"Will you pray for me? I can't afford to make a mistake at this point in my life."

The vicar smiled at Lucy and then turned a slightly sadder smile to Hilda. "Don't be too cautious, Lucy. Sometimes hesitations keep you from experiencing *all* of the blessings God intends for us."

After the washing up had been done and the dishes were placed back in the cupboards, Vicar Todd and Hilda prayed that God would give Lucy wisdom in the days ahead. She was so grateful to them, and as they prayed, she felt increasingly confident that everything would work out. At last she bade them good-night and made for her cottage.

CHAPTER 21

Decisions

On Friday evening, Lucy was flying about her kitchen, banging pans and slamming doors. She had invited Gordon over for dinner at eight o'clock, and nothing was going right. The Aga was acting up, and she was getting rather cross and flustered. It would be their first chance to spend an evening together since her return from London, and Lucy wanted everything to be just right. Things had changed between them, and she wanted to talk about what she was feeling—and then there was Africa. *Help me, Lord. I want this night to be perfect. I need you to get me through it.* Lucy was relieved when everything was finished with five minutes to spare. She even had a chance to sit down and put up her feet before Gordon arrived promptly at eight.

"It smells wonderful, Lucy." He kissed her on the forehead. "I have been waiting for this evening all week."

"Me too." She took his coat and hung it in the hall. "You certainly have been busy. Is this typical?"

"Well, things usually pick up after the holidays, and I was at the seminar for a good portion of December, but I am adding many patients. I may need to take on an associate soon. In fact, I have already started making some inquiries."

"How exciting!"

"Yes, it would mean fewer hours and more flexibility."

"Wonderful. You could use a break once in a while." Lucy felt a slight tightening in her chest. She couldn't help wondering what his having more free time meant for their relationship. *Here goes, Lord. Please, direct our path.* "Well, the food is ready. Shall we?"

Gordon grinned. He took Lucy's arm and graciously directed her toward the dining room. "Yes, we shall. I am ravenous."

Lucy was pleased when, after a quick prayer of thanks, Gordon began eating eagerly.

"This is delicious, Lucy." He spoke with his mouth half full of chicken and bacon in cranberry sauce. He pointed toward the plate with his knife. "This sauce is incredible. Did you make it yourself?"

"Yes, a secret family recipe!" The way Gordon returned to his meal made Lucy wonder if he had stopped his work to eat at all during the week. So much for heartfelt dinner conversation. Lucy shrugged and took another bite of the chicken. There would be plenty of time for conversation. And Gordon was right, the food was very good. She'd have to cook more often.

After the meal, Lucy insisted they leave the dishes for later and steered Gordon into the sitting room, where she already had a fire going.

"Well, isn't this cozy." Gordon took Lucy's hand as they sat down on the sofa. "So now that you've decided you aren't too old for me, where do we go from here?"

Lucy was a bit surprised by Gordon's abrupt beginning—he was incorrigible at times.

"Well, I guess I would like to spend more time with you—get to know you better. I care for you very much."

Gordon smiled at her briefly. "That's a good start. I feel the same way. In fact, I am looking forward to spending a lot of time with you. Let's make sure we get together at least two times a

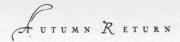
week—no matter how busy we get. And road trips! There are some wonderful drives we can take. And I would like you to join the small group I lead—if you are interested. It would be a great way for you to meet more of my friends, as well as get to know me better. Oh yes, it might be helpful to meet with Vicar Todd. I think he would be happy to talk to us as our vicar *and* our friend. And, of course we must pray constantly. We need God's guidance. This is a big step." Gordon took a breath. "So what do you think?"

Lucy was taken a little aback. Gordon had it all worked out. He certainly was a go-getter—and she loved that about him. But she wasn't quite ready to get swept up in their relationship. She had one last obstacle to face before she could pursue anything with him.

"It sounds wonderful Gordon, but I need to talk to you about something." She gently pulled her hand from Gordon's grasp, not because she didn't want to be near him—she just wanted to be able to think straight.

"I'm sorry." Gordon drew back a bit. "Am I going overboard? I just wanted to do this right."

"No, it's fine. I want to do things right, too. That's why I need to make a little detour here." Lucy rose to put another log on the fire. She didn't want Gordon to think she was shutting down their relationship, but she knew she needed to tell him what was on her heart before moving on. *Please, Lord. Give me the right words.* She sat beside him once again and stared into the yellow flames as she gathered her thoughts.

"Gordon, I need to go to Africa. I must confront my fears and come to peace with the past—this time with God's help. I'm not certain when I will leave or how long I will stay, but God is calling me there, and I need to go soon." Lucy was surprised when she saw a huge grin break out on Gordon's face.

"Lucy, this is great, perfect! I agree you should go. It's just what you need." He wrapped his arms around her and they sat for a moment, with only the sound of the crackling fire in the background.

Lucy could feel the pounding of Gordon's heart. *Thank you, Lord. He understands.*

Gordon pulled away from Lucy. "The best part of it is that I'm planning to go to Africa myself. I have fought against going, as you know, but God has been working on my heart lately. Jane's baby is due at the end of April, and it would be wonderful to see my family again. If I can bring another doctor into my surgery soon, I know I can take the time." Gordon hugged Lucy again. "Why don't we go together?"

Lucy's heart skipped a beat. What could she say? Didn't he understand she had to do this on her own? It was between her and God.

Gordon continued. "We could go to Kenya first. You could meet my family. We could spend some time there and then fly down to Mozambique to see Luke and Karen—or the other way around. I'd love to see the orphanage and the clinic. I can give you your jabs!" He grinned. "Or would you rather have that lady doctor in Redruth do it for you? What do you think?"

Lucy had never seen Gordon so excited. She tried to scramble her thoughts together. The last thing she wanted to do now was hurt his feelings or derail their relationship, but she also knew—beyond a shadow of a doubt—what she needed to do. For once Lucy had to be strong—she took a deep breath.

"Gordon, as much as I'd love to go to Africa with you—I can't. I have to go alone."

"I don't understand."

"It's my last hurdle, the last step in my journey back to God. You have been an important part of the process, but now it is between me and God. I have to step on that plane alone. I need to land in Mozambique without fear and hatred. I need to look into the eyes of the orphans of Mozambique without remorse. I need to live in the orphanage without Ruth and Tom—without regrets. I can't lean on anyone. I just want to lean on God."

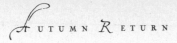

Gordon looked a little shell-shocked. Lucy wasn't normally given to such speeches. But she continued. "I need to visit Grace's grave, Gordon. I need to go to it with peace in my heart—and I need to do it alone."

Gordon stood, took Lucy's hands into his own, and drew her to her feet. He held her close with her head rested on his shoulder. It was a safe and wonderful place for Lucy to be. She never dreamed that something so wonderful would happen to her for a second time.

"I understand, Lucy. You're right. I should have known. Forgive me."

"There is nothing to forgive." She kissed him softly—just long enough to bring the spark back into his eyes. "Now, let's get to those dishes."

Lucy and Gordon spent the rest of the evening making plans for and praying about Lucy's trip. They also discussed how they would spend their time until she left. Gordon, it seemed, had some wonderful suggestions for adventures they could undertake. Lucy was surprised by his ideas and attention to detail. She laughingly insisted that if he ever gave up practicing medicine he should consider becoming a travel agent or tour guide!

Just before midnight, Gordon said he needed to leave since he had an early morning appointment.

"I had a wonderful time, Lucy. Thank you."

"You're welcome, and thank *you*—for your encouragement and support."

"My pleasure. Anytime. If I don't talk to you tomorrow, I'll see you at church. Say, if you'd like, I'll stop by and we can walk there together."

"That would be great. Call me."

"I'll do that." Gordon moved as if turning to leave, but before he reached the door, he turned to face Lucy. "I love you, Lucy Summers."

Though Gordon's declaration was not unexpected, it took Lucy

263

by surprise. Was she ready for this? Did she love him? What about Tom? "Why, thank you, Gordon. I . . . I care for you very much. But I . . ."

Gordon smiled and kissed the tip of Lucy's nose. "It's okay, Lucy. I understand. We have plenty of time." He shrugged his shoulders. "I just wanted you to know."

As Lucy left the gates of the orphanage compound, she was struck by the incredible peace she felt. Had the atmosphere of Mozambique changed so much, or was it her? *It's me, Lord. Thank you!* Luke had asked if she wanted him to walk out to Grace's grave with her. The cemetery was quite a distance from the compound, and he was concerned she might lose her way. But she politely insisted she would have no problem.

"I could find your grave with my eyes closed, Grace." Lucy had taken this walk so many times in her dreams, she almost knew the number of steps it would take. But those dreams had been nightmares, and now, though Lucy was sad, she also felt peace. *Only one more field to cross. Only one more pain to overcome! Help me, Lord.*

As she reached the cemetery, Lucy was surprised to see how much it had changed. When she and Tom had buried Grace, the orphanage had been in its infancy. Only a few graves had flanked Grace's at the crown of a treeless hill. Now they had been joined by what seemed to be hundreds of graves—a sad testimony to the innocent victims of Mozambique's civil war. The sapling they had planted in hopes of providing a bit of shelter from the blazing sun had grown to a massive tree—and had been joined by many others of varying sizes. They formed a shady canopy that shielded Lucy as she started her ascent to her daughter's grave.

It was marked with a simple headstone and bathed in golden dappled sunlight. Lucy bent to trace the words with her fingers:

Grace Summers

Cherished daughter of Tom and Lucy
Now in the arms of Almighty God

As her hand lingered on the warm stone she began to weep, and with her weeping the last dregs of her grief subsided. She was free from the regrets and anger. Free to recall the good memories—once crowded out by pain and resentment. Free to begin life again in the power of the Holy Spirit. "It's you Lord. Only your love and strength has brought me to this place. Thank you, Jesus."

Lucy knew Grace could not hear her. She was with God, but she still spoke as though her precious daughter sat next to her. "I love you, Grace, and have thought of you every day since you left me. I struggled for a long time, trying to make sense of life and loss. But I am letting you go now—along with the regrets. I will still remember, but I can't hold on. You're with Daddy now—safe in the arms of Jesus."

As she rose, Lucy carefully laid a bouquet of bright pink bougainvillea at the foot of the headstone. She had gathered it from the garden outside the bungalow she and Tom had called home so many years before, and it seemed a fitting memorial to her little girl and her daddy.

The bougainvillea seemed to glow like a fire as its bright paper-thin blossoms caught the sunlight and fluttered in the breeze. Lucy stood for a few moments, remembering. And then she was ready. "I loved your daddy so much, Grace. He was everything to me—my strength, my support. But he is gone and I need to go on. Jesus is my support now. It is infinitely better this way. He is leading me to a new life, Grace, and to a new love."

Lucy slowly began her descent down the dusty pathway, but turning back toward her daughter's grave she said softly, "I hope to bring him to visit you someday."

A new beginning and fresh start,
is what God wants for his children.
We must not live in the past,
We must learn from it.

Author Unknown

In his heart a man plans his course,
but the Lord determines his steps.
Proverbs 16:9 NIV

SALLY BRICE WINTERBOURN lives with her family in suburban London, England, and is very involved in her church and community. She and her husband, Graham, have four sons, Ben, Toby, Noah, and Sam. While writing is her favorite pastime, Sally also enjoys painting watercolors and gardening. *Autumn Return* is her first novel.

ACKNOWLEDGMENTS

Everyone needs encouragement, and I am no exception.

I could never have known when my neighbor Stan Benton gave me a little book for my fortieth birthday that it would be so significant to me in later years. Thanks, Stan! I prayed the poem on its first page when I sent my manuscript out.

Go, little book! From this my solitude;
I cast thee on the waters—go thy ways:
And if, as I believe, thy vein be good,
The world will find thee after many days.
Be it with thee according to thy worth:
Go, little book! in faith I send thee forth.

Robert Southey

Little did I know then that my little book would literally travel across the Atlantic's vast waters to find a publisher in Bethany House—God knew!

First, I would like to thank Gary and Carol Johnson for their kindness and encouragement to me. And a very special thank you to David Horton, who has been so understanding and kind, and to Karen Schurrer and the Bethany team for their patience in helping to make the book better. A big thank-you to Sharon Madison for her kindness and for believing in my work. You have all helped make my dream a reality!

Thanks so much to Chris Head, my agent and friend, and to his wife, Jackie. God knows the right people for the right time and Chris was just the person I needed to help my work get published.

To Linda Hill—thank you from the bottom of my heart for your inspiration as a writer.

I would like to thank my very dear friends and prayer partners Moira Hughes and Enid Claxton for their invaluable love, prayer support, and encouragement through many difficult times. You are precious!

Special thanks to my friend Pam Lucas for showing me what a difference a computer could make and for encouraging me with my work, to Tony Tidey for finding me a job that would help me with my computer skills, to John Evans for helping me choose my first computer, and to his wife, Karen, for helping me out with some typing when my typewriter went wrong! A big thank-you to Jean Duguid who had the faith to lend me her electric typewriter at the very start of my writing.

My grateful thanks to my colleague at work, Michelle Jones, for without her help I would never have conquered the computer, and to my manager, Iris Mills, who is always encouraging me with "You can do it!" God bless you both. Your kindness and patience over-whelmed me at times. I will never forget what you did for me.

I would also like to thank my elders and their wives—Ken and Barb Swan, Mick and Mary Lebaigue, and Andrew and Peggie Ray—for their constant love and care over the last eighteen years.

Thanks to all my dear friends at Chase Fellowship, particularly Christine Edgington; Barbara and Robert Green; David Lyon; Tony, Sheila, Evette and Janine Roper; Leslie Dufton; and Vicki Barnes—such faithful friends who took the time to read this manu-script for me!

I also want to thank others who read my work, including my dear friends Jenny and Steve Howard, Jan and Beth Morrison, June Frances (now with the Lord) and her daughter Catherine (a big encouragement to me), and Doreen West.

I would also like to thank my oldest and dearest friends, Christine Hargreaves and Jane Cutts, for fun and for being there. I love you!

Love and thanks to my sister, Wendy, and her husband, Clive, and my brother, David, and his wife, Nicky. I love you all. Thanks also to my brother- and sister-in-law, Barrie and Carole Cockayne, for their love and kindness to me and mine, and to Uncle Cliff and his wife, Joyce, who also read for and encouraged me. Love to all my California cousins, especially Linda Forsheē for her incredible kindness to me.

And at very last, thank you to all my wonderful relatives, the Brices, the Elmores, and the Winterbourns, for being such brilliant family—you are all very precious to me!

Escape With Janette Oke and T. Davis Bunn's
SONG OF ACADIA

With more than 20 million books sold between them, Janette Oke and T. Davis Bunn are two of the most beloved writers of Christian fiction. SONG OF ACADIA is their first historical series written together and represents a powerful combination of their storytelling strengths.

A Chance Encounter Will Forever Change Their Lives

At the beginning of *The Meeting Place*, two young women, their lives shadowed by nations in conflict, begin a friendship that will propel them on a journey from which they can never turn back....

Worlds Apart

The year was 1753, and the lines of separation were firmly drawn. The French had named the region Acadia, their "beloved home." When the British came soon after, they battled with the French on the new continent as they had in Europe for centuries.

The settlers of Acadia were either French or English, and though their villages might be but a stone's throw apart, most could go an entire lifetime without speaking to someone from the other side.

And then the chance encounter of Catherine Price and Louise Belleveau in a meadow of wild flowers... From this unexpected friendship, Oke and Bunn spin a tale of devotion, loss, renewal, and bonds stronger than blood and faith stronger than tragedy.

The Meeting Place
The Sacred Shore
The Birthright

BETHANY HOUSE PUBLISHERS
11400 Hampshire Ave. S., Minneapolis, MN 55438
www.bethanyhouse.com • 1-800-328-6109